Summer in CRANBERRY Harbor

Cranberry Harbor Series Book 3

CANDACE HAMMOND

Sea Crow Pre

To my granddaughter, Niah. You are a beacon of light and hope in this world. I'm so grateful for you, and love you to the moon and back. xo

ALSO BY CANDACE HAMMOND

Christmas in Cranberry Harbor

Spring in Cranberry Harbor

Summer in Cranberry Harbor
Published 2026 by Sea Crow Press
Barnstable, MA

www.seacrowpress.com

First Edition

Paperback ISBN: 9781961864566
Ebook ISBN: 9781961864573
Library of Congress Control Number: 2025950394

www.seacrowpress.com

Summer in CRANBERRY Harbor

Cranberry Harbor Series Book 3

CHAPTER 1

In the fourteen months since Lizzie and Jack had gotten married a lot had happened. A whole lot a lot.

Terra Marique is now complete, and the commercial spaces are hopping. After only being open for six months, Bert's Veggie Burgers; Vera's Vegan Cakes, Cookies and Pies; and Washashore Soups were in regular rotation using the commercial kitchen, with more folks lining up to use it. The community center is already becoming a town hub, hosting an improv group and a very popular weekly open mic. Lizzie had no idea how many people in Cranberry Harbor were secretly wonderful actors and musicians!

Lizzie and Jack had toyed with the idea of finding a space for themselves at Terra Marique; it was everything they could have wanted—eco-friendly, totally off the grid, a wonderful community of artists, farmers, tech people, families, older people and local workers—but they'd instead seized on another great opportunity. The Terra Marique project had inspired the town to revise its zoning rules, and due to those changes, they'd been able to build a wonderful, very-green and energy efficient house on a portion of her parents' one-and-a-half acre lot, creating the family compound Gabby, Lizzie's mom, had always dreamed of. And it ensured that Jack was not living where he worked, always a good idea when possible.

Everything was perfect. And that terrified Lizzie. She'd never been particularly aware of what a worrier she was until there was, well, nothing pressing to worry about. She'd married the love of her life, thanks to some wonderful angel investors the Cranberry Harbor Gazette was in good shape, they had a home they loved, and her parents were healthy and happy, as was her brother, Matt, his wife Shannon, and their now-kindergartner, Sophie. And that made Lizzie very nervous.

"Lizzie? Are you listening?" her best friend Alexis asked. They'd agreed to meet for coffee at Sea Coast, the best (and only) coffee shop in town.

Lizzie shakes her head. "Oh, Alexis, I'm so sorry," she says, taking a gulp of her now-lukewarm latte. "I zoned out for a moment there. You were talking about the Salty Dogs?"

"Are you okay? Getting enough sleep?" Alexis asks, concerned. "It's not like you to space out, though I know talking about Cape League baseball and the Cranberry Harbor Salty Dogs is not exactly what gets you excited," she teases.

"Really? I'm surprised you, as my best friend, seem unaware of my deep, unwavering love for collegiate, wooden bat baseball," she laughs. "How do you not recall that summer in middle school where my mother signed me up to be a bat girl?"

Alexis laughs. "I think I forgot because you were a bat girl, for, let me think… maybe two games total?"

Lizzie laughs too. "Oh, you're mistaken, it was three. I lasted three whole games. And hated every minute of it. I was petrified about getting hit with either a ball or a bat that was flung after a hit. I've rarely attended a game since."

"I stand corrected, my apologies," Alexis kids.

"Accepted." Lizzie finishes her coffee. "So what do you need from me?"

"Well, as you know, Terra Marique is a sponsor, the main sponsor—we've even got our name on the jerseys," Alexis says.

"Oh, believe me, I know, I've been sorting through fonts with Jack for weeks…"

"I like the Merriweather choice, by the way—your influence I imagine?" Alexis asks.

"Yes, left to his own devices it would have just been Times New Roman, so anyway, you want to talk about ad sizes? A feature story?" Lizzie asks, trying to ignore the nagging feeling that something bad is going to happen.

"Yes and yes, please," Alexis says.

"I've already got an ad designed—I'll email it to you—and our new full-time reporter, Eric, has already done an interview with Paul, and the new head coach. We're on it," Lizzie says.

"I should never have doubted that for a second. Thank you, thank you. I can now totally take those off my list," Alexis says, sitting back in her chair and picking up her coffee cup. "I did not know that being the community coordinator for Terra Marique was going to involve sports."

"It's a multi-tasking world, my friend. I'm not saying that's a good thing, but in the last week alone, as the now-editor of the Gazette, I have unclogged a sink, caught a mouse in a Havahart trap and released it into the wild, and posted 68 photos to social media about a horseshoe crab named Spike who was brought home by a child whose parents somehow thought *that* was a good idea. Really? A pet horseshoe crab? And they then brought it to Safe Haven for Animals when it inevitably became sick."

"What? How did I miss that story?" Alexis asks, shaking her head. "How dumb are people?!"

"Apparently, pretty dumb!"

"Is Spike going to be okay?" Alexis asks, immediately rooting for Team Spike.

"Yes, he was dehydrated and very hungry. He'd been out of the water for two days, and they can die within 4. The whole thing was just so aggravating and showed such a disrespect for animal life. You know? Jeez, the kid, who was six, was feeding him Cheerios and strawberries."

"Wow. Well, I'm sure Dr. Amanda gave them a good talking to," Alexis says.

"Oh you know it. They ended up making a big donation, I think out of fear of repercussions, and I'm betting they never bring any wild creature home again."

"When we were little we all took classes at the First Light Natural History Museum and we learned from such an early age about looking out for animals, sea life, birds. Hmmm."

"I know that look," Lizzie says, studying her friend. "You're having a lightbulb moment."

"Yeah! What if with some of the grant money we have at Terra Marique for education, we had naturalists at the beach a few times a week offering some free classes to people about wildlife on the Cape? They could talk about how we can observe and learn about animals, birds and fish without harming them. And why taking hermit crabs, et cetera, home with you..."

"Don't forget horseshoe crabs," Lizzie interjects.

"Yes, and horseshoe crabs, is not a good idea. And using poisons to kill rats and mice also kills the birds and animals who then ingest them, because even though we have thankfully banned all these chemicals in Cranberry Harbor, a lot of people come from places that haven't." Alexis is getting excited.

"Sounds like a very good idea, and one I am sure my husband will also like," Lizzie says, smiling.

Alexis jots down a few thoughts, and they're both quiet.

"Do you ever get a feeling of existential dread?" Lizzie asks, piercing the silence rather dramatically.

"Whoa, that's random," Alexis says, putting down her pen and looking intently at Lizzie. "Okay, what's up? This feels like when in the movie *Barbie* she asks the other Barbies if they ever think about dying."

Lizzie laughs and shakes her head. "No, it's not that dire, but I don't know... everything is going so well, it's scary."

"Ah yes, I've been there," Alexis says, nodding thoughtfully. "Looking over my shoulder, like somehow I don't deserve all the good things in my life so something bad has to happen to balance out the universe? It's the worst!"

"Yes! Ugh, it's the absolute worst! And I feel so ungrateful. I'm so fortunate, so how can I of all people feel this angst?" Lizzie says. "I feel like I'm disrespecting the gifts given to me."

"First of all, you are someone who is always very conscious of others, of being generous, grateful, and thoughtful, so stop beating yourself up about that right now," Alexis says. "Heck, last week when I had a sore throat, within an hour you were on my doorstep with hot soup from the Washashore Soup folks. Do not do that, my friend; I won't hear of it."

Lizzie laughs."Maybe it's kind of a normal letdown that you feel when something you've put everything into is completed, and you think, now what?" she posits.

"Hey, it's not like you're doing nothing, Lizzie. Jeez, you just took over running the Gazette without your dad like six months ago, and I'm sure his heart attack really threw you for a loop. That was scary for all of us. Cranberry Harbor doesn't work without Peter Martin."

"*My* world sure wouldn't work without him, and I'm very happy for him that he decided it was time to just have fun." Lizzie smiles. "Have I told you what pickleball fanatics my parents have become? It's crazy! They keep trying to get Jack and me to play with them and I just don't have the time right now, but I'm so happy that after almost 40 years of running the Gazette he's not stressing about bylines and deadlines."

"Maybe you're just waiting for the next new thing that will spark you," Alexis says. "A new passion. You always did like having that next thing to work on."

"Yeah, that's true. A lot of people seem to think that the next thing should be a baby, but I'm not so sure it's the right time. I'm absolutely amazed by the number of people, many who hardly know me, asking when we're going to have a baby," Lizzie says.

Alexis can tell she's sussing out her feelings on the matter. She shakes her head. "That's ridiculous. Only you and Jack can know if that's the right thing for you both or not. It's not anyone else's business. You will never get any pressure from me."

"I appreciate that, more than you can know," Lizzie says, looking wistfully out the window. She takes a deep breath and sighs. "Well, I'd better get back to work. This has been lovely, and thank you," she says, taking Alexis's hand, "you've helped me more than you can know." She stands up. "I feel terrible that other than horseshoe crabs and the Salty Dogs this has been all about me. Let's meet up tomorrow. I know Ian is due back from being on location soon, and I want to hear all about you, okay?"

"Very okay." Alexis stands up and gives Lizzie a hug. "We take turns in friendships," she says as she keeps hugging Lizzie. "When you're best friends you know it's going to be you who may need to talk another time. No one's keeping score, Lizzie. Love you."

Lizzie squeezes her harder. "Love you too," she sniffles. "Man, my brother is so right when he calls us the schmaltz family," she says, wiping her nose with a paper napkin.

"Matt is correct, and I love it," Alexis says. "Now scoot before I cry too!"

"Fine, see you later," Lizzie says, walking out the door, dabbing her nose, and feeling so incredibly grateful to have Alexis as a friend and to be in Cranberry Harbor, and wondering what her next project will be, other than, you know, running the Cape's only independent newspaper.

CHAPTER 2

"Well, this is a nice surprise," Lizzie says, happy to see her dad sitting at their old partner's desk when she walks into the office. "Are you itching for a deadline?" she teases.

Peter laughs. "Hardly," he says, running his hands over the edge of the desk. "I cannot even begin to estimate how many hours I spent at this desk, some of them making me want to tear my hair out, but most of them quite happily."

Lizzie sits down across from him in her old spot. It had taken a while, but about six weeks ago she had started working in his chair, on his side of the partner's desk, giving Eric her side.

"So what brings you in today, Dad?" she asks, smiling at him and resting her elbows on the desk, chin on her interlaced fingers. "Freelance work? Looking to cash in your percentage of the ownership?"

He laughs, "No, none of the above. I had an appointment across the street with Dr. Myers."

Lizzie sits bolt upright. "You're feeling okay, right?"

He smiles at her. "Yes, it's all good. She was very pleased with all my tests, and I have to say, not being so stressed about the paper has helped, along with exercising a lot more. Between pickleball and the hiking group, I haven't been this active since I played tennis in college."

She sits back in her chair. "Thank goodness it was all good

news," she says. "You are not allowed to give me, or any of us, any more scares—you got that, Martin?"

"Yes ma'am," he says, smiling at her. "Anyway, I did have one ulterior motive for coming in…"

"I knew it! I knew you had something up your sleeve," she teases him. "What's up? What can I do for you?"

"Through pickleball your mom and I have met this lovely couple from Boston who moved here last year so their son could be part of the day program at Coastal Horizons, you know, the residential center for young adults on the autism spectrum," he says.

"Yeah, we did a story on them when it opened last year. That's great that they've started having programs for non-residents as well. Oh, you want me to do a story about it? Done and done," she says.

"No—well, sure, that would be great, but no, the real reason I'm here is because their son, Andrew, who's 20, really wants to get a job at Sea Coast. He loves creating latte art, and he's really great at it. He's made your mom and me some fantastic lattes at their house, with hedgehogs, llamas, all sorts of things," he says. "Anyway, you're such good friends with Leah I thought maybe you could put in a good word for him?"

"Of course, I'd be happy to," she says. "I'm so glad you and Mom have made some new friends, too; that's wonderful," she says. "The next time I'm at Sea Coast, probably tomorrow, I'll mention Andrew to Leah. What's his last name?" she asks, grabbing a pen and a scrap of paper.

"Oh, it's Wilder. His parents are Paul and Olivia. We'll have to have them over sometime soon and have you and Jack come," he says.

"That sounds nice," she says, "I'll make sure to talk to Leah as soon as possible," she says. "I'm betting she'd love to have someone who can create great art with steamed milk in her employ."

Peter can see by the look on Lizzie's face that she has a lot of work to do and can't sit around chatting all day.

"Okay, I'm off," he says, standing up and pushing the chair in.

Lizzie stands up too and gives her dad a big hug.

"It was so good to see you. Don't be a stranger," she says.

He stops and looks around. "It's funny, I always thought it

would be so hard to walk away from this, that I'd never be able to give it up, but it's been pretty easy. You know why, right?" he asks.

Lizzie shrugs her shoulders, "Because you were ready?"

"No, because I had you to turn it over to," he says, beaming at her.

"Oh, that!" she says, smiling at her dad. "Well, seeing how you're thinking it was the reason for your heart attack, all I can say is thanks a lot for handing it off to me!"

"You'll be fine, sweetheart. You've got secure backing. You've got Eric, who's an amazing reporter, and a bunch of freelancers now." He kisses her on the head and walks to the door. He turns around before leaving. "You are doing a fantastic job, in case I haven't told you," he says.

Lizzie smiles and cocks her head, "You tell me quite often, and I never get tired of it," she says. "Now off with you; go play some pickleball or take a hike!"

Peter laughs, "Wow, being in charge has sure made you bossy. See you later!"

Lizzie waves and walks back to her desk. As she surveys the piles of notes, books and newspapers on her desk, she's not sure what to tackle first.

Her peaceful contemplation is pierced by the sound of a car horn blaring, sounding like it is going on for the entire block. Then she hears some voices yelling,

"What the heck?" she says, getting up and going to the window.

She can't really tell what's going on. The car is long gone, but there are some people milling about. She sits back down at her desk. This has become a frequent pattern, the loud car horns blowing off and on throughout the day. Everyone seems so impatient and in a hurry. Cranberry Harbor never used to be like this. She shakes her head and laughs. She may only be 35, but she winces at the thought of saying to a teenager or 20-something, "Back when I was young..." That said, she may have to write something about the increase in crankiness. It's not good.

Lizzie was snapped out of her inner rabbit hole of wondering what was making people so cranky by Eric breezing in, smiling and excited. It was a nice change of energy in the office.

"Hey, you sure look excited. Where have you been?" Lizzie asks, curious.

'Remember? I went on that ghost tour put on by the Cranberry Harbor Historical Society at the cemetery this afternoon. It was surprisingly fun!" he says.

"Oh right! Was it really interesting?" Lizzie asks, now very curious.

"Yeah!" he says, sitting down in the seat opposite her at the partner's desk and pulling out his laptop from his backpack. "They had actors at graves scattered throughout the cemetery telling the stories of people who had lived here, and wow, some of the stories were harrowing: fishermen lost at sea, women who started businesses on their own back when that rarely happened..."

"Wow, Eric, I grew up here and didn't know about that. Maybe you can do a little more digging and find out more about them? This would be a fantastic story," Lizzie says, feeling so happy that she was able to hire such a great journalist for the Gazette.

"Oh, I'm already on it. I made some calls on the way back, and actually, I have several ideas I want to explore," he says.

"This story feels a little evergreen. We don't need to run it this week, right? So take your time and do all the research you want and need to do. And don't forget about Christie, the head of research at the library. She might be of help if you need anything more. She's full of information about this town."

"Great idea, and more time would be good. I think there could be some really interesting stories to uncover," Eric says.

"I probably don't tell you often enough, but I'm so happy to have you here. You add so much to this paper, and your enthusiasm makes me feel better." She sighs and looks out the window. "Right before you came in, I was feeling very discouraged about the impending summer season, sitting here and already hearing car horns blaring. You helped me move on from obsessing about that. Thank you."

"I am very happy to help, but yeah, I hear you. I've only lived here year-round for about four years and I'm starting to gird myself for the summer people to arrive, even though not that long ago I was one. What is it you call newbies?" he asks.

"Washashores," Lizzie says, smiling at him. "But some

washashores immediately become part of the community and fit right in. You're one of those. You totally have a local vibe."

"Why thank you, I appreciate that," he says. He shuts his computer and starts gathering his notebook and other items. "If it's okay with you I think I might run over to the historical society before they close, ask them some questions, and then see if I can track down Alexis to see if her grandfather would be interested in talking to me. From things she's said in passing I think he could be a great source."

"Of course! Go! Research! I can't wait to see what you uncover," Lizzie says. She glances at the clock on the wall. "I think I'm going to leave too. I am feeling like a yoga class would be a good idea." She packs up her computer and picks up her bag with her yoga clothes in it.

"See you tomorrow!" Eric calls as he leaves. Lizzie takes her yoga clothes into the bathroom, changes, puts her hair in a ponytail, and zips up a lightweight hoodie. She then slips on her best recent thrift shop find - her almost-new Birkenstocks.

She's happy to see Justine from Toy Works, Leah, and even her sister-in-law, Shannon, all had the same idea of cutting out from work a little early and hitting the 5:00 Yoga Flow class.

After they roll out their mats all near each other, Leah immediately lies down and takes a deep breath.

"Long day?" Lizzie asks her, sitting down on her mat, beginning to do some twists and stretches to warm up.

"Yes," she says, not sitting up. 'Is it too late to decide I don't want to own a coffee shop and become a pop star instead?"

"Hmmm, you really think that being Taylor Swift would be less stressful than selling lattes and scones?" Lizzie asks, lying back herself. She pulls her knees into her chest one at a time.

"Yeah, you're probably right, and I stink at singing and can't write songs, so there you go." Leah moans slightly and sits up.

"So what's got you feeling like you want to trade in your business for the road?" Lizzie asks.

"Just a few too many people coming in and not being very patient," she says, finding a nice downward facing dog. "It's not even really summer yet, but they're here—"

"Ah, the 'what do you mean, I have to wait for five minutes for my coffee' people? The 'oh the inhumanity' people?"

Leah sighs again, and shakes her head. "Yup, and I don't have enough help. The college kids aren't here yet, and I need someone who can make lattes, who won't need a ton of training." She lies down again. "Ugh."

"Oh! I might have someone for you! Apparently he's very into latte art, and loves doing it," Lizzie says.

Leah sits bolt upright, "Really? Who is this unicorn?"

"His name is Andrew Wilder, and he moved here not too long ago with his parents to go to the day program at Coastal Horizons. He's 20, and loves making lattes, apparently," she says.

"Okay, yeah, have him come see me tomorrow sometime," Leah says. "We've had some residents from Coastal Horizons work at Sea Coast before and they've been awesome employees. I'd love to meet him."

Leah is looking a little happier and less stressed than when she came in, and by the time the lights are slightly dimmed and the relaxing ambient music begins to play, both she and Lizzie are feeling much more zen.

She looks over at Shannon as they flow from down dog through a vinyasa to warrior pose. "I didn't mean to ignore you—you okay?" she whispers, not wanting to disturb the class or get a glare from the teacher.

Shannon nods, and tilts her head toward the instructor, who doesn't look happy. Jeez, even yoga teachers seemed to be having a tough day.

By the end of class the trio are all feeling much better, more relaxed and better about life.

Lizzie is rolling up her mat. "I don't know what it is about yoga, but it's always the perfect recipe for me to calm the heck down and take a beat," she says, putting her mat in the carrier her mom gave her for Christmas.

"Me too," Leah says. "When I walked in here I sort of hated the world. Well, maybe not the *whole* world. Vermont was looking pretty good to me, but now I'm feeling much more like myself."

"You're awfully quiet, Shannon—everything okay?" Lizzie asks as they exit the studio into the lobby.

Shannon looks at both of them, causing Lizzie and Leah to exchange a look of concern.

"What's going on?" Leah and Lizzie say at the same time.

Before speaking Shannon moves them away from the others who are putting on their shoes and exiting.

"You can't tell anyone yet, but I'm pregnant," she says. Preemptively she shushes them and motions them to calm down.

Shannon and Matt had been trying to have a second baby, had gone through a miscarriage last year, and were ready to give up and have Sophie as their one and only. Lizzie and Leah both understood her trepidation at getting too excited too soon.

Lizzie hugs her, and quietly says, "I'm so excited for you and my brother, and I won't breathe a word to anyone."

"Thank you. Of course you can tell Jack; we're all family," she says, squeezing Lizzie back. "I did tell your mom and dad. It's very nice to have a doctor in the family. She's been so supportive and reassuring," Shannon says.

Leah gives her a hug too. "I'm very happy for you both. Let me know if I can do anything, okay?"

Shannon nods. "Thanks you two. I'm trying not to get too excited, but we've made it to 16 weeks now, so my doctor in Boston is cautiously optimistic that it's going to be okay. The two miscarriages I had before were at 10 and 12 weeks, so this is looking good."

"Fingers and toes all crossed for you. Does Sophie know?" Lizzie asks.

"No, we're waiting a bit longer. We don't want her to be disappointed again," Shannon says.

They all head to the door as the next class trickles in.

"Well, this ended my day on a very nice note," Leah says, walking to her car. While talking and not looking where she's going, she walks right into a guy who's looking down at his phone, headed into the yoga studio, dumping both her yoga mat and his to the ground.

"I'm so sorry," he says, picking her mat up and handing it to her before retrieving his own. He grabs his mat and stands up. "Are you okay?"

Leah doesn't recognize this very nice looking guy. Owning the only coffee shop in town, she generally knows everyone. Lizzie and Shannon elbow each other as they witness this potential meet-cute.

"Oh yeah, I'm fine," Leah says. "It was my fault 100 percent. I was talking to my friends." She points to Lizzie and Shannon, who give a quick wave and then, not wanting to intrude, go to their cars, raising their eyebrows and smiling to each other.

"I was looking at my phone, so totally my bad. I'm Jonathan," he says.

"Leah," she says back.

"Well, I guess I better get to class," he says. "It's my first, and I don't want to be late."

"Oh no, that wouldn't be good; the teacher might make you do extra cobras or tree poses," she jokes.

"I have no idea what those are, but I better get in there," he says, walking toward the door. "Nice bumping into you, Leah," he says, walking backward, smiling at her.

"Very nice meeting you," she says, feeling very happy she decided to come to yoga tonight.

CHAPTER 3

When Lizzie walks in her front door, she discovers Jack already at home, a very rare occurrence, and already cooking dinner. It smells delicious.

"Well, this is a nice surprise," Lizzie says, putting her arms around Jack's waist as he slices some avocado.

He turns his head to give her a kiss, and then keeps cutting.

Lizzie surveys the kitchen, lifting the lid off the cast iron skillet. "Oh, Bert's veggie burgers," she says. "Hmmm, with avocado, tomato and cheddar cheese… this is just what I wanted."

"I also made some sweet potato fries. They're in the oven," he says.

She steals a slice of tomato and pops it in her mouth. "You are definitely my favorite husband," she says. "Want a glass of wine?" she asks, walking over to the cupboard and taking out two glasses.

"I'd love one, thanks. I think the Chianti we had the other night still has a few glasses in it." He points to the bottle on the counter.

"Perfect," she says, uncorking the bottle and pouring them each a glass.

She sits down on a stool across from him.

"So tonight after yoga Shannon told Leah and me that she's 16 weeks pregnant," she says, leaning over and pilfering a piece of avocado as Jack plates their veggie burgers.

"Wow, that's great!" he says, sliding a perfectly plated meal in front of her. He walks around the island to sit next to her. "Is she feeling okay?"

"Yeah, she seems to be. She's worried, of course, but this is farther than she's made it the last couple of times," Lizzie says, then picks up her veggie burger and takes a bite. "Oh my gosh, this is fantastic. Thank you."

"You're very welcome," he says, taking a bite himself. He nods in agreement.

They both eat in silence for several minutes until they're done.

"I think we were both very hungry," Lizzie says, pushing her empty plate away from her. "That was perfect. Thank you, sweetie," she says, kissing him on the cheek.

She gets up and takes their plates over to the sink and rinses them.

"How was your day?" she asks, putting the dishes in the dishwasher.

He sits back and exhales. "It was good. Really good. I realized today that so much of the time I'm so wrapped up in the day-to-day running of things at Terra Marique that I don't get to really see what we've done, but something happened today that kind of broke that tunnel vision."

She pours them each another glass of wine and sits down next to him. "Really? Tell me about it."

"I was walking from my car to my office and I saw this little boy and his mom walking what appeared to be a new puppy around the green. It had a bow on its collar, so I stopped and bent down to pet it." He sits back and seems emotional.

"You okay?" Lizzie asks, putting her hand on his.

"Yeah, it just really got me. I asked him what the dog's name was, and he said Terra, and made sure I knew it wasn't Tara," he says.

"That's so sweet," Lizzie smiles, thinking that's the cutest thing ever.

"I asked why he wanted to name her Terra, and he said because he loves Terra Marique, and because before they got their house there he couldn't have a dog, and now he can." He's teary and choked up. "Wow, it just really got me, you know?"

Lizzie nods. "What you created has changed lives, Jack. You've given him a place to call home forever and ever, and he gets to have the dog he's always wanted."

"You know what it's like to get so wrapped up in the day-to-day and minutiae that you lose sight of the big picture?"

"Oh yeah, it's really easy to forget the real mission of what we're doing," Lizzie agrees.

"Totally, but in that small exchange, I got pulled back to Earth and away from spreadsheets and Zoom meetings, and it snapped me back to reality, and seeing this incredible thing that we all created so that this little boy can have a home and a puppy..." he says, choking up.

Jack shakes his head and laughs. "Look at me," he says, pointing at himself, shaking his head. "I've turned into the biggest mush!"

"That's what comes from marrying into the schmaltz family," Lizzie says, hugging him. "And I love that about you. And I'm so proud of you, and everyone who made Terra Marique happen, so that little boy and so many others can make their dreams come true," and then she gets teary. "Ugh, see what you started?" she teases.

There's a knock at the door as they're both sitting there teary-eyed.

"Come in," they both call out at the same time.

Lizzie's mom Gabby walks in carrying half a pie, but then looks concerned that she's come at an inappropriate time.

"I'm sorry," she says, placing the pie on the counter. "I don't want to intrude, I just wanted to leave this—so sorry to bother you." She heads to the door.

"Mom," Lizzie says, getting up and stopping her mother from leaving. "You don't have to hurry out. We were choked up about a sweet little boy and his new puppy at Terra Marique. You know," she points to all three of them, "the schmaltz family?"

"Oh phew, I was worried I interrupted something serious," Gabby says. "Oh, kids and animals? They get me every time."

"And the little boy named his new puppy Terra," Jack says, looking emotional again.

"Oh my goodness, that's the sweetest thing ever," she says. "Now you're going to make me cry." She takes a deep breath. "Anyway, the nice thing about having you both next door is I can give you our leftovers so we don't eat them all," she says, gesturing to the pie. "It has no sugar, the crust is 100 percent organic whole wheat, the apples are organic, and I used local honey, so it's pretty healthy, as desserts go."

"Thanks, Mom," Lizzie says, giving her a hug. "Can you stay for a minute?"

"Sure, just a quick minute. Your dad was cueing up some new streaming series he wanted us to try. How was your day?" she asks, taking a seat.

"Good. Oh! I mentioned your friend's son, the one who makes latte art, to Leah. She said for him to come by tomorrow," Lizzie says, filling the electric kettle with water. "Tea?" she asks her mom and Jack. Gabby shakes her head.

"I'd love some with my pie," he says, getting out two plates and some forks along with the mugs.

"So Shannon told me at yoga class tonight about the baby. That's pretty exciting," Lizzie says, placing two green tea bags in the mugs.

"It's very exciting," Gabby says.

"Are you worried?" Lizzie asks.

"As a mom? Of course, and a bit as a doctor, but she's in good hands and 16 weeks is good. And she's been having morning sickness, always a good sign. I've got a good feeling about this," she says, which reassures Lizzie.

"If you feel good, then I feel good," Lizzie says.

"Well, I should get back. There's a 1950s British detective with mysteries to solve, and a retired editor waiting for me. I hope you enjoy the pie," she says. "See you later, you two."

Jack takes a bite of the pie. "Oh my God, this is so good!" he says. "Your mom totally missed her calling. She could have had an amazing restaurant if she'd wanted."

Lizzie laughs. "Yeah, so much time wasted being a family practitioner, right?" she jokes, taking a bite herself. "Damn, that's some fine pie," she says, And despite their attempt at restraint, by the end of the evening, that half pie was gone.

As they sit on the couch, both rubbing their tummies, Lizzie turns to Jack.

"Does all this talk about babies and pregnancy make you think about wanting to have one?" she asks.

"Uh…not really. Not yet. You?" he asks, a little nervous.

She shakes her head. "I mean, it's not like we haven't had this talk many times, like, we'll know when the time is right, but I just want to make sure you're still okay with where we're at, you know?"

"Oh definitely, we should always feel like we can talk about it and yeah, things change, circumstances change," he says, looking at Lizzie a bit quizzically.

"It does feel a bit like we're outliers sometimes. I'm in my mid-30s. What if, like Shannon, I have a hard time getting pregnant? But I haven't felt ready to put my work on the back burner, and you're so busy…I hope we don't regret waiting a bit longer."

Jack emphatically shakes his head. "I don't think we will, honey. It's got to feel right. Though I think I was a pretty big surprise for my parents. So, I guess you can make all the plans you want—"

"And sometimes life has its own ideas…" Lizzie says, smiling at him. She lets out a deep sigh. "Good talk." She puts her head on Jack's shoulder. "We'll know when it's right."

He kisses her on the head. "I'm glad we checked in on this," he says, kissing her a bit more passionately.

She nods, and standing up, smiles and pulls him up and starts leading him upstairs, turning out the lights as they go.

"Hey, just because we're not ready doesn't mean we can't practice," Jack says, happily following her.

"Yes, indeed," she says, leading the way, also feeling very happy and very much in love with her husband.

CHAPTER 4

When Lizzie wakes up the next morning, feeling happy in their cozy bed, and moreover, happy in her life, Jack has already gotten up and upon hearing her stirring, magically appears with a lovely, steaming mug of Sea Coast roasted coffee, fresh from their kitchen.

"Hey," she says, happily accepting the coffee. "Thank you. What a lovely treat—coffee in bed." With her free hand she fluffs the pillows behind her and leans back, taking a sip of the coffee.

"Hmmm, this is so good. Thank you. This is a perfect start to the day," she says.

Jack, his own coffee in hand, crawls in next to her. "I agree. We should do this more often," he says, snuggling in.

"Yeah…the only problem with that is…"

"We both work for ourselves and have terrible people for bosses who make us work all the time and never allow us to take a morning off and come in late?" Jack says, teasing her.

"You took the words right out of my mouth," she says, drinking more of her delicious coffee. "We need to talk to those people, or maybe just ignore them."

"I vote for ignoring them. I mean, what? Like we're going to get fired? We're the damn bosses, right?" Jack offers.

"Hell yeah." She sits up and looks at the clock. It's 7:42. "What do you say to each of us going in a little late and taking a walk on the beach before work?" she asks, looking very excited, and Jack knows he'd better not say no.

"Yeah! Let's do it," he says, downing the rest of his cup of coffee, throwing the covers off and getting up. "I'm just going to take a quick shower, send two emails, text a delivery guy, and then, heck yeah!"

Lizzie laughs, "I'm blown away by the spontaneity," she says. Then she's quiet. "Yeah, I just need to check in and post a link for the print edition of the paper, and then, yeah, I can throw caution to the wind. Oh, and make one—no, two—calls, and send an email to the printer about a change in an ad for the Salty Dogs..."

Jack walks over and kisses her. "We really stink at letting the day take us where it wants, don't we?"

She throws back the covers, stands up and hugs him, patting him on the back. "Baby steps, sweetie, baby steps. We'll get there. Maybe by the time we're 60 we'll figure out how to take an entire day off."

"Whoa, that's crazy talk!" he says, laughing. "I'll be ready in say... a half hour?" he says, walking into the bathroom to shower.

"Sounds perfect," Lizzie says, "And very spontaneous," Jack rolls his eyes, laughs and closes the bathroom door.

They do pretty well. They both showered, dressed, did a little work, shared a smoothie and were out the door in 50, not 30, minutes, but it was a start.

As they drive down to Sea Meadow Beach Lizzie can feel the tension she's been holding begin to leave her body. It was the perfect time. It was still early in the season so the beach wasn't packed, the tide was out, far out, perfect for walking, and it was sunny, barely a cloud in the perfect blue sky. They could not have designed a more idyllic time to walk. June and September were her favorite months on the Cape. It was warming up in June, but not too hot and humid. The crowds that had descended for Memorial Day weekend had lessened and it wouldn't be that crowded again until after the Fourth of July. September she loved for the fewer people, the beginning of fall and endless blue skies. "Shoulder season," also called "locals summer," had long been a well-kept secret but over Lizzie's lifetime more people had learned of how dreamy it was in the fall, and it wasn't quite as quiet as it used to be. There's a push and pull when you live in a tourist destination. It's fun to see new faces, to see people love the place you love so much, but it's also nice to see them go back to their hometowns, leaving you to yours. But for many of the people in Cranberry Harbor, it is those eight to ten weeks that support them for the year. And as so many locals were priced out of the housing market, it was more vital than ever to earn as much as you could.

They both slip their shoes and socks off and start walking from the parking lot to the beach.

Lizzie stops for a moment. "I know I have lived here my entire life, save a few years in Boston, but I am never not awed by this. Look at this! Have you ever seen anything so incredibly beautiful?"

Jack puts his arm around her. "I have not. How fortunate are we?" he says as they start walking.

When the tide is fully out in Cranberry Harbor you can walk out on the sand for about a mile. Lizzie always loves watching people coming here for the first time and seeing their total awe at the experience. It's something never to be taken for granted.

They walk in silence for a while, both taking in the salty air, the sounds of all the gulls, and then...the refrains of the Grateful Dead? Out on the flats? They look at each other, not really believing what they're hearing and now seeing. An older gentleman and his dog, happily encamped on the beach, with a huge old-school boombox, absolutely blaring *Friend of the Devil* at a decibel level that would scare fish.

"In an era when anyone can listen to anything they want, at any volume they want, with earbuds or headphones, why on Earth would someone need to come and disturb everyone's quiet morning on the beach?" Lizzie asks.

Jack shakes his head as they get closer. They can see that the guy is just itching for someone to complain so he can lecture them about his freedom and public space, and they silently agree not to give him the satisfaction. Still, it's impossible to ignore and has kind of spoiled their nice, quiet morning walk. Lizzie might not feel so annoyed if she got to do this all the time, but it's a rare moment that they get to enjoy the morning together at the beach, and this guy is ruining it.

"Have you thought of perhaps headphones?" Lizzie yells over the music, and Jack immediately knows it's not a good idea.

"Have you ever thought of minding your own business?" the guy counters, not very cleverly.

"I have, but with your music invading the space for a good quarter of a mile, you've kind of made your music choice everyone's business. We just thought maybe you could turn it down a little, so we could all enjoy listening to the water, the wind, the birds..."

He shakes his head. "Nah," and turns it up even louder.

"Let's go, honey," Jack says, taking her hand. "He's not worth stressing over," and they begin to walk away.

"Have a great day you two. Maybe go hug a tree," he yells.

"I swear." Lizzie is getting mad, and Jack pulls her hand, urging her to keep heading back to shore. "Ugh!" she exclaims. "What an inconsiderate weasel."

"That's one word for him," Jack jokes.

Lizzie laughs. "Sorry, I just can't stand selfish, entitled people."

"Oh, I'm well aware, and I'm 100 percent with you, but getting into a shouting match with some random guy on the beach isn't going to change him, and it's going to ruin your day. I know you; it would eat away at you all day, and he's just not worth it," Jack says, putting his arm around her.

"Do you ever get the feeling that people just aren't as nice or thoughtful as they used to be?" she asks as they keep walking.

"Yes, and I think it's partly technology and social media. People shout at each other in all caps and say things they'd never say in person, and then they bring that energy into the real world and they just aren't as nice to each other," he says.

"I agree. I think smartphones broke our brains," she says, teasing but not really.

"Broke them, huh?" Jack queries.

"I watched a young woman completely ignore a toddler—not hers, mind you, but still, it was a little kid—stuck behind her chair trying to reach a napkin on the counter at Sea Coast the other day, and the holder almost fell on him. She never looked up from her phone, didn't turn, nothing. I was about to hurry over to him when the mom, carrying an infant she was nursing, ran over to rescue him. Like I said, broken brains."

"Wow, that takes a special level of obtuseness even I haven't mastered," Jack says.

Lizzie keeps thinking and talking as they walk back to their car. "And I've noticed that people don't wave 'thank you' as often when you let their car in when you're driving. I tell you, it's an epidemic. I just thought Cranberry Harbor was kinder than other places."

"It's a cold, cruel world out there, Lizzie," Jack says, "but I refuse to join in." He runs over to her side of the car and opens her door, grandly gesturing for her to get in. "I will try to do better at noticing my own little lapses in kindness." He closes her door and walks over to the driver's side and gets in, after brushing the sand off his feet, of course.

They each fasten their seatbelts, and Jack starts their still fairly new electric car. They'd moved up from two hybrids to one hybrid and one EV, hoping in the next year or so to go electric for them both. Lizzie thought that guy on the beach would have had a heyday with seeing them in an electric car. They were indeed very much tree huggers. She is proud of that.

Lizzie is quiet as they drive home.

"You okay?" Jack asks as they pull into their driveway. "Don't let that guy ruin your day; he's so not worth it." He leans over and kisses her.

"I know, you're right." She kisses him back. "I'm not going to give him that power, and I'm going to make this a wonderful day."

As she gets out of the car at home, her niece Sophie comes running over to her.

"Aunt Wiz!" she yells, wrapping herself around Lizzie's legs.

Lizzie picks her up, though now at 5-years-old it's getting a bit harder. "What are you doing here, sweetie? Aren't you supposed to be in school?"

"Oh, I'm sick. I throwed up two times!" she says, throwing her arms around Lizzie's neck and squeezing her.

"What were you saying about having a great day?" Jack asks, smiling at her.

Lizzie sighs. Having a positive attitude is going to be a bit of a challenge today, she thinks.

CHAPTER 5

By the time Lizzie gets to Sea Coast, Alexis is already there with Ian, her boyfriend of the last almost-year.

Ian MacFayden was a documentary filmmaker who'd been working on a film about the climate crisis. A part of the film had been following the building of Terra Marique, and he'd just returned from the Arctic filming the scary decline of sea ice, also stopping in Portland to see about a growing initiative there to combat climate change. He was a busy guy.

"Hi, you two," Lizzie says, not planning to sit down with them, instead thinking she'd get her coffee to go and head to the paper, giving them some space. "Welcome back, Ian. How was the trip?"

"It was great, and exhausting, depressing, and inspiring," he says, shaking his head and smiling. "Please, sit. What do you want? I was just going to get a refill; let me get yours," he says, always such a good guy.

"I don't want to intrude. You two haven't seen each other in weeks."

Alexis stops her. "Lizzie, sit down, we'd love to hang out for a little bit." She turns to Ian. "She'd like a latte," she says, smiling, then turning back to Lizzie. "Latte okay?"

Lizzie nods. "Yes, that would be perfect, thank you." She leans toward Alexis. "So Ian seems good," she says. "Did he get back today?"

"No, he got an earlier flight, so he got in early last night." She looks dreamily at Lizzie. "I really missed him. These trips are getting harder the closer we get."

"I'm sure. I know I'd miss Jack if he went away." She looks wistful for a moment. "Wow, come to think of it, we haven't been apart for even one night since we got married. That's crazy."

"Well, consider yourself lucky. Being with an international documentary filmmaker is..."

"Is what?" Ian says, arriving back at the table just then.

Alexis is flustered. "Uh...it's amazing?" she says, trying to gracefully recover.

He raises his eyebrows and looks at Lizzie. "Really? 'Amazing?' Is that what she *really* thinks, Lizzie?" He's on the verge of laughing but is doing his best to keep it in. "I'm not sure that's what I'd say."

"Okay, I'll bite," Alexis says, being a little flirty. "What would you say?"

"I'd say it's a pain in the butt having a partner who's away a lot, often out of touch, distracted, taking calls at all hours because his sources and partners are all over the world. He can be grumpy because of the jet lag when he gets back, and then spends hours and hours in the editing studio ignoring me."

Alexis bursts out laughing and points at Ian. "Yes, and yes! What he said!" And then they kiss, because none of that really matters, because they're crazy in love, and somehow they make it work.

"How's the film coming?" Lizzie asks, taking a sip of her coffee. "Do you have a deadline?"

"I do not have a deadline yet, but the person I'm working with at the U.N. probably does but just hasn't told me for fear of freaking me out," he says. "I think I've shot most of what I need. Now it's a matter of finding the narrative and a cohesive way to tell the story of what's happening to the planet. And to tell it in a way that compels people to actually do something about it, not to give lip service on one hand, while taking money from oil companies with the other."

"But no pressure, right?" Lizzie says, feeling for him. "That's a lot to put on a film. And in turn you," she says. "Having seen your other work I have no doubt it's going to be incredible, but I also can't imagine what it's like to try to pull together all these threads and tell a story that will inform and move people."

"Like you said, no pressure," Ian laughs.

"Oh! Alexis," Lizzie says, quickly pivoting.

"Yes?" Alexis sits bolt upright, and turns to her.

"Did Eric reach out to you about getting in touch with your grandfather?" Lizzie asks. "Apparently he found some relatives at the Cranberry Harbor Cemetery and wanted to talk with him."

"He did! I actually think they were meeting early this morning. Pop was super excited about it," Alexis says.

"Oh good. I'm so grateful that he's willing to talk to Eric. There could be parts of Cranberry Harbor history we don't know much about that he might be able to shine a light on," says Lizzie.

"He was stoked about it. I'm looking forward to learning more about our family myself," Alexis says.

"Yeah, me too," Lizzie says. "I am so happy you introduced me to Eric. He's been such a great addition to the paper. Thank you!"

"My pleasure," Alexis says.

"Well, on that note, I'd better get myself to the office and see what is waiting for me there," Lizzie says, picking up her coffee cup and standing. "Thank you, Ian, for the coffee. I will return the favor next time."

"Happy to do it. Glad to see you. Give my best to Jack," he says. "Tell him we need to work on that baseball team idea. And I want to shoot some more footage about what he's doing at Terra Marique, just for fun."

"Oh, this is the first I'm hearing of baseball, and that would be great to have some film to document what he's done at Terra Marique," Lizzie says. "I will certainly pass that on." She pushes in her chair. "See you two later! Maybe dinner sometime soon? With Ben and Sean too?"

"I'm totally down for that," Alexis says. "I'll reach out to them and set a date."

"Awesome!" Lizzie turns to leave, and then turns back. "So glad you're back safe and sound, Ian," she says.

Lizzie is surprised to find Eric already hard at work when she gets to the paper.

"Hey, I thought you were meeting with Richard Johnson this morning," she says, glancing at the clock. It's only 10:20.

Eric laughs. "Yeah, when he said 'early' I was thinking maybe 9?" he offers, gesturing with his hands. "But no, he meant 7:30, and walking through the cemetery while we talked so he could point out some family gravestones."

"Wow, so you got in an interview and a workout," Lizzie teases. "Very efficient."

"I wouldn't exactly say a 'workout;' he is 87, after all. But it was an amazing time spent with a man who is very interesting, smart, and funny."

"I'm so glad!" Lizzie says, getting herself settled at her side of the partner's desk. "I can't wait to read the story."

"I had no idea that his family used to own Bradford's," he says.

"Wow, I had no idea either!" Lizzie says.

"Mr. Johnson told me that his great grandparents opened a market, the Emporium, now Bradford's, like 150 years ago. They sold everything from food staples like flour and dried fruit to clothes, kerosene for lanterns, and animal feed."

"Wow, I always wondered why there was that huge old barn around the back parking lot. It seemed a little less than sanitary for storing food, but I can see how it would work for horse, chicken and cow feed. That's so interesting. Is the Bradford family in any way connected to the Johnsons?" she asks.

"Yes, apparently someone in the Johnson family, a distant cousin of Richard's, married a Bradford, and eventually their son and daughter took it over after the elder Johnsons had passed, and they changed the name, which is kind of sad. The Emporium is a pretty damn cool name," Eric says.

"Oh, so cool. I'd love to do my grocery shopping at the Emporium. It sounds very fancy and a little whimsical," Lizzie says. "Grocery shopping could use a bit of whimsy for sure."

"And apparently they—the Johnsons—bought goods to sell from several Wampanoag locals, like furs, handmade artwork, clothing," Eric says.

"That's very interesting," Lizzie says, wondering if this is really true; there's so much lore around the early days that isn't. And it's often designed to make the settlers who took so much land from the Wampanoag people look better.

They're both quiet for a minute.

"I always wish Cranberry Harbor was more diverse," she says. "I hope that you've found it to be mostly welcoming?" she posits, unsure of his experience. "I hope you'll find a way to work that into the story as you delve into some of the history of the town."

Eric nods. "Of course, and thank you for the encouragement to relay my experience. It's mostly been good, but there are a few folks around who haven't exactly been welcoming. There aren't a lot of Black folks here, for sure," he says, shrugging.

"I'm really sorry about that, Eric, and I feel awful that I've never really talked to you about it, about how you have been treated here. Talk about clueless—I'm really sorry." She shakes her head.

"Stop, Lizzie, don't beat yourself up. It's been fine, like ninety-percent of the time fine. You have nothing to apologize for, but thank you for saying that, and caring," he says.

"There are so many wonderful things about the Cape, and Cranberry Harbor in particular, but diversity is an area that isn't great, and I'm really glad you're writing about it. We've grown a lot in the last couple of years, in lots of ways. We're the home to a cutting-edge eco-friendly and proactive community. We're actually going to be showing the world, thanks to Ian's film, how we can live better and do better by the planet. So I think it's great to speak to another area where we could do and be better as well."

"I agree 100 percent," Eric says. He takes a deep breath. "If you don't mind, I think I'm going to take my laptop, my notes and myself over to Sea Coast." He starts putting his things in his backpack. "All those years of freelancing and not having an office had an impact on me. I still write better in a busy coffee shop," he says, smiling at her.

"No problem. Write wherever it works best for you," she says. "You're never tethered to this office, that's for sure."

After Eric leaves Lizzie is unsure of what she needs to do next. Being the editor often means having less time to write the kind of stories she wants to write, but right this minute there's nothing pressing and she doesn't know what to do with herself, not having a to-do list a mile long. Eric has his new passion project, and she is feeling a little envious about that.

After metaphorically twiddling her thumbs for 20 minutes—which in this era means scrolling through social media—she decides that she also needs to get out of the office and get a change of scenery.

And where do you go when you don't know what to do with yourself? To visit your husband at his work, of course.

"Well, this is a nice surprise," Jack says, getting up from his chair and coming over to give Lizzie a kiss. "To what do I owe the honor?" He gestures to a comfy chair near his desk and sits down again. "Everything okay?"

"Yeah, everything's fine. I just didn't know what to do with myself, so I..."

Jack laughs, "Ah, you were bored so you came to see me."

Lizzie laughs too. "No, it's not like that. I wanted to come see what was new here, and what was happening. I'm looking to feel inspired, and this seems like a good place to be around inspiring people. I don't feel like I'm doing anything all that important lately."

Jack shakes his head. "You run a very successful weekly newspaper, have tons of subscribers from around the world, you write about a third of the content for that paper, but you don't think you're doing enough in the world? I find that pretty unbelievable. Heck, they wrote a piece about you in the New York Times a few months ago. Do you think it's possible you've set the bar a little too high?" Jack teases.

"I know, it sounds weird. You're right, it's not like I'm not crazy busy, but I like feeling passionate about something. Like when we were fighting to build Terra Marique. I loved fighting the good fight." She pauses. "Wow, do I sound ungrateful? Like it's never enough? Because I don't want to be that person," she says.

"Hardly," Jack reassures her. "You sound like someone who likes a good cause to sink their teeth into. Me? I feel like I have more than enough right here to keep me going for a while."

"I envy that," she says, a little wistful, getting up and sitting on his lap, giving him a big kiss.

"Oh, I get it. You're bored so you came over to my workplace to flirt with me and to try to get me to leave early," he says, smiling at her.

"Nah, I'm just fooling with you." She gets up and heads to the door. "I'm going to go get another caffeine jolt. Maybe that will help."

"Okay, well, remember, some down time isn't necessarily a bad thing," he says.

"I will remember that, but I'm still going to keep looking for my next passion project."

CHAPTER 6

When Lizzie arrives at Sea Coast she is happy to see Sean, Ben, and Ollie, now a very busy two-and-a-half-year-old, sitting at a table by the window.

"Hey, guys! This is a nice surprise!" Lizzie says, giving each of them a hug.

"Wizzie, look at my new toy!" Ollie says, showing her a very cute little stuffed tiger, just the right size for his little hands. Ollie had been taught by Sophie to call her Aunt Wiz, which over time in Ollie's world had become Wizzie. She had grown rather fond of it.

"Oh my gosh, I love him!" she says, crouching down near his chair. "Does he have a name yet?"

Ollie purses his lips, and looks at the ceiling, and then at the tiger again. "Tiger," he says very proudly, hugging the little toy. "Hi Tiger," he says, kissing it over and over.

"It's very nice to meet you, Tiger," Lizzie says, patting its head. She stands up.

"We went to Toy Works first, and Justine was so sweet and gave it to him. It was so kind of her," Ben says. "Please, sit down—I mean, if you have the time."

"I'd love to," she says, plopping down and sighing.

"Long day?" Sean asks.

She shrugs. "Kind of, but not really."

"I know that look. I remember that look from high school, when you'd be cooking up some new project or something to do," says Ben.

Lizzie laughs. "Wow, the people here really have known me for a long time. I can't hide any feeling!" She shrugs again. "I'm looking for something positive for the town to sink my teeth into, you know?"

"Huh, so running a newspaper and being a part of tons of community events isn't quite doing it for you?" Sean asks. "Hey, anytime you want to take care of a toddler, we are very happy to oblige, no charge! You will be so happy to be bored or at loose ends after two hours, you will never say you're looking for something to do again."

Sean and Lizzie laugh.

"Oh, I know, which is why I'm not quite ready to do it." She looks at Ollie, now happily walking Tiger across the empty tables and chairs around them, talking to him, under the very watchful eyes of his dads. "You two are not the people I should complain to, that's for sure."

"It did not sound like complaining," Sean says. "Not at all, more like longing. And I get that, though I don't know the last time I had enough bandwidth to long for anything other than a cup of coffee and a nap," he says, laughing.

"Oh, I cannot begin to imagine the 24/7 existence of parenting a very bright and active toddler. My hat is off to you both. And you run a very successful inn, and you, Sean, somehow manage to be an accomplished artist as well. It's amazing," she says.

"Accomplished might be a bit generous, but thank you," Sean says. "I haven't produced much new work at all since Ollie came into our lives, but I also know that before we know it he'll be in school, and I'll have a lot more time."

"How are things at the Marshview?" Lizzie asks. The Marshview Inn was a gorgeous historic inn at the other end of town that Ben, a chef, and Sean had taken over from Ben's parents, who had very happily retired from innkeeping four years ago.

"Good. We're pretty much booked solid for the season. It's crazy. It seems to happen earlier and earlier each year," Ben says.

"I'm thinking that all the rave reviews have something to do with that, and the fact that you had several celebrities staying there two winters ago when they were shooting that series in Provincetown," Lizzie says.

"That certainly didn't hurt," Sean says.

"Yeah, it's good, don't get me wrong, but I do find myself missing slower times, the off-season being a little more quiet. It's sure not like when we were kids, Lizzie," Ben says.

"Right? Gosh, it used to be Labor Day, the sidewalks rolled up, everyone left, and it was so, so quiet," she says. "I miss it in some ways, in others it's nice to have some more people, but I do miss how I used to know everyone at the post office, or heck, here at Sea Coast! Now I come in and sometimes I don't know anyone. It's very weird."

Ben nods in agreement. "Totally, and we used to know so many of the people coming to the inn, generations of people coming back each year. That's really changed. Along with the attitude, sometimes."

"Oh no, really? Leah was talking about people being impatient here at times. You're finding the same thing?" she asks.

"Oh yeah. Leah too? So it's not just us, Ben," Sean says.

"I don't think so. I don't know, I've come to think that way too many people have forgotten their manners," Lizzie says. "We all spend so much time on our screens that when people are actually interacting with another human they don't know how to behave."

Just then, Lizzie pauses, seeing the very handsome guy from yoga the other night coming in and making a beeline for Leah. She knows she shouldn't stare, but she can't help herself. He's so good looking, and she'd love for Leah to meet someone wonderful. From where she's sitting she can't see anything other than Leah, and smiling, and maybe even blushing. She sees him entering info into his phone, some nodding, maybe some more blushing on Leah's part, and then he's gone, but not before Leah insists on giving him an iced coffee.

As soon as the door has closed behind him and the coast is clear, Lizzie motions for Leah to come over.

"Hey, that was yoga guy, right?" Lizzie asks. "From the other night?"

"Yes, it was Jonathan, or as you know him, 'yoga guy,'" Leah smiles.

"Oh, I know that smile," Ben says. "You like him," he teases her.

"I hardly know him. He's been in here a couple of times, nitro iced coffee, black, and he seems to like the new plant-based breakfast quesadilla," Leah says, smiling slightly.

"Is he new in town? What's he do?" Sean asks, in between helping Ollie navigate his blueberry muffin.

"He's the new assistant coach for the Salty Dogs," she says. "He came here from the Berkshires. He's been working the college baseball circuit for a couple of years and got recruited to come here for the summer." She shrugs. "That's all I've got. Oh, and he's also been a middle and high school math teacher."

"He's very cute," Lizzie says. "We might have to go check out a Cape League game or two. I think Ollie would like that, don't you?" she says to Ben and Sean.

"I think he'd mostly like the Salty Dog mascot, and probably the ice cream truck," Ben says. "We're a few years out from him being a bat boy," he jokes.

"Well, I still think it would be a fun, early evening out. We could bring a picnic. It would be just like a Norman Rockwell painting," she says, smiling at her friends. "And hey, it sounded like from what Ian said, you've all been talking about playing some baseball yourselves. Maybe you can get some tips from watching the best college players in the county."

"I think mostly what we'd get is a big reality check as to how old and out of shape we are," Sean says, laughing. "But hey, I'd love to go to a game."

"We are not old; heck, we're only in our mid-30s," Lizzie says. "We aren't even considered middle-aged yet, though that's right around the corner," she says, feigning dismay at the thought. "Leah, it's up to you. You may not want a flock of your friends showing up to a game where a cute guy you kinda sorta like is coaching. Totally your call."

Leah shakes her head. "If this was a few years ago I might have been mortified, but somehow, now that I'm 28, I don't care so much. To hell with it, let's pick a date and all go to a game. Let's ask Alexis and Ian too, because, hey, why stop at just us? Let's bring a crowd!"

"And someone has to go scout a good spot and put out the

chairs and blankets early in the day," Ben says. "Someone who doesn't own an inn or have a toddler." He looks around the table.

"And doesn't run a coffee shop that opens at 6 am," Leah says.

All eyes turn to Lizzie.

"Fine! I will go and lay out blankets, set up some chairs, and stake a claim on some acreage at Sparrow Park," she says.

"No matter how long I live here I will never stop being amazed how the honor system works at that park for the games," Sean says. "The first summer I was here and saw all the chairs and blankets all over I had to ask Ben about it. I couldn't believe no one just up and moves other people's stuff, or worse, takes things."

"Oh, that would be total sacrilege," Lizzie says. "I've never seen it happen, but I can well imagine Septa Unella yelling, 'Shame!' if anyone did anything like that."

Everyone looks at her quizzically.

"What? No *Game of Thrones* fans here? If you were you would have totally loved that joke," Lizzie says.

Ollie is starting to get antsy, and there's now more muffin on the floor than his plate. Ben scrambles to pick up the pieces. "I'm so sorry, Leah. If you get me a dustpan I'll clean this all up." Ollie is now starting to vocalize his being over time in a high chair.

"Don't worry about it, Ben, I've got it," Leah says. "You have clearly overstayed his interest in being here, go, shoo, have fun!" she teases, grabbing a dustpan and cleaning up the table and floor.

Sean and Ben quickly gather up all their paraphernalia, hoping to avoid a pre-nap meltdown. "Thank you!" they both say. "And let us know about that game. It sounds like fun, especially if we can do it soon, before the season really gets going after the Fourth of July," Ben says, as they quickly hustle themselves and their tired toddler out the door.

"Will do!" Lizzie calls after them.

She and Leah sit down at the now mostly clean table.

"Phew, those guys never stop," Lizzie says, taking a sip of her coffee. "I have such admiration for all they do. Parenting, running the inn, Sean's painting career—I'm exhausted just watching them."

"Yeah, I see people in here all the time with kids, and I don't know how they do it," Leah says. "Of course, there are those who just seem to have given up on any semblance of actually parenting those kids, the ones who torture the other customers while their parents scroll their phones, blissfully unaware that little Matilda or Duncan is running around the place disturbing every human being in here," she says, sounding a bit burned out, and it's not even fully summer yet.

"Wow, does that happen a lot?" Lizzie asks. "I've seen it a few times when I've been here, but is it like a daily occurrence?"

"I wouldn't say daily, but several times a week, for sure," Leah sighs. "I actually had to ask a family to leave last week because their kid was so loud that all the other customers were leaving. Literally, people were walking out the door."

"Whoa, that's crazy. I bet that went over well," Lizzie says.

"Oh, you know it," Leah rolls her eyes and laughs. "I think the final words from the dad were, 'I'm going on Yelp and am going to ruin you!'"

"Wow, grace under pressure," Lizzie jokes. "What is happening to people?" She pauses and looks around Sea Coast. "Have they gotten more obtuse, more clueless? I don't get it. Sean and Ben seem to be finding it too, and I've noticed a weird thing lately…"

"What?" Leah asks.

"How often when I let someone in while I'm driving, they don't do the little 'thank you!' smile and wave, they just barrel in. I can't tell you the number of times I've said out loud in my car, 'You're welcome!'" Lizzie shakes her head. "When I'm walking and crossing the street, I always wave and say thank you when someone stops to let me go."

"People—they're the worst," Leah says and they both laugh.

"They totally are!" Lizzie agrees.

"You know your mom's friend's son? Andrew? The guy I hired who loves making latte art? Thank you, by the way, for that lead..."

"Oh yeah! Is that going well?" Lizzie asks.

"He's awesome. He started working immediately. He's such a hard worker and is so good at it. But the other day someone snapped at him for taking too long, was being really impatient, and it made me so angry, and I could see it hurt Andrew's feelings. I gave the guy a hard stare, and when Andrew proudly handed him his latte with an adorable koala on it, he shut up and walked away," she sighs. "Why can't people just be nice?"

"I don't know, but it seems to be everywhere," Lizzie says. "Given how much we work, Jack and I don't get to travel too much, but a few months ago, when we went to North Carolina for his college roommate's wedding, people in the airports and on the planes we took were so crabby and impatient."

"We need to fix this, Lizzie," Leah jokes with her.

"Hey, if anyone can solve this problem it's us. Two ladies sitting in a coffee shop with all the answers." Lizzie smiles. "Hey, civility has to start somewhere; why not in Cranberry Harbor?"

CHAPTER 7

A sure sign that the summer season is coming on the Cape is the rollout of existing businesses opening back up, along with some new ones as well. Lizzie is surprised to see some signage for a new gelato place on her drive home and thinks how that could be a dangerous temptation to drive by every day. There was always a mixture of feelings as people returned—excitement and anticipation of lots of outdoor music, theaters opening back up, but there was always a little sadness as well. The closeness the local community feels in the off-season tends to get pretty strained with the influx of thousands of people coming to their town.

Living in a resort area isn't the same as a typical small town with a steady population. Cranberry Harbor has about 6,038 year-rounders, at last count. People do come and go. But in June, July and August that number swells to about 20,000. That's a big difference.

Long-time Cranberry Harbor folks know the drill—it's part of the price you pay for living here. The Cape depends on those tourist dollars. It does not mean, however, that they always love it, or even like it. It is an internal battle for many a Cape Codder.

As she drives through town, Lizzie wonders what the overall tone of this summer will be. Will people be coming bringing their best selves, or something else?

When she pulls into her driveway, she's surprised to see her parents carrying a box and a bottle of wine over to her and Jack's house.

"Hey, are you two reverse burglars? Bringing things from your house to others?" she calls out to them after she parks and gets out of the car.

"You caught us," Peter says. "We're slowly getting rid of junk in our house and giving it to you to deal with," he says, laughing. "I think it's a great plan!"

Lizzie laughs. Peering into the box, she can see it's full of very yummy smelling food.

"What's all this about?" she asks, intrigued.

"We were supposed to host our pickleball friends, but at the last minute one couple had to babysit their grandson, and the other couple, Fran and Dave, he badly sprained his ankle, and they're on their way home from the ER," Gabby says. "Anyway, there's a lot more here than we can handle, so we thought we'd share."

Lizzie thinks for a minute. "Hey, we haven't gotten to hang out with Matt, Shannon and Sophie in a while. How about we all have a party? We can do it here, if you like. I'd love to see my annoying little brother and his family," she jokes.

"That's a great idea," Peter says, pulling his phone out of his pocket. He walks toward their yard talking and laughing, and turning back seconds later. "He said they'd love to. They were just thinking about ordering out, and he told me that he knew pickleball was entirely too dangerous and that we should stop playing immediately," he says, laughing and putting his phone back in his pocket.

"And?" Gabby says.

"Oh, they'll be here in about 10 minutes," Peter says, having buried the lede.

"I'll call Jack," Lizzie says, "so he doesn't stop and get something for dinner on his way home."

As they gather around the table at Lizzie and Jack's house, Lizzie is once again struck by how lucky she feels to be able to, at the drop of a hat, have her whole family together.

"Before we know it the summer season is going to be full on,"

Lizzie says. "I'm so glad we were able to do this. Spontaneity is the way to go with all our busy lives. To family, and never being too busy to get together," she says, lifting her wine glass and clinking it with Sophie's glass of milk.

"Oh! Before things get too crazy with summer people and activities, Leah, Sean, Ben, and hopefully Alexis and Ian were talking about going to a Salty Dogs game—you know, bring a picnic and have a fun, early evening?" Lizzie offers. "Any of you interested in joining us?"

"That sounds like a lot of fun," Shannon says. "We're actually having some of the players come to the library next week to talk to the kids about their favorite books when they were growing up. We're also going to have some outdoor games, and story time. They were so amenable about coming. That's not always the case," she says. As the head of children's services at the Cranberry Harbor Library, Shannon had more activities going on there for kids and teens than anyone there has ever had. From yoga to art to pajama parties, there was always something cooking for young people, and yes, literally, they even had cooking classes for kids.

"I want to go watch baseball, Mommy," Sophie says, starting to look a little tired and crawling into Matt's lap with her beloved blankie. "Do we have to go now?"

"No, sweetie, not tonight, but soon," Matt says, hugging her little curled up body.

"Good, because I'm tired," she says, sucking her thumb.

"Yeah, we should probably head home," Shannon says, standing up and starting to gather plates and glasses from the table.

"Please, Shannon, don't worry about it. You all get going. Sophie's so tired. We've got this," Gabby says, taking the dishes from her.

"Okay, but you know, I'm pregnant, not an invalid, but that said, I will milk this for as long as I can to get out of doing things," she teases.

"Right, says the woman who volunteers for absolutely everything," Peter says.

"Not so much lately," she says, gathering up their things. "I'm trying very hard to take it easier, you know, as a precaution."

"That's a very good idea," Gabby says, giving her a hug. "If there's anything more we can be doing to help you, please let me know, okay?"

Matt, now standing, still holding Sophie, shakes his head. "Mom, you and Dad are practically co-parents at this point. I don't think there's any way you could do more. We honestly don't know how we'd get by without you," he says, giving his mom a kiss on the cheek. "Thank you."

"We love doing it, honey," Gabby says. "We can only play so much pickleball, you know," she jokes.

"Speak for yourself. I could play every day," Peter chimes in. "I don't know why, but it's incredibly addictive."

"We still haven't tried it, you know?" Jack says to Lizzie.

"I don't know, isn't there an age limit or something? Aren't we too young?" Lizzie says, laughing. "I thought you needed to show an AARP card at the courts to be granted entrance," she teases.

"Very funny. We'll get you and Jack out there to play some doubles sometime and we'll see how you do," Peter says, teasing right back.

"I'd love that," Jack says. "Oh! Matt? Did you have any interest in playing some baseball? Sean, Ben, Ian and I were talking about starting a Cranberry Harbor team to play some games in the older men's league. Wanna join?"

Matt takes a deep breath. "It will depend on how big a time commitment it is, but if it's not too much time, yeah, that'd be fun. But with the business, suddenly everyone wants solar panels—not that I'm complaining—Sophie, and a new baby on the way..."

"I get it. Yeah, Terra Marique keeps me pretty tied up too, and we don't have any kids." He pats Matt on the shoulder. "I'll keep you looped in. My feeling was the folks involved wanted to keep it pretty loose and easy. Everyone's so busy here in the summer, but we thought it could be fun to have a few games, you know?"

"Definitely! I never get to play ball anymore. It would be fun," Matt says, Sophie squirming while he holds her.

"I'll make sure he gets out to play," Shannon says, joining them at the door. "Thank you, everyone, for such a fun evening and delicious dinner! Love you," she calls as they head out the door.

"Love you!" Sophie yells back to the house as they walk to their car.

Gabby starts cleaning up, with Peter right behind her, and Lizzie stops them.

"You two have done enough. We've got this. As soon as you go we'll clean it all up," she says. "And we will return all your serving dishes to you tomorrow. We know where you live," she says, smiling at her parents. "Really, you go home and put your feet up. We've got this."

"Speak for yourself," Jack says, laughing. "Seriously, Gabby, Peter, you made this night happen; the least we can do is some dishes. Go home and watch the Red Sox. We've got this. And thank you once again," he says, "for feeding us another incredible—and healthy, I might add—meal. I don't know how you do it, Gabby. You should write a cookbook."

Lizzie stops what she's doing. "Oh my God, yeah, Mom, you definitely should! So many people want to eat well, and eat more healthfully, but think it means eating salad seven days a week and never having anything fun. You make eating healthy fun," she says.

Gabby shrugs. "I don't know, you and your dad are the writers. I was a doctor for 35 years. I only write chart notes."

"Do me a favor and at least think about it," Lizzie says. "And Dad and I can help with edits, and as you know, anything you want to learn how to do, like writing a cookbook, you can find a video online to teach you how."

Gabby kisses her daughter and gives her a hug. "I promise I'll think about it," she says. "Love you both."

Lizzie and Jack collapse on the couch as soon as her parents leave.

"How about we refrigerate the leftovers, put the serving dishes in the sink to soak, and deal with the rest of it in the morning?" Jack says.

"Oh my God, it's like you read my mind," Lizzie says, leaning over and hugging him. "I knew there was a reason I married you."

"Great, lazy minds think alike," he says, groaning as he gets off the couch. "They say every pot has a lid, even if it's a dirty pot," he jokes.

Gabby starts cleaning up, while [illegible] around her bed. Lizzie stops her.

"You two have done enough. We've got this. As soon as you can, we'll clean it all up," she says. "And we will return all your serving dishes to you tomorrow. We know where you live," she says, [illegible] at her [illegible]. "Really, you go home and put your feet up. We've got this."

"Thank you so much," Jack says to Lizzie. "Seriously, Gabby, [illegible] you made that [illegible] was [illegible] and [illegible]. [illegible] going and [illegible] and [illegible] ... [illegible] was the [illegible] I [illegible]. I don't know how you do it, Gabby [illegible]."

Lizzie [illegible] she [illegible] [illegible] [illegible] [illegible] [illegible] [illegible] [illegible] [illegible] [illegible] well, and [illegible] [illegible] [illegible] [illegible] [illegible] [illegible] [illegible] [illegible] never [illegible] anyplace [illegible]. "[illegible] [illegible] [illegible]," she says.

Gabby [illegible]. "I don't know [illegible] your [illegible] [illegible] [illegible] [illegible] [illegible] years [illegible] only [illegible] [illegible]."

"Don't [illegible] and [illegible] about it," Lizzie says. "And [illegible] I [illegible] [illegible] [illegible] [illegible] [illegible], [illegible] will want to [illegible] [illegible] [illegible] [illegible] [illegible] [illegible] [illegible] [illegible] [illegible] [illegible] [illegible] to [illegible] you [illegible]."

[illegible] [illegible] [illegible] [illegible] and [illegible] [illegible]. "[illegible] [illegible] [illegible] [illegible] [illegible]. Love you both."

[illegible] [illegible] [illegible] the couch [illegible] [illegible] [illegible] [illegible].

"[illegible] we [illegible] [illegible], [illegible] the [illegible] [illegible] [illegible] [illegible] to [illegible] and deal with the rest of it in the morning," Jack says.

"[illegible] [illegible] [illegible] you [illegible] my mind," [illegible] says, [illegible] over and [illegible] [illegible]. "[illegible] [illegible] [illegible] [illegible] [illegible]."

"[illegible] [illegible] [illegible] [illegible] [illegible] [illegible] [illegible] [illegible]. [illegible] [illegible] [illegible] [illegible]. [illegible] [illegible] [illegible] [illegible] [illegible]. [illegible] even [illegible] [illegible] [illegible], [illegible]."

CHAPTER 8

Somehow all the friends and Lizzie's parents managed to find a game date where they could all meet, just three days later.

As planned, Lizzie went early to place their blankets and beach chairs on the hill next to Sparrow Field, though she was joined by her dad, who insisted on helping.

"Boy, this sure takes me back," Peter says, pausing to look out at the field.

"Yeah?" Lizzie says, straightening out the last blanket. They were taking up a lot of acreage, but there were about 12 of them coming. Ben and Gabby had been busily texting each other, insisting they wanted to take care of the food. The fact that she was relegated to picking up sourdough bread and grapes made Lizzie wonder if her culinary abilities were not so subtly being judged. But ultimately she didn't really mind because she was on deadline and Jack had meetings with investors, so being off the hook for cooking was not a bad thing.

"Yeah, I told you I was a ball boy back in the day, right?" Peter says, still wistfully looking out into the field.

"You've never said too much about it," Lizzie says, now standing next to him.

"I did it for two summers when I was 11 and 12. It was so much fun, and to be that close to these college players, the best of the best

—as a little kid, it was pretty big stuff." He pauses. "A few of the guys I handed bats to went on to the majors. I was so proud of that, like I had something to do with it somehow," he says, smiling at Lizzie.

"You know, here we were talking to Mom about writing a cookbook, and you've got so many stories, as witnessed by the monthly story slam at Tall Tales. Maybe you should think about writing a book, Dad."

Peter shakes his head and brushes off the idea. "Nah," he says.

"You can certainly say no because you don't want to write any more—Lord knows you've written more than your fair share of words in your lifetime—but if you're saying no because you don't think it's interesting, I think you're dead wrong. You have been a witness to so much growth and change in Cranberry Harbor. We need someone to record the history of the town, of our community."

"I'd be lying if I said I'd never thought about it. I have journals full of notes and rough drafts of stories." He pauses again. "You really think people would be interested in the history of this town? In what I've seen?"

"Dad, you started a newspaper here, all by yourself in the 1980s when that was a really crazy thing to do. The Cape had a daily paper, but you had this idea of telling stories of the Lower and Outer Cape in a more personal and in-depth way. And over 40 years later, in the midst of so many independent newspapers being bought up, and many dying, what you started is still living on—thriving, actually. You definitely have a story to tell, not to mention decades of columns you wrote for the paper that would work for a book with a little tweaking," Lizzie insists.

"So you think your mother and I should both be writing books, huh?" he laughs. "You must really think we're playing way too much pickleball."

Lizzie laughs too. "I think pickleball is good for your health, but I also think that you both are integral to this town, and you've got stories. Great stories. The one you told a couple of years ago at the Tall Tales story slam about not only writing the paper, but getting it printed, and then having to deliver it yourself on Christmas Eve is a classic. I'm sure Matt, Shannon, and Jack would agree with me."

He sighs, looking out as the Salty Dogs begin to arrive for their morning practice. "I'll think about it, okay?" he says.

He may be saying he's going to think about it, but Lizzie knows her dad very well, and the smile he's got on his face is clearly evidence of the fire in his belly. Oh, he's going to write that book and she's going to make sure it gets published.

It is a perfect early evening for a game. The summer season hasn't fully hit, so it's mostly locals, and everyone's so happy to be there.

Ben and Gabby have outdone themselves with a spread worthy of a Roman banquet. They have a bit of everything, from tapas to hummus, fruit, tiny burritos, and it's all delicious. Lizzie, of course, makes certain everyone is aware of the sourdough bread she picked up at Bradford's, pointing it out to everyone in her most self-deprecating fashion. Theirs is the blanket and beach chair section to be envied by all those attending the Cranberry Harbor Salty Dogs versus the Chatham Sharks at Sparrow Park.

"We should have known it was the Martin/Cahoon family that everyone has been speaking in hushed tones about. This looks magical!" says Anika Patel, who along with her husband Jay owns Tall Tale Books.

"Please! Jay, Anika, sit down, there's more than enough!" Gabby says, with everyone else concurring.

Anika is shaking her head no, but Jay has already made himself at home next to Jack.

"Jay, we shouldn't impose," Anika says, looking a bit embarrassed.

""Don't be silly. You're going to help save us from having to schlepp all this home after the game, so please, do us a favor and eat!" Peter says. "It's the least we can do for all the times you've hosted us at the bookstore with the story slams, book signings…"

"And don't forget the Booklovers Singles events," Alexis says, smiling at Ian.

Anika relents and sits down. "That's right, you two met, or at least re-met there, didn't you?" she says, accepting a plate and napkin from Gabby, who gestures to her to fill up.

"Where are your kids?" Lizzie asks, surprised to not see them.

"They're both down on the field," Jay says, pointing to their son and daughter in Salty Dogs uniforms. "They're both bat kids this season. We said they could both do it, but only if they worked the same games, and the assistant coach was very understanding about it."

"Oh, that would be Jonathan, right?" Lizzie says, looking at Leah, who's giving her the look of death, or at least the 'don't you dare saying anything about me kind of liking him' look.

"Yeah, he's been so wonderful. He's the one working with the kids. He's so patient and positive We're really happy so far with their experience as part of the team," Anika says.

No sooner have those words left Anika than Jonathan comes sprinting up the hill from the field, eyes right on Leah, which Lizzie can't help but notice.

"Hi," he says, a little winded, looking directly at Leah. Then quickly looking at everyone else, he gives a little wave and says hi. He squats down next to Leah. "So, I was wondering if after the game, maybe, if you're not doing anything, but you probably are, but if you're not..."

Lizzie so wants to help this poor guy out. It's hard enough to ask someone out if they're alone, never mind in front of a whole bunch of her friends, not to mention two parents of kids you're working with.

"I was thinking, um, maybe we could go get some ice cream? Maybe sit on the beach for a little bit, post sunset?" he finally chokes out.

"I'd love that," Leah says. "When the game's over I'll come down to the field."

"Perfect!" he says, an obvious look of relief on his face and in his body language as he springs down the hill and back to the team.

"Go Dogs!" Lizzie calls out, smiling. She elbows Leah.

"What?" she says, both smiling and blushing.

"He's so cute!' Lizzie says, very quietly. "That took a lot of guts asking you out in front of everyone. He must really like you."

Leah waves her off, but then says, "You think so?"

"Uh, totally!" Lizzie says.

"We concur," says Ben, who's just arrived back from the playground with little Ollie.

Lizzie is so happy to see Leah happy. In a community where the median age is 65 it's not easy to be single and in your 20s. Or 30s—heck, even your 40s. Slowly but surely word of Terra Marique was spreading, the tech innovations coming from the work being done there, along with organic farming, local food companies and artists of all types, and it was helping to attract young people there, many of whom had grown up and left the Cape, who hadn't thought it would ever be possible to live here, to think about building a sustainable life in Cranberry Harbor.

They watch the game a little bit, Leah now barely paying attention, until Ryan Woods, a second baseman from North Carolina, launches a ball right out of the park and onto a windshield in the parking lot, and seconds later the crowd's cheers are punctuated by the car's alarm system blaring. A very upset man seated near them begins hurling a string of expletives as he runs to the parking lot, obviously going to check his car.

"He said some bad words, Mama," Sophie says, taking a break from eating her vegan cookie, homemade by Gabby.

"Ah, the sounds of summer," Peter says. "The thwack of the bat hitting the ball, and the crack of a windshield. Poor fella."

By the seventh inning stretch Sophie is starting to fade, and so is Ollie. The folks with the little kids start to pack up.

"It's been wonderful," Ben says. "Thanks so much for including us, but we need to get this guy home."

Lizzie gets up to give Ben and Sean hugs and get a high-five from Ollie.

"Thanks so much for meeting us, guys," she says. "Ben, that hummus and homemade pita bread were incredible. We will be coming by the Marshview for your Sunday brunch sometime very soon."

Ben hugs her back. "We'd love that. I don't want the summer to go by without seeing you and Jack. It does get to be a blur," he says, trying to corral Ollie while Sean gathers their things.

"If you like, just leave your dishes. I can drop them off tomorrow. It will be less stuff to carry now," Jack says. "And besides, I want some more of that hummus, so completely selfish motive," he teases.

"Yeah, finish it up, and no hurry on the dishes," Ben says, literally being pulled by Ollie to go.

"Papa, we have to go before the ice cream truck leaves. Dad promised."

Sean shrugs his shoulders and smiles at Ben as he gives him a look. "Well, I guess we have one stop to make," Ben says. "Love you guys," he calls out as they all walk away.

"I want ice cream too, Mommy," Sophie says. "Please?"

"Darn, I was hoping she didn't hear that," Shannon says, moving to get up.

"Shannon, I'm already up. Can I take you to get some ice cream, Peanut?" Lizzie asks her niece.

"Sure!" she says, skipping over to Lizzie and taking her hand, gently pulling her off the blanket.

"Okay, let's go, sweetie. What are you going to get?" she says, thinking maybe she'll get something herself.

"I want a popsicle, please!" she says, sounding so cute that Lizzie just wants to freeze time.

"That sounds perfect," she says, looking at the choices on the side of the truck. "They have grape, orange, and cherry. Which would you like?"

"Cherry! No, grape! Oh, maybe orange? Choosing is so hard, Aunt Wiz!" she says, looking sad.

"How about since they're double popsicles you can break in half, I get a grape and you get a cherry and we share?" Lizzie says, feeling like the peacemaker of popsicles.

"Great idea, Aunt Wiz!" Sophie says, jumping up and down.

If only every one of life's problems were so easily solved, Lizzie thinks, smiling.

She pays for the popsicles and convinces Sophie to not break them in half until they get back to the blanket, lest a half gets dropped in transit.

Jack was happy to take the cherry half, and Sophie enjoyed having two popsicles now to eat. Even though she was not a particularly big baseball fan, or any sport for that matter, Lizzie loved being there with Jack, and her whole family. Once in a while she missed the energy of Boston, but not often enough to make her think of going back. Moments like these made the slower pace of the news all worth it.

By the end of the game the Salty Dogs had bested the Chatham Sharks 4-2 and remained undefeated so far in the season. It was early in the season still, but bragging rights had been earned, and all of them happily cheered on their home team.

CHAPTER 9

The Fourth of July was only three days away, and Cranberry Harbor was a beehive of activity. Every year Lizzie thought this was the busiest summer ever, but this year she was convinced she was right. She surmised it was partly due to an economy that had folks feeling a bit more flush, along with an article in the Boston Sentinel, her former employer, about the town, about Terra Marique, and what a wonderful small community it was. Though today, as Lizzie navigates Main Street on foot, dodging drivers who weren't really paying attention, the town isn't feeling so small.

Lizzie is also aware of the energy she was feeling around town. It didn't feel happy, and relaxed, it felt frantic and annoyed. There were signs at all the crosswalks that drivers were supposed to stop and let pedestrians cross, and they mostly did but, it appeared more often than not, begrudgingly.

On this day, she was walking from the Gazette offices to Sea Coast to get a coffee when a person, distracted by their phone, almost hit her as she was crossing the previously empty street, until they'd come speeding along. The person then proceeds to yell at her for being in the street. She shakes her head in disbelief, resists giving an angry, international hand gesture, and takes note of the out-of-state license plate as it speeds off.

When she walks into Sea Coast, Eric and Alexis are sitting and talking, and she plops herself down with a thud of annoyance and a loud, "Ugh!".

"Whoa, you're sure coming in hot, what's up?' Alexis asks, wide-eyed. "Bad day?"

"My day was going great until this, this jerk almost hit me as I was crossing the street, and then she yelled at me! Me, the person she almost nailed with her car. I don't know, if this is what the summer is going to be like, I'm not sure I'm up for it." She lets out a big sigh.

"Wow, I'm really glad you're okay," Eric says. "Let me get you something. Coffee? Tea? Baseball bat?" He smiles at her.

Lizzie laughs. "Could have used that bat about five minutes ago," she says. "Maybe from now on I'll walk with one and whack cars that don't stop. Maybe the message will get out: 'don't stop for pedestrians, and you could end up with a dented bumper.'"

"Seriously, what can I get you?" Eric asks, standing up.

"Really, you don't have to get me a thing, Eric." She starts to get up, but he shakes his head.

"Lizzie, you buy me coffee all the time; let me return the favor. It will make me feel better," he says. "And you need to sit and chill for a bit."

"Okay, I won't fight you," she says, glancing over at the menu on the wall. "I'm thinking some iced chamomile tea, one squeeze of honey, and, hmm, I've definitely earned a cookie. A raisin oatmeal? Thank you!'

When Eric leaves, Alexis leans forward, shaking her head. "What the heck? People are so angry, so impatient," she says. "I was here the other day and watched a grown man lose it over getting rainbow sprinkles on his ice cream instead of chocolate." She shakes her head again. "I wanted to go up to him and say, 'Dude, if this is the worst thing that happens to you today you are doing very well.'"

"Seriously, everyone needs to turn it down a notch," Lizzie says, leaning forward on her elbows and chin in her hands. "It's not even the Fourth yet. We don't usually see this much bad energy until August at least."

"I hear you. This whole place needs to take a chill pill," Alexis says. "We need to make Cranberry Harbor a no-anger zone."

Lizzie sits bolt upright. "Oh my gosh, Cranberry Harbor can become a 'Kindness Zone,'" she says, her mind suddenly going a mile a minute.

Alexis knows her best friend well enough to just sit back and let her brain do its thing, so she just smiles and nods.

"Think of it—we can have banners and signs, and every local business could participate. We might even be able to get some national press," she says. "Wow, this could be really cool."

Eric returns, tea and cookie in hand. "Okay," he says, noticing the energy shift at the table. "Clearly I missed something. What could be really cool?" he asks, returning to his own coffee and muffin.

"Lizzie wants to make Cranberry Harbor a 'Kindness Zone,'" Alexis says using air quotes. "I like the idea, I'm just not sure how we could make it happen."

The table is quiet for a moment or two.

"I know!" Lizzie blurts out. "There's a special Town Meeting on Tuesday. I say let's talk to the Selectboard and see if we could be given a few minutes to speak, and that's like what, four days away? That's plenty of time to formulate a plan to present to the town, right?"

Eric and Alexis don't want to be buzzkillers, but as they look at each other they're not as sure what they could actually do, or how they'd make anything happen.

"Um, I love the idea, I'm just not sure what that looks like," Eric says, wanting to be supportive. "How do we get to people who are just visiting and aren't invested in the town the way the locals are?"

"Okay, good point, but, maybe, just maybe, people will want to come visit the place where everyone is kind, and good behavior is, I don't know, maybe rewarded in some way?" Lizzie offers. " I know being kind should be its own reward, but to kick it off, it might not hurt to incentivize it?"

"Huh, interesting, like having a running log somehow of random acts of kindness?" Alexis says. "Oh! Maybe on the town's social media have people posting about when they witness random acts of kindness?"

"I like that, a lot. It's getting people not to just perform acts of kindness, but to be on the lookout for them," Lizzie says.

"I love it—things like when a lost dog is reunited with its family," says Eric.

Lizzie's quiet for a minute. "Is this a dumb, or super Pollyanna-ish idea?" she says, starting to doubt herself.

"Yes, it's very Pollyanna-ish, in the best possible way. I think it will take a little planning, and getting people on board, but I can see this town totally getting into it," Alexis says. "Listening to all our friends who own businesses around here, I think they'd love to have a message of being kinder, more patient and just taking it down a notch."

"I agree," Eric says. "And we have a platform with the paper to be able to present it in a really positive, fun way, but also as something we all need. The world is a really challenging place a lot of the time, and how nice it would be to have a place to go where it's expected that you will be a steward of kindness. I think it could really catch on."

Lizzie nods, thinking. "And maybe it could culminate with a philanthropic gift of some sort at the end of the season. Being kind for kindness's sake is good, but if everyone could see something like a donation to a community organization, or Habitat for Humanity—something like that—it might help motivate people. We could have a big party on the town green and hand over a check to whatever organization has been chosen."

"I'm always all-in for a town party," Alexis says. She takes out her tablet. "Okay, if we're going to bring this to Town Meeting next week we have some work to do."

"I don't want to give either one of you a whole bunch more to do. I know you're both incredibly busy," Lizzie says. "The last thing you need is me giving you a lot of homework."

"No worries, Lizzie," Eric says. "Cranberry Harbor is really my home now, and thanks to what you two and Jack created with Terra Marique, I have a permanent home, and I want to give back in any way I can to this community. And I think it could be really fun. Except for the grumpy folks who will want to tell us we can't tell them how to act," he says, laughing.

"Oh yeah, be prepared for some pushback," Alexis says, smiling. "But we can handle a few grumps, right?"

"Wow, you two are the best. You really don't think I'm crazy?" Lizzie says.

"Oh, we didn't say that," Eric says, laughing. "It's totally crazy, but most innovative, impactful ideas are. Nothing changes without envelope-pushers."

Lizzie is excited. She hasn't felt this excited about a project in a while. Cranberry Harbor and the people in it mean everything to her, and she's not liking the shift she's been seeing in the way people are treating each other.

"Wow," she says. "We're really doing this." She points to Alexis's tablet. "Put me down for contacting the Chair of the Selectboard. I know Connie; she does yoga with us sometimes. I bet she'd be open to at least talking about this."

"Okay," Alexis says, typing briskly.

Leah walks over from behind the counter, intrigued by the intense work that seems to be happening at table five.

"You three look very energized about something," she says, "Can I ask what's got you all so jazzed, and can I get in on it?"

"You tell her, Lizzie, it was your idea," Alexis says, typing some more.

Lizzie takes a deep breath, "So you know how we've been talking about how impatient, grumpy, and downright rude some visitors—and locals, I'm sure, to be fair—have been?"

Leah nods and rolls her eyes. "Heck yes, it's not even the Fourth yet and people are coming in here agitated and disappointed before we even say hello."

"Right?" Lizzie says. "We're thinking about starting a kindness initiative, making Cranberry Harbor a 'kindness zone.' We'll have banners and signs and various reminders around town that unkindness won't be tolerated and that this is a place where people only beep their horn if an accident is about to happen, if there's a mistake with your coffee order you *kindly* ask for something else, you hold the door for others, say please and thank you, wave thank you when someone lets you in while driving, or crossing the street...."

"Stop texting and driving so you see those people crossing the street," Eric offers, circling back to the origin of this whole idea.

"Lizzie almost got nailed walking here by a car driven by someone looking at their phone."

"Wow, first, I'm really sorry that happened, and am glad you're okay," Leah says, putting her hand on Lizzie's arm, "and double wow, I think this is such a cool idea! I love it." She sits back and looks around the cafe. "I can totally see putting up signs and banners. Oh! And buttons! We can all wear *Cranberry Harbor is a Kindness Zone: Be Kind* buttons. Oh! And have a really cute bumblebee, you know, 'Bee Kind' on it! Bee kind could maybe be the motto and logo?"

"Yeah! I love it, Leah," Lizzie says. "I'm so glad you don't think it's a silly idea!"

"Silly? No way, this town needs a kindness intervention asap!" she says. She glances over to the counter and the line that's getting longer. "I'd better get back to work," she says, standing up. "Let me know what I can do. I think the company that prints our t-shirts also makes buttons. I'll look into it and get back to you."

"Thank you, Leah," they all say in unison as she walks away.

"Okay, so what do you want me to do?" Eric asks.

"Hmm, is there something that's coming to mind for you that you'd like to work on?" Lizzie asks, wanting everyone to feel some agency in choosing what they're doing.

"I'm not sure if this fits in or not, but when I went to the doctor a couple of months ago for a checkup I noticed there was a woman who was all alone, and she looked so scared, and I felt so bad that she didn't have anyone there with her. I wondered if, for people who are alone, no family, or friends nearby, if there could be volunteers who would drive people to appointments, wait with them, distract them a bit, maybe, and if the patient wanted it, even go in with them and take notes for them. It can be so stressful. I know I always worry I'm missing half of what they're telling me, and I'm a young guy, with thankfully nothing serious going on," said Eric.

"That's an interesting thought," Lizzie says. "You know who would be perfect to ask about this?"

"Your mom," both Alexis and Eric say at the same time.

"Yes! As a retired doctor she'd know about the appropriateness of something like that, but you're so right, it can be so hard sitting in a doctor's waiting room all alone." She writes herself a note to call her mom when they're done and ask her what she thinks.

"I think this is a good start," Alexis says. "After you contact Connie about bringing this up at Town Meeting let us know, and we can meet up again. And in the meantime, I'm sure in our everyday lives we're going to encounter situations that will give us more ideas and more places to spread kindness."

"Oh! The library!" Lizzie suddenly calls out. "I bet Shannon would love to do some kindness projects with the kids, and read books about being kind. I'll call her."

As they all begin packing up their papers, tablets and computers they are startled to hear a man at the counter raising his voice at Leah.

"I called in that order almost an hour ago, and it's not ready?" he fumes. "Must be nice to run a business so casually," he says, sarcastically.

Leah, holding a piece of paper, says, reading it, "Actually, you called in an order only 14 minutes ago, and the specialty coffee orders you placed take some time so we told you the order would be ready in a half hour. It hasn't been a half hour." The guy doesn't say anything.

Eric, Lizzie and Alexis look on from their table at Leah's gracious yet brutal calling out of this guy's rudeness. Leah looks over to them and gives a wink.

Leah turns to take the large order, all placed in a carryout box, from the barista and pushes it across the counter to him.

"There you go, sir," she says, and glances at her watch. "In just 20 minutes we have," she says, reading the order, "24 coffees, including four decaf, two oat milk lattes, 3 soy lattes, 2 almond milk lattes, 3 espressos and 10 regular coffees with creams and sugars on the side for anyone who wants them." She pushes the box over to him. "And there are two dozen fresh-out-of-the-oven cookies on us, because, well, that's how *we* do business." And then she smiles.

The man doesn't apologize, doesn't take out his wallet for a tip, nothing, but nonetheless, Leah definitely won that round. As soon as he's out the door Lizzie, Alexis and Eric start clapping, causing everyone in the place to turn. Leah laughs and takes a bow.

"Hey, deflate them with kindness," Leah says from behind the counter, giving them a smile and a shrug.

"I like that, Leah. I may steal it," Lizzie says. "You are totally my hero. I would never have been so patient or kind. I would have gladly shown him the door."

"Nah, then he wins, I like being true to who I want to be and not letting someone like that ruin my day or who I want to be," Leah says.

"I feel like I just watched a master class in grace," Eric says, putting his messenger bag over his shoulder. "Kudos to you, ma'am."

"Okay, we are out of here," Alexis says. "To be continued?"

"Yes," Lizzie says. "And I think we just had a first-hand lesson on why this is so important."

"For sure," Alexis says, holding the door for someone coming in, who does not say thank you. They all look at each other and laugh.

"We've got our work cut out for us, that's for sure," says Eric.

"We sure do," Lizzie says, shaking her head. "We sure do."

CHAPTER 10

Lizzie couldn't wait to talk to Jack about spreading kindness in Cranberry Harbor, and when he comes in the door he hardly knows what hit him.

"...And we're going to promote it in the paper. I already have some ideas for columns I want to write, and I'm sure Eric will write some too," she says as she paces around the living room. "Oh! And Leah is going to have buttons made that say, 'Bee Kind,' with you know, a bee on them, and, and," she pauses and takes a breath. "And yeah, I have to get the Selectboard to support the idea, but that shouldn't be hard, right?" she says, smiling so hard that Jack feels like he can't be anything but 100 percent on board.

"Wow! You've sure been busy," he says, feeling a little overwhelmed at the end of a long day at Terra Marique, and taken a little aback by Lizzie's energy. He's also had lots of experience dealing with the red tape of Cranberry Harbor and knows that while it's a wonderful place, the wheels of change can move not just slowly, but glacially. When he was trying to get the town behind letting him build Terra Marique he experienced it firsthand. But the last thing he wants to do is rain on Lizzie's kindness parade, so he rallies. "What can I do?"

"Really? You really want to help?" she asks.

"Of course I do," he says, putting his arms around her in a big hug.

"You looked a little freaked out. I didn't mean to overwhelm you," she says. "I just got so excited at the thought of doing something that could make Cranberry Harbor a kinder place to visit and live, and maybe make things better for all the people who work so hard all summer. I don't want anyone spending their summer working hard and getting snapped at by grumpy people."

"Or almost getting run over by angry, distracted drivers," Jack says, squeezing her more tightly. "I'd like to have a word or two with that driver."

"And I can only imagine those words," Lizzie jokes.

"Whatever do you mean? I am always the epitome of decorum and patience," he says, smiling at her.

"Uh huh," she says, taking his hand and leading him to the couch. "Yeah, I know you too well to believe that," she says, kissing him.

""Ah, now you're resorting to using your wiles to get me to do something. What do you need me to do? Spill it, honey," he says.

"Fine. I was thinking Terra Marique, and all the amazing creative people there, would be a perfect place to be a bit of a hub for the kindness project, maybe?" Lizzie says, looking very unsure of what she's asking for, and tipping toward panic.

"Okay," Jack says, seeing Lizzie is starting to spin. "Hmm, well, you're right that we've sure got our share of creative and generous people there. I'm sure when they get wind of this plan they're going to want to get involved. Maybe a good first step is actually asking people how they'd like to help? Ask for ideas of how to spread kindness, and how they'd like to help. I think people are much more excited to help when they have a stake in it, right?"

"Very true, people get much more excited when they feel like they're really a part of something," she pauses. "I think I need to talk to people around town so I don't just seem like I'm steamrolling everyone into something I'm planning. That doesn't land like the most kind thing, does it?"

Jack laughs a little. "As always, you're very well intentioned, and everyone would certainly know that. But it's true, I think if you make this something that everyone feels a part of they will be much more apt to get excited about it and be committed."

"You're so right," she says, slowing herself down a little and bringing herself back down to Earth a bit. "So overall, you think it's a good idea?"

"I do! And I love the idea of getting all the businesses involved, because if people are being kinder and more generous it's a total win/win for everyone." Then he stops.

"I know that look. What are you thinking?" she asks, smiling at him.

"Well, I was just thinking that maybe some of the food businesses that operate out of Terra Marique would be willing to coordinate their offerings and donate meals to people who could use them. You know, maybe some older folks, or people who've been sick. We could get an idea of who could benefit from a kind of local Meals on Wheels operation. All the folks working out of our kitchens are great people who I know would like to help."

"That would be amazing, honey! I love that!" She throws her arms around him. "Thank you for being on-board with this." She curls up and snuggles into him. "You are totally the best husband anyone could ever want, you know that? Like really, on a scale of 1 to 10, you're an 11."

Jack turns and looks at her skeptically. "You want something else, don't you?" he asks, smiling at her.

"Whatever do you mean? Can't a woman just appreciate her husband without it being suspect?" she asks,

"Ah, I know what it is. You want me to make dinner—that's it, right?" he teases, pushing her back on the couch, kissing her, and they both laugh.

"Yes!"

"You know that I am a man of this century, right? That I don't expect you to work fulltime and do all the home stuff too. You do know this?" Jack asks.

"Of course I know that. I wouldn't have married you if you were some throwback guy from the 1950s. You probably make dinner more than I do," she says.

"I'm betting your mom makes dinner more than the both of us," Jack says, getting up off the couch. "I will go and assess the situation in the fridge and see what we have to fashion something edible."

"I looked earlier, hence my punting it to you," Lizzie says. "The proverbial cupboards and fridge are quite bare," she says, getting up off the couch as well. "I was so excited about the kindness project I forgot all about practical things like...food!" she jokes. "We could order some takeout, maybe some bibimbap from Whistle Pig Korean? And some of those delicious hoduk hand pies for dessert?'

"I was thinking of something we could do here to use up some of the odds and ends we've got, but now, thank you very much, you've got me thinking that sounds awful and that I want Korean. Thanks, Lizzie," he teases, pulling out his cell phone to call in an order.

"You will be very happy I suggested that," she says, turning on her heels and walking back into the living room. "I'm so nice, I'll even go and pick it up," she says, slipping on her shoes.

"It will be ready in 20 minutes," he says, walking over and putting his shoes on too. "Why don't we both go and have a picnic at the beach?"

"I love that idea. Yeah, let's do that," she says, grabbing her purse and keys. "And it's on me," she says.

"Well, since we're married, and have joint accounts..." Jack says as they walk out the door.

"Shhh, let me pretend I'm being very generous," she says, walking to her car.

"Fine," he agrees, getting in and fastening his seatbelt. "Wow! Thanks, that's so thoughtful of you! And for driving too!" he says, playing along.

As Lizzie starts driving she pats him on the knee. "Happy to treat you; you're a sweet guy." They both laugh.

They arrive at Whistle Pig in about 10 minutes and both go in. They love the owners, Jin Park and her husband, Ethan Miller, a couple in their 40s who opened the restaurant about 15 years ago, after they'd both fallen in love with the Cape. Jin had grown up outside of Boston, and Ethan was from New Jersey. Lizzie and Jack liked them so much, and they were both very involved in town events and issues.

Lizzie and Jack notice as soon as they walk in that something feels off, and as they approach the counter, both Jin and Ethan look irritated, which is not at all the norm.

"What's going on? Everything alright?" Jack asks, worried they'd been robbed, or hurt.

Jin sighs and shakes her head. "It's okay, no big deal; it's just someone came in to pick up an order, and he had to wait for a minute or two for it to be ready, and he was just not very nice," she says.

"I'm so sorry. Sadly, it seems to be going around," Lizzie says, getting angry herself seeing her friend upset.

Jin shakes her head. "I just can't believe how pissy people get over something as silly as picking up food. I just get frustrated and wonder if it's worth it sometimes. Like maybe I'd rather just make art, which was my original life plan," she says. "Being alone in a studio and not having to deal with grumpy customers sounds kind of nice."

"I am so sorry that happened to you, Jin," Lizzie says, wanting to track that man down and let him have it. "He wasn't local, was he?" she asks.

"No, he was a tourist. I saw an out of state license plate as he drove away," says Ethan. "Anyway, enough about that; I don't want to give him any power to ruin our evening." He turns and takes two bags off the counter behind him. "Here you go," he says, handing them to Jack.

"If it's any consolation, Lizzie is starting a kindness project in town, making Cranberry Harbor a 'kindness zone,'" Jack says, using air quotes.

"I love that!" Jin says. "Let us know what we can do. I'd love to help!"

"Can we make it legally binding? You know, like if someone comes in all huffy we can make a citizen's arrest?" Ethan jokes. "Punishment could be having to work for two days at the establishment where you had an attitude."

They all have a good laugh about that. The idea of a huffy customer having to smile and be polite to other grumpy customers feels very satisfying to all of them.

It hits Lizzie that this kindness project isn't just some silly idea. Dealing with people who are less than kind, or downright mean, like the man Leah said was going to leave a terrible review online, really impacts people who own businesses and the workers, and really affects the morale of individual businesses and the town.

"Please let both or either of us know if anyone else gives you a hard time," Jack says. "You are our friends and beloved members of the community. We want to back you in any way we can, okay? We care about you both."

Both Jin and Ethan smile. "Thanks, guys," Ethan says. "You're the best. And I mean it, let us know about the kindness project. We definitely want to be a part of it."

"Will do," Lizzie says.

"Unfortunately, with summer coming, we need to remember that not everyone is going to be nice, and be prepared for it, and not be shocked when it happens," Jack says.

"Yeah, but no one should have to accept being disrespected, no one," Lizzie says. "We're bringing some things up at Town Meeting next week. Hopefully, they will pass. I'll keep you looped in."

"Thanks, now go and enjoy your food and your night!" Jin says, smiling as they leave.

Lizzie and Jack put their seatbelts on in silence, both a little sad about how it's not even the Fourth of July yet and the summer is looking less-than-joyful.

"I think this idea of mine is a whole lot bigger than I thought. The impoliteness, the selfishness is even more pervasive than I thought, " Lizzie says.

"Ideas are like that, aren't they? Nothing is ever as simple as it might seem at the outset," Jack says, putting the car in reverse.

"You just said a mouthful there, honey," Lizzie says, looking out the window as they drive to the beach. "We've got a lot of work to do to make Cranberry Harbor kinder for everyone."

CHAPTER 11

When Lizzie and Jack arrived at Sea Meadow beach, well before sunset, they were surprised to see Leah and Jonathan there as well. It appeared great minds think alike, though they had a selection of Sea Coast paninis and iced coffees. Lizzie was very happy to see Leah having some fun, and also wanted to make sure to not intrude on their date, so after a brief exchange, she and Jack walked on, planning on choosing a spot far away from them, but then the pair called after them, asking them to join them.

Now out of earshot, Lizzie stops walking and looks at Jack. "What do you think? Should we join them, or say no thanks?"

"I'm good either way," Jack says. "I don't want to wreck their date, but they're inviting us. But I also thought it would be nice to just hang with you, too. We could say rain check, though I have kind of wanted to talk baseball with Jonathan."

"Okay, come on," Lizzie says, turning around and walking back. "Let's join them. They wouldn't have asked if they didn't want us to, so let's go talk baseball," she says, teasing him.

Jack laughs. "We don't *have* to talk baseball, and I don't want to bug him, so don't bring it up unless he does," he says, catching up with her.

"I make no promises," she says, giving him a look he knows all too well.

"I know you. You're totally going to out me as a baseball nerd, aren't you?" he says, laughing. "I don't care, I am a nerd and I don't care who knows."

"Hey guys!" Lizzie says, as they arrive back at Leah and Jonathan's beach picnic site. "Are you sure we're not crashing your date? We don't want to be third, and well, fourth wheels here."

"No, not at all," Leah says, moving some of their things around to make room.

"Oh, we have a blanket, you don't have to rearrange all your stuff, " Jack says, unfurling their blue plaid beach blanket.

"How have the bugs been?" Lizzie asks, sitting down, and settling in. "Some nights those noseeums are such jerks, not to mention the greenheads."

"So far so good," Leah says. "But I also have some natural bug spray I bought at the farmer's market if you want to use some."

"Thank you, I may take you up on it if they start making a meal out of me," Lizzie says, turning to Jack. "So Jonathan, Jack loves baseball and has been trying to get some guys together to play a few games—not a formal league or anything; they're all too busy to commit to that—but I wondered what we would have to do to maybe use the Sparrow Park field when the team has an away game? Do they even let that happen?"

"Yeah, for sure, they'd definitely let you guys use it," Jonathan says. "The high school team uses it sometimes, so you'd just have to clear it with their coach. I can help you with that. I really wish I could join you. I'd love to hang out with some local guys," he says, looking at Leah.

"Need a break from college kids?" Lizzie asks, as she opens up her bibimbap.

Jonathan and Leah both laugh.

"Yeah, I was just saying to Leah that I'm only maybe ten years older or less than a lot of these guys, but sometimes it feels like a very big difference," he says, laughing and shaking his head.

"There's a very big difference between 18 and 28," Jack says. "A lot happens in those ten years to grow you up," he says, looking quizzically at Lizzie. "Not sure if that's proper grammar," he laughs.

"I'm not sure either, but I like it. I feel like a lot has happened to 'grow me up' in the last few years," Lizzie says, smiling.

"Me too," says Leah. "Nothing like running a business to smack the youth right out of you."

They all laugh at that.

"I may only be in my mid-thirties, but I swear, some days I feel a whole lot older," Jack says.

"Being a responsible adult really can take the fun right out of life, that's for sure," Lizzie says.

"I think I was born old," Jonathan says. "I like the idea of owning a house, having a dog, all the things that tie you to one place. I've spent the last five years moving from town to town, job to job, so being in one place and having one, maybe two jobs at the most, sounds very good to me."

"Where did you grow up?" Lizzie asks, very much enjoying her delicious Korean food.

"Ohio," he says. "A small town outside Cleveland. But I've been in New England for a while. I went to Boston College and have been working the college baseball circuit at various schools around Massachusetts, Vermont and New Hampshire, and doing some teaching along the way."

"Have you figured out, with all these moves, where you'd like to settle?" Lizzie asks, suddenly feeling like a mom asking what a boy's intentions with her daughter are.

Jonathan looks down at his plate and moves his food around a little with his bamboo fork. "I'm kind of liking it here," he says. "The people are really nice, it's obviously beautiful," he says, looking out at the bay as the tide is coming in. "The Cape has a lot going for it." Lizzie swears she can see him blushing a bit.

"Yeah, but maybe before you commit you should spend a winter here and see what you think, right guys?" Leah says, to Lizzie and Jack.

"Yeah, Cape Cod winters can be a little…" Jack is searching for the right word when Lizzie interjects.

"Bleak?" she says. "But what it lacks in sunshine it makes up for in bone-chilling dampness," she teases.

"Wow, do you two work for the Cape Cod Chamber of Commerce? Because you really know how to sell this place," Jonathan says, smiling.

"I've tried telling him what it's like," Leah says, "but I think he thinks I'm exaggerating."

"Sadly, thanks to climate change it is a little warmer than it used to be," says Lizzie. "But I will be the optimistic voice here, and say…"

"Finally! Something positive!" Jonathan says enthusiastically.

"There's a sense of community that really happens after the summer people leave and the place is once again mostly locals. It's the time of year when people aren't so flat-out busy, the places that stay open aren't as crowded, and you know most of the people when you go to Bradford's to grocery shop, or stop in at Sea Coast," she says, smiling and gesturing to Leah, "and you feel, I don't know," she stops for a moment, thinking, "you feel safe, like people have got you, and it's a wonderful warm and cozy feeling."

"Well, now I think the Chamber totally has to hire you to write their next brochure," Jack says, leaning over and putting his arm around Lizzie, giving her a hug.

"Aw shucks," she says, waving him off. "I know it sounds schmaltzy, but after living in Boston for several years, and sure, making friends and having a bit of a community, it felt really good to come back here. To come home. And of course I know it's different for me because I grew up here and do have my family, but I think if you get involved in some local groups, make an effort to join in, you can find community and friends here. I wasn't ever able to recreate that in Boston, and that may be just me, but I wouldn't trade being in the city again for anything. Though a trip to someplace warm and sunny in February would be a very nice thing."

"From what I've seen it's not easy to find a place to live and make a living here, though," Jonathan says. "Real estate prices are crazy."

"They are, which is why we created Terra Marique," Jack says. "And I realize how that sounded like a totally cheesy intro to an infomercial," he laughs. "But seriously, it has made a big difference. We do have places, small houses, little bit bigger houses, and apartments, so if you ever decide to seriously look into moving here, just let me know. I will help you out for sure."

"Wow, that's good to know, thanks so much," Jonathan says. "So what's this about wanting to play some baseball?" he says, ready to move on to another topic.

"Please, Jonathan, he needs to find something to do other than work, even if it's only once in a while," Lizzie says.

"Oh, like you don't work, what? Sixty hours a week?" Jack counters.

"Hey, I do yoga at least," Lizzie rebuts.

"I can vouch for that," Leah says, "since I go too."

"Me too," Jonathan says. "I'd never done it until this summer, and the PT person on the team suggested it for my hip flexor, and it's really helped. And it's helped slow me down a little bit. You should try it, man," he says to Jack.

Jack scrunches up his face. "Yeah, it's never been my thing. I'm more into running and biking."

"Cool, we'll have to bike sometime," Jonathan says.

"I'd like that. I can show you the best trails in the state park," Jack says.

Leah stands up. "I'm going to run to the bathrooms, be right back," she says.

"Hold on, I'll join you," Lizzie says, also getting up.

The bathrooms are a little bit of a hike from where they're sitting, so they have a few minutes to chat.

"So, it sounds like Jonathan is pretty smitten...you know, with the Cape," Lizzie says, elbowing Leah.

"Ah, so that's why you wanted to come. You don't have to pee, you just wanted the scoop," she teases back.

"Oh no, I have to pee like crazy," Lizzie says, "but I did find it interesting that he seems to have fallen so hard for the Cape, but something tells me it's more than this sandbar that he's fallen for."

They reach the bathhouse, and Leah holds the door for Lizzie. There's no line and they keep talking as they go into neighboring stalls.

"I guess you're right," Leah says through the wall. "You really think he wants to stay because of me?"

"Heck yes," Lizzie says, standing up, flushing and heading for the sinks, where Leah joins her as they both wash their hands. "Leah, a man doesn't talk about moving to an entirely new place unless he's got a reason. And I don't think the reason is because of how much he loves the Salty Dogs."

They dry their hands, head outside and begin walking back to the blanket.

"It's just, I don't know, I've been single for a while now, and I don't even know how to read the signals, and whether to really let someone in," Leah says. "Sometimes it just seems simpler to be alone, you know? No disappointment, no annoyance."

"I get it. When I was in Boston it seemed a lot easier to be single. I kept meeting people who weren't a good fit, and when I came back here again and ran into Jack, I was convinced I really didn't want to risk getting hurt again. And I was positive he was not the person for me. And, well," Lizzie says, looking at Leah, and then looking over at Jack as they reach the guys, "look how it turned out." She leans over and says to Leah before they sit down, "I'm not saying you're not complete without a guy, or that you have to be with someone, I'm just saying stay open to what happens."

Leah smiles and nods as they both sit down. "So, what did we miss?" she says.

"You missed the part where we decided that after sunset we should all go and get some ice cream," Jonathan says.

"Sounds perfect," both Lizzie and Leah say, looking at each other and smiling.

CHAPTER 12

The next morning, while still in her jammies and snuggled on the couch, coffee at hand, Lizzie texted Alexis and Eric to find a time to meet up to discuss next steps for the Kindness Project. She was also following up on her email to Connie, the chair of the Cranberry Harbor selectboard. Nothing gets done in this town without the go-ahead and blessing of the selectboard. Thankfully, Connie had also been Lizzie's mom's receptionist and right-hand person in her medical practice for years. She was as important as Dr. Gabby Martin was to their patients, and Lizzie had known her since she was about six-years-old. Hopefully those warm and fuzzy memories would get her a spot on her calendar.

"Hey, you're sure up and at 'em this morning," Jack says, rubbing his eyes and walking like a zombie to the couch to give her a kiss on the head. Lizzie laughs at the sight.

"You certainly look sleepy. You should have stayed in bed a bit longer," she says to him as he stumbles toward the kitchen. "There's coffee," she calls, as he emerges from the kitchen, mug in hand.

"I can't stay in bed, unfortunately, even though I was wide awake from about 1:30 until 5. I hope I didn't disturb you, though you seemed out for the count," he says, yawning.

"You stressed about something?" she asks, putting her laptop and phone on the coffee table. "Everything okay at Terra Marique?"

"Yeah," he says, stretching, then taking a large sip of coffee. "Ian wants to come to do some interviews. He's getting to the end of his film, so I want to make sure everything looks good, that we're presented in the best light, and there's some deadlines for grants from some of our backers that are dogging me."

"Do you need to hire more help? Maybe it's all too much for just you and Alexis? I know her Master's was in community development type stuff, but you've both seen your jobs evolve and take twists and turns over the last couple of years. Is it time to bring someone else in to help carry the load?"

"I'm not sure. It may be. I've got a Zoom meeting later with one of the VC's, and she could be a good person to bounce ideas off of. I don't really know her yet—Amanda something..." he says.

Lizzie hates seeing him look worried and wishes she could help him, but running an environmentally based housing, jobs, art, business and research nonprofit is not exactly in her wheelhouse, so she feels pretty useless. If he needs a story written about something, she's the right person, but running a nonprofit? Not so much.

"I don't like seeing you worried," she says, wrapping him in a hug on the couch. "I wish I could help."

He shrugs. "Don't worry about it. These are good problems to have, the problems of this project growing and evolving into more than I ever could have imagined are pretty amazing. It's just that my knowledge is limited too, and I worry the investors will want to replace me with someone better."

There, he said it—what he's really worried about. "Someone better than the person who came up with the idea? Who got the town to go along with the plan? Who secured all these investors and got so many people on board? No, there's no way they'd want anyone else at the helm of Terra Marique. This is your creation, your baby."

She's curled up with her arms around him, trying to make him feel okay, but she knows she can't. All she can do is support him and let him know she believes in him.

"When is your meeting?" she asks, finishing off her now-cold coffee.

"At one o'clock." He glances at the clock on the wall; it's now 7:48. He stretches and hugs Lizzie back. "Thank you for listening and for not thinking I'm a loser."

"What? Where did 'loser' come from? Is that what you were saying to yourself all night?" Lizzie asks, visibly upset.

"Kind of," he says. "Sort of, I mean, not totally, but the word pops into my head sometimes."

"Well, tell it to pop right out," she says. "No one, absolutely no one, thinks that, okay?"

"Okay," he says, giving her a kiss and getting up off the couch. "Thanks coach," he says, smiling at her.

"Anytime," she says back. "Go get 'em, tiger!"

Alexis, Eric and Lizzie had all agreed to meet at Sea Coast at 11. They picked Sea Coast hoping Leah might be able to pop in and be part of the meeting since she'd be there working. It was hard during the summer, and even during the off-season with a much smaller staff, to capture her for a meeting off-site. Lizzie had learned the hard way trying to wrangle her for various town-related meetings off-site rarely worked.

Lizzie is the first one to show up for the meeting, so she grabs a table and is already on her laptop with her green tea and bag of mixed nuts when the others arrive.

"Well, you're way ahead of us," Alexis says, putting her backpack on a chair. "I'm just going to get an iced coffee and will be right back," she says, then turns back. "You good?" she asks Lizzie, to which she nods as she chews some nuts. "Eric?"

He waves her off. "Thanks, I'm just going to get myself a box of water. I'm too caff'd up already." He sits down and silently opens up his laptop.

"You okay?" Lizzie asks, he looks so serious.

"Me? Yeah, sorry, I've just been on deadline for that story about Alexis's granddad, and his family's history in Cranberry Harbor, and want to do a good job. I'm a little distracted, that's all," Eric says.

"It's truly an evergreen story," Lizzie says. "There's no hard deadline, so don't pressure yourself. We've got plenty of content for this and next week's issues, so take your time. I can't wait to read it."

Alexis comes back, not just with her iced coffee but with a paper plate full of cookies. "I tried to say no, but Leah insisted on giving these to us," she says, feigning sadness. "Guess we're going to have to humor her by eating them," she says, picking one up. "Hmmm, oh my gosh, these are so good!" she says just as Leah walks up to the table.

"You like them? It's something new we're trying out. So many people are going plant based, no sugar, no dairy, I wanted to try something new. It's a challenge. I've been baking the traditional way for a long time, but you think they're good?" she asks.

Alexis emphatically nods her head. "Heck yes," she says after swallowing. "Try some, you guys," she encourages Lizzie and Eric to take one.

"I used whole grain flour, coconut sugar and dried dates, dried cranberries, oatmeal, and applesauce. There's no butter and no eggs. It's a first time experiment, so be honest if you think they're awful," Leah says.

All three of them are chowing down on the cookies now, and are all clearly loving them.

"Wow, these are so good, Leah," Lizzie says. "There's so much more to them than a regular cookie. They taste...I don't know, more satisfying? Regular cookies are so full of sugar and refined stuff that there's nothing substantial to them, but these have some weight to them, in a good way." She takes another bite and shakes her head. "There's probably a reason I'm not a food writer," she says. "I stink at describing food. I just know they taste good, have a good mouth feel, and I like them."

They all laugh. "I think that sounds just like a food writer," Leah says, smiling. "Eric? You eat the cookies here fairly often—how do they compare?"

He's chewing and obviously thinking. "It's a very different animal than the regular more processed cookies, but I think the customers who would choose a healthier cookie would know that going in, you know? They know they're not going to get a traditional Toll House cookie, or hermit, and that's what they want. So I think that population would love these."

"So you don't think the average Sea Coast patron would like it as much?" Leah asks.

"I think you're always going to have the folks who are like, 'I like my cookies, I like my white sugar,' and that's cool. I think, though, as the culture has been shifting toward less processed food, and less or no sugar, those people would love something to have as a treat that doesn't mean they've messed up their eating plan, you know?" Eric takes another bite. "I for one really like these."

Alexis concurs. "Two thumbs up from me," she says.

"Okay, as long as you're not just trying to be kind," she says, to which they all feign moaning. "I know, I couldn't resist." She stands up. "I have to attend to a few things, but if I can I'll come back for some of your meeting. Thanks for the feedback, guys," she says as she walks back to the kitchen.

"Maybe along with getting everyone to be kinder we should make Cranberry Harbor into a Blue Zone," Lizzie says. "You know, those parts of the world where more people live to be 100 because they eat good, whole food, have lots of friends, and get regular exercise? Probably because they don't sit and work on computers all day," she says, laughing and shaking her head.

"I'm thinking we will have more than enough to contend with creating the Kindness Project," Eric says. "People will come out swinging if we encourage them to be nicer and then take away their sugar," he jokes.

""Oh, I think you're so right. Hell hath no fury like a person getting off sugar," Alexis says. "Ian went sugar free for several months last year, and in the beginning it wasn't pretty. I don't think we can ask people to do those two things at once."

"Alright, you've convinced me, one project at a time," Lizzie says, looking down at her notes. "I was thinking about all the ways we can get kids involved. If they're excited about something, it will be much easier to get their parents on board. After this I'm going to go to the library and talk to Shannon to see if she has some ideas, which I know she will."

Eric is going through some notes. "Oh!" he says. "I saw this amazing house on TikTok where they had a little free library cupboard, a mailbox to leave notes of inspiration to put on display for all to share, and there was a bench for people to sit on with heart shaped pavers around it, and signs that had messages like, 'You Are Loved,' and 'How Do We Change the World? One Random Act of Kindness at a Time.' It was just so nice, you know? It made me wonder about creating a little 'kindness space,'" he says, using air quotes, "somewhere on Main Street?"

"That's a really cool idea," Lizzie says, leaning forward on her elbows, thinking. "Maybe we could get permission from the town to set something up on the Town Green? A kind of kindness station? We could have water for dogs, maybe some little treats for them, a place for kindness notes, like you mentioned, Eric. A box where you could take out a random act of kindness you could perform? Like 'take back someone's grocery cart,' 'buy coffee for the person in back of you,' 'pick up litter on the beach,' or "say thank you to everyone you interact with today,'"

"Hold a door open," Alexis says. "Help an older person put their groceries in their car."

"This is a great idea, and I'm thinking this could also work for kids. I'll run this by Shannon at the library when I see her," Lizzie says. "Speaking of which," she says, glancing at the clock on the wall, "I should get over there before lunch." She pauses. "You both have me thinking... I'm going to bring her some decaf coffee, and a couple of those plant-based cookies—you know, to be kind," she says, smiling.

"Very good idea," Alexis says. "You are walking the talk, my friend."

"Thank you both so much for being so on-board with this crazy idea," Lizzie says, closing up her laptop and putting it in her bag. "This isn't something that would be doable, or as much fun to do, alone. It really takes a few people to make things happen, and I really think that just by setting a tone and putting out a message that we could make a change in how people interact in this town."

Those words are no sooner out of her mouth than a woman at the counter begins raising her voice to the young man working behind it.

"I clearly said almond milk, and this is oat milk. I can taste the difference! How hard is it to take an order and get it right?!" she says emphatically. "This isn't a hard job! How dumb are you?"

The young man, who looks at best 17, is near tears as she continues on, complaining about the service and asking to speak to the manager.

Leah, like a superhero, appears out of nowhere.

"Yes? You wanted to speak with me? I'm the owner, how can I help you?" she says with a tone somewhere between respectful and suppressed rage.

She gestures to the offending coffee cup like it contains toxic sludge. "He messed up my order and I am very upset," she says.

"I can see that," Leah says. "What exactly is the problem?"

"I asked for an almond milk latte and he gave me oat milk, and it's disgusting. It's undrinkable," she says in a tone usually reserved for truly offensive acts.

"Well, I will tell you what we are going to do." Leah goes to the register and takes out a five-dollar bill and hands it to her. "Here you go, take your money back, get in your car, and go to the next town, and get yourself another coffee." She stops. "Oh, and please, never come here again, because no one, absolutely no one, speaks to anyone who works here that way. Have a great day!" Leah says, a big smile on her face.

"Well, I never!" the woman says, picking up the money and the offending coffee cup. She turns on her heel and struts out of the place, as several patrons applaud her exit.

"You okay, Tyler?" Leah asks the young man at the center of the drama, who's a bit stunned by all the commotion.

He nods, and then turns to Leah. "Man, you were amazing! You were so cool. Thanks for having my back."

"Anytime. No one is ever allowed to speak to anyone working here like that." She puts her arm around him. "We've got you, okay?"

Tyler hugs her, and nods his head into her shoulder.

"And that, my friends, is why we are doing this," Lizzie says. She shakes her head. "What makes people act like that? Entitlement? Frustration? Anger at the world?"

Alexis and Eric both shake their heads.

"I have no clue, but I do know if anyone ever talks to me like that I want Leah there. Wow, she's a total badass," Eric says, grinning.

"Heck yeah," says Alexis. "She is amazing!"

Right then, Leah appears at their table. "Well, that was fun," she says, dramatically wiping her brow. "Jeez, could you believe that woman? Tyler started yesterday, the poor kid. I'm surprised he didn't quit on the spot. No one deserves to be treated like that. But I don't know, I kinda wish I'd, I don't know, maybe not reacted and responded with more grace, I guess?" she says, scrunching up her face a bit. "I mean, if we're going to be doing this kindness initiative, shouldn't we be modeling how to be kind and not being mean right back? I don't know," she says, slumping down in a chair at the table.

"Well, first of all, you did the right thing in looking out for Tyler, and for taking a stand for how people are expected to act in your shop," says Eric. "I mean, you didn't yell at her or swear at her, you refunded her money, and you told her she was not welcome in your business if that was how she was going to act. I think you handled it really well."

"I agree," says Lizzie, "but I also understand where you're coming from. I don't know the best way to deal with a situation like that, because you don't want to placate them and therefore let them think it's okay to act like that. I think this is something we need to think about maybe?" she asks the group.

They all nod.

"Yeah, there's got to be a way to defend your employee and take control of the situation, but not resort to also being a jerk. You, my friend, were just the opposite, an example of kindness for us all. You handled the situation beautifully, Leah," Alexis says. "I would have wanted to show her the door and slammed it behind her."

"You were perfect, Leah," Eric agrees. "I would not have been so cool. It's funny, and maybe everyone is like this, but I feel so much more protective of others than I do myself. As a young Black guy I let a lot of stuff go, but if I see someone dissing someone else, I am all over it."

"That's because you're a very kind and compassionate person," Lizzie says. "Let's all think about this if we want to try to come up with some strategies to share with other business owners for dealing with jerks, or rude people, if we're trying to be kinder," Lizzie laughs.

"Gee Lizzie, how dare you call someone yelling at my help a jerk —how mean are you?!" Leah teases.

"I think we're going to find that being kind isn't always easy," Alexis says.

"And that sometimes, like today, people do need to be called out for their behavior," Eric says.

"Totally!" Lizzie concurs. "You handled a very rude person with about as much grace as I've ever seen, Leah, so kudos to you. The more we talk about it, the more I think you handled it perfectly. Tyler knows you have his back, as does everyone else who works here, and by the applause she received on her exit from the people hanging out here, I think it's pretty clear that all these lovely people here agreed with you."

"Yeah? Thanks, guys," Leah says to the trio. "I think I've gotten better at it. I used to use a lot more hand gestures and expletives in the past. I have calmed down a bit and I think show more tact and maturity than I did in the past. So that's good."

"It's very good," Lizzie says. "I am not sure I would have been as polite to that woman as you were."

"This has been an interesting morning, but I now need to get to Terra Marique, because, well, I don't have to tell you about how my boss gets," Alexis teases.

"Ooof, that Jack guy?" Eric says, packing up his things. "It's all rude hand gestures and swearing all the time," he says laughing. "I don't know how you do it, Lizzie; he's a lot."

They're all laughing as they head to the door, which feels good. It is a much-needed diffusing of that tension they all just experienced.

"Okay friends, until we meet again, thank you," Lizzie says, walking to her car. "Stay kind, people," she calls out.

"I'm going to try!" Eric calls back.

"Me too," says Alexis.

Lizzie starts her car and begins driving to the library to see Shannon. This isn't going to be easy, she thinks, and that's what makes it necessary, she decides. She puts on her blinker, wanting to take a left to the library, and no one is letting her in, until a very nice young man in a plumbing truck smiles and waves her in. She smiles and waves back and thinks there may be hope yet.

CHAPTER 13

Lizzie finds a parking spot right in front of the library. The Cranberry Harbor Library was so beautiful. The town had voted to approve a big renovation project five years ago, before Lizzie had moved back home. It had long outgrown its very limited space, and it had been 40 years since the previous renovation, so it was more than time. Now there was a children's garden, a beautiful patio for outdoor groups, and the building was awash in light from all the windows.

She walked past the circulation desk to the children's library area and found Shannon, cross-legged on the floor with a little girl reading, of all things, a book called, *Kindness is My Superpower,* by Alicia Ortego. Lizzie recognized the book because it was one of the ones she'd seen at Tall Tales when she was looking for children's books about kindness.

Shannon spots Lizzie, and signals her that she's almost done, and Lizzie lets her know it's no problem. She loves wandering around the library, and unless she's there to see her wonderful sister-in-law, she doesn't always make it to the very bright and cheery children's wing.

There truly could not have been a better person in charge than Shannon. Since she'd taken on the job as Children's Library Director, she'd done remarkable things. Not just with the space, the collections of books, but with all the opportunities she provided for kids and families. Every single day there was something happening for kids after school. There were yoga classes, arts and crafts, visits from companion dogs, and so much more. In the summer she had created a very fun, very active and interactive summer reading program that every kid in Cranberry Harbor participated in. She even had high school students who loved it so much when they were younger that they now mentored younger kids and started their own book club. It was amazing to see.

As soon as her young companion scurried off with her mom, Shannon came and joined Lizzie at the child-sized drawing table.

"Having a nice time drawing?" she asks, smiling at Lizzie. "You know, we could go sit at a bigger table," she says. "We don't have to scrunch in here."

"I don't know, I rather like feeling large. It makes me feel more powerful," she jokes.

"Wherever you're most comfortable," Shannon says. "I'm used to sitting in tiny chairs off and on all day!"

"That was so sweet that you were reading to that little girl," Lizzie says. "You are very hands-on. I love that."

"Her mom, dad, and sometimes her grandmother are frequent fliers here. I know them well. Her mom wanted to get a book for herself so I told her to go look and I'd watch Sky. I know how hard it is with a three-year-old to do anything for yourself, so I'm happy to help."

"You are very kind," Lizzie says. "Which is why I'm here."

"I've been hearing bits and pieces from your mom about this kindness project," she says, raising an interested eyebrow.

"Yes, we want to turn Cranberry Harbor into a kindness zone, a place where people are polite, and well, kind to each other, where from town line to town line you're going to see signs that say you've entered a 'Kindness Zone,' and that kindness is requested, if not expected, in your interactions while in our borders."

"That's such a sweet idea," Shannon says. "I'd love to do something with the kids around kindness. We often touch on that anyway, well, like you saw in the book I was reading to Sky. We talk about it a lot here, because, well, especially with the older kids, middle school or so, it definitely becomes an issue."

"In what ways do you see that happening?" Lizzie asks, ever the journalist.

"Well, kids not being included, left out, some bullying, things like that," Shannon says. "With littler kids it's not sharing toys or books, some pushing with toddlers. Nothing too terrible, but little things I like to nip in the bud when I see them happening." She pauses and looks around the space. "I'd love to put up some signage about it being a 'Kindness Zone.' I think the kids would really like that."

"Yeah? I'm so glad! Not being a parent myself, I haven't been sure how to broach this with kids, so I was counting on you, and perhaps Anika and Jay at Tall Tales, to help with maybe some signs, and book displays of books about being kind, and maybe story hours around it?" Lizzie says.

"Certainly, I'd love to do that," Shannon says. "Oh! And maybe a jar where you can pull an idea for a 'random act of kindness' you could perform, like putting a toy back that you didn't take out, helping a younger child with a puzzle, offering to play a game with someone who's there alone."

"Oh! I love that!" says Lizzie. "And maybe a jar where you can write down a random act of kindness you performed and feel good about?"

"Yeah! And maybe have a party at the end of the summer where we celebrate all the acts of kindness we've collected over the summer!" says Shannon.

Lizzie is busy taking notes, and Shannon gets up to grab her laptop and starts typing.

"If I don't make a Google Doc and keep track of my ideas they will disappear from my brain and I will never remember them!" Shannon says.

"Glad to hear it's not just me!" Lizzie says. "I swear, if I don't write down something either on paper, in my Notes app or on my laptop within minutes, sometimes seconds after an idea occurring to me, it can be gone forever."

"The worst is when I go to look something up on Google and as I'm waiting for it to load, something else, like news about some celebrity, will pop up, and the original reason I went to Google is gone, vanished," Shannon says.

"You are not alone, and jeez, we're young, Shannon! By the time we're in our 50s will we have any brain cells left?" Lizzie laments.

"I sure hope so!" Shannon says, typing away. "So do you have a starting date?"

"Well, I'm meeting with Connie at town hall tomorrow, to see if at the special Town Meeting next week I might be able to say a few words and get everyone on board. My goal is to roll this out right before the Fourth of July. I know it's coming up fast, but we can get signs made fast, and be ready to go, right?" Lizzie says, partly to reassure herself, since that deadline is looming.

"I think so," Shannon says, looking a little worried. "Yeah, heck yeah, we've got this," she says, looking more energized.

Lizzie sighs in relief. "Good," she says, standing up. Shannon stands up too, and they hug. "Thank you so much for being on board with this crazy idea. You will be a crucial asset for sure."

"I think it's a great idea, and I can't wait to roll it out!" Shannon says.

"Fingers crossed the town agrees," Lizzie says, turning to go. "I'll call you after my meeting at town hall tomorrow."

"Good luck!" Shannon calls after her. "You've got this!"

Lizzie gives her a thumbs-up as she walks out, hoping against hope that Shannon is right.

If, as they say, timing is everything, then Lizzie showed up at the Cranberry Harbor town hall, at exactly the right moment. When she approaches the office of the Chair of the Selectboard, she hears loud sighs, a few "goddammits," and the forceful landing of said person in their chair, along with a "humph!"

Lizzie, a bit reluctantly, knocks on the door. "Bad time, Connie?"

"Oh, perfect time to have the press arrive," she jokes.

Connie has always been very open and transparent with her, but Lizzie understands for most public people the press is looked at warily, though Lizzie has never been a journalist that tried to catch politicians, CEOs, college presidents, or anyone in 'gotcha' scenarios. She preferred doing her homework, asking tough questions, and being upfront to tricking anyone, and that had earned her the respect and appreciation her dad always had when he started and ran the paper. Thankfully, the respect went both ways.

"Tough day? I can come back later, or tomorrow if that's better for you?" Lizzie wants to talk to Connie when she's feeling generous and happy, not if she's upset.

"No, it's not a big deal, it's just...people!" she says, shaking her head.

"Ah, can't they just be the worst?" Lizzie says, smiling.

"It's not even full-on summer season yet, and people are being so grouchy, demanding, rude, it's crazy," Connie says.

"I'm sorry. That's a pain. Is this about building permits or something?" Lizzie asks, curious as to what has so many people in a dither.

Connie laughs and shakes her head. "No, it's people having meltdowns about beach stickers."

"Really? Beach stickers? Huh, that's interesting," Lizzie says, curious because as far as she can recall no one has complained to the paper. "Is this something new?"

"Yes, second home owners who aren't happy about not paying the same rate as year-round residents, and are feeling taken advantage of," she says.

"Even though they are fortunate enough to be able to own a second home in Cranberry Harbor, the fact that they're paying more than someone who lives here all the time offends their sensibilities?"

Connie nods, and jokingly bangs her head on her desk.

"How much is the difference?" Lizzie asks, now curious.

"They pay $300 more, for the whole year, which also includes being able to recycle, compost, and get rid of trash at the transfer station, though when I mentioned that, the four people complaining the loudest said that was of no consequence to them because they had private companies that dealt with that."

"So clearly, it's not like they're not going to eat this summer because of their beach sticker cost," Lizzie says.

"Hardly." Connie sits back and sighs. "I don't know what it is. It seems the people who used to come here were nicer, less entitled and demanding."

"You're not alone. All the businesses in town have talked about it, and well, that's why I'm here. We have an idea," Lizzie says, getting excited.

"Really? I'm all ears," Connie says.

"We want to make Cranberry Harbor a 'Kindness Zone,' have signs up at the town's borders, in various spots, maybe a banner across Main Street, and just set the tone that rudeness and unkindness are not acceptable." She pulls out a proposal she's written up with all the different ideas she, Alexis, Eric, Leah and Shannon have all come up with.

"Huh, the 'Kindness Project'—boy, if this town could use anything right about now, it's a big dose of kindness," Connie says. "What can I do to help?"

"Well, funny you should ask," Lizzie says.

By the time Lizzie leaves, she's been granted 15 minutes to speak at Town Meeting in just a few days, and has the full backing of the Selectboard—more than she ever could have hoped for. It seems everyone is up for a bit more kindness.

CHAPTER 14

When Lizzie gets back to the Gazette office she is surprised to see Jack there, sitting in her chair, talking with Eric.

"Hey! Oh no, did we have plans I forgot about?" Lizzie asks, suddenly worried they had a date she'd spaced out on.

"No, I was just in the neighborhood and thought I'd stop by to say hi, and bring you a late afternoon decaf green tea, with a squeeze of honey." He smiles at her. "Though I've been sitting here for 20 minutes or so keeping Eric from his work, so I'm not sure if it's still hot."

She walks over to him and gives him a kiss as he starts to get up out of her chair. She presses his shoulder down and shakes her head, and pulls a chair on wheels up to the shared partner's desk.

"Stay put. It's good for me to get a change of perspective once in a while," she jokes. "I don't want to interrupt if you two were in the middle of something," she says, taking a sip of tea. "The temperature is perfect, thank you so much."

"We were just talking Red Sox, Salty Dogs, and finding a time to go have a pick-up game ourselves sometime," Eric says. "What have you been up to, Madam Editor?"

"'Madam'? I feel so unworthy of the title," she says. "I've actually had a really good day and am grateful I had most of my deadlines met since I've been gone all day." She takes another sip of her tea. "After you, Alexis and I parted ways," she says, looking at Eric, "I went to see Shannon at the library, and as we assumed, she was completely on board with looping the kids and the children's wing of the library into the kindness project, and then I went to town hall. I admit I was kind of nervous about that. After all you went through getting Terra Marique built," she says, turning to Jack, "well, ever since then I've been a little wary when I have to go there and broach something with them."

"And?" Jack asks.

"And Connie was completely on board. We've got 15 minutes Tuesday night at the special Town Meeting to bring it up to the people, let businesses know, hopefully get permission and maybe even some money for signage. Truly, it couldn't have gone better," she says, drinking more of her tea, and feeling so glad Jack brought it.

"That's amazing!" Eric says. "I mean, I wasn't really worried, but I've been to enough Selectboard meetings to know that a lot of times they have their own agenda and don't really appreciate people coming in with theirs. Bravo," he says, clapping.

"I think it helped that she had just been dealing with some irate part-time residents about the cost of beach stickers, who weren't very easy to deal with, so she had gotten a taste of what we've been seeing and what this is all about," says Lizzie. "I would send those people a thank you note if I knew who they were," she laughs.

"Hey, timing is everything, and if the people who hold the power have experienced the issue you're coming to them with, all the better," Jack says. "Oh, that reminds me, I talked to the food vendors I could capture at the Terra Marique community kitchen, and they'd love to help out with some food donations. Most are operating on narrow margins, so it can't be a tremendous donation, but they were saying they'd love to help out with lunches for kids who depend on free lunch during the school year, and maybe do some Meals on Wheels type of thing for older folks in need. They were very excited to pitch in."

"Oh, that's so great. Thank you for doing that, sweetie," Lizzie says.

"And I talked to Jonathan, I think it is? The guy from the Salty Dogs?" Eric says, "And he was saying he wanted to try to get the team to donate some time giving kids, teens or even adults some baseball tips."

"Wow, we may actually pull this off, guys! I can't believe how it's coming together," Lizzie says. "And without a lot of rancor."

"Well, I would hold off celebrating until you get past Town Meeting. There's usually a couple of curmudgeons who need to be naysayers no matter what," Jack says. He laughs. "Do you remember the woman from East Cranberry Harbor, who had to make sure we knew she was from *East* Cranberry Harbor..."

Lizzie interrupts, "Which by the way, isn't even a thing; there's no different zip code, or post office situation. It's just a way of letting people know you are rich and live on the water," Lizzie says. "Sorry, I didn't mean to interrupt, that just always makes me crazy."

"Oh, it's ridiculous and haughty. I hate it too," Jack says. "Anyway, she got up because someone who had passed away had donated funds to have water bowls for dogs in their memory at various places like the town green, in front of a couple of stores on Main Street..."

"Yeah, there's one in front of Sea Coast," Lizzie adds.

"Yes, it was sweet, and she complained that they looked bad and took away from the ambiance of downtown Cranberry Harbor," Jack says, shaking his head. "Oh! And that they'd attract mosquitoes and make people sick."

"Really? That's so crazy!" Eric says, hardly able to believe what he's hearing. "That was actually one of the things that I noticed about this town when I first moved here. I thought it was really cool, and pretty sweet that the town put that much thought into caring for the dogs in town. Crazy what gets under some people's skin."

"Yeah, so my only caveat is, just be prepared for some sanctimonious person to get up at the meeting and say being kind is unfair, or goes against town bylaws," Jack says, and both Lizzie and Eric start laughing.

"That's a very good, tried and true deflection," Lizzie says. "You bring up the town bylaws and everything stops while they madly search for something written down in the 1700s that is somehow applicable to this issue in present day Cranberry Harbor."

"I love this place, but it's sure got its characters who don't want to be ignored," Jack says.

"It's always so interesting to me," Eric says, "having only moved here a few years ago, and having come from a large city, how identified people can be with being from here, and the way eyes roll at the 'washashores,'" he says, using air quotes. "A term, by the way, I had never heard of until I moved here. It's interesting how often that gets levied against someone. But I can understand, you don't want someone who moved here from New York six months ago telling you how you're doing something wrong, or that they don't like—that's got to be annoying. I try hard to keep lots of thoughts to myself."

"Yeah, it's the 'last one over the bridge' syndrome, we call it," Lizzie says, shaking her head. "I mean, I'm all for people who want to come here, make Cranberry Harbor their home, but when they bring their ideas about suburban lawns and the way it was done where they came from, etc., it is annoying. We're trying so hard to preserve the environment for the future, and they're just thinking, 'I want a green lawn that looks like a golf course,' or they want all the conveniences here that they moved to get away from. Sorry, buddy, we're not going to get that big box store in town; you're going to have to drive a little ways to get your discounted housewares." Lizzie stops herself. "I digress, and I am not sounding very kind about the newly relocated Cranberry Harbor residents. Wow, it's way too easy to fall into complaining, isn't it?!"

Eric looks at the clock and jumps up. "Damn, I'm supposed to be on my way to the high school to talk to the baseball coach about this year's team," he says. "If you two will excuse me, I have a story to cover," he says, grabbing his bag, notebook and water bottle.

"Later, Eric, it was nice hanging out," Jack calls after him. "He's a really good guy. I'm so glad you were able to get him to come on board full time. I'm sure he helps take the stress off you."

"Oh, I can't imagine not having him," Lizzie says. "I give him assignments for sure, but he's so self-motivated and smart, and he knows a good story. It's amazing to me for someone who hasn't lived here that long how he just understands the community and has such great instincts."

"I'm so glad," Jack says. He sighs and starts to get up.

"What's that sigh about?" Lizzie asks, a little concerned.

He sits back and runs his hands through his hair. "That Zoom meeting I told you I was going to have with one of the VCs?"

"Yeah, did that not go well? What's going on?"

"She was cool and everything, but the sense I'm getting more and more is they think I did a great job creating the concept, getting Terra Marique built and launched, but they aren't sure a tech guy is the best person to be running something as complex as this," Jack says.

"What the heck? None of it would be there without your vision, creativity, ability to find the best people to work with." She's getting angry. "I can't stand these stupid venture capitalists." She says the word with such contempt, it makes Jack laugh.

"I know, they can be pains in the ass, but they're also why this happened in the first place. Without their money it's just a cool idea," Jack says. "And a million people have great ideas that never see the light of day." He's quiet for a minute. "I have to admit, they've kind of gotten in my head a bit though. Am I the best person to run Terra Marique? Could someone with more of a managerial background do better? Is my lack of experience holding it back from being all it could be?"

"Okay, now you're just psyching yourself out, honey." She gets up and hugs him. "Like you said, you're letting her get in your head, and it's messing with you." She squats down next to the chair. "You have done an incredible job, not just getting it passed by the town, but getting it built, in record time I might add, and the diverse people you've got doing everything from growing turnips to making veggie burgers to working on microchips. It's remarkable. Not to mention the recording studio that's coming for music and podcasting, the artists, the classes, the community and kids' gardens—you made all of that happen. And most importantly, you've given so many people here a place to live that they can afford."

He leans over and kisses her head. "Thank you, babe, you are a very convincing cheerleader," he says, grinning. "I also give much credit to Alexis. Her Master's in community planning has really helped. But you're right, we have done a really good job. I mean, if they want me to take some courses in management, or anything else, I can. I'm sure I could even do that online."

"Of course you can. And the other thing, the thing that can't be replicated, is that you come from here, you know the Cape, you know Cranberry Harbor. It's why this was even permitted to happen. If some random person from California had come here wanting to develop this piece of land and proposed this off-the-grid, multi-use, mixed-use community, no one would have been sold on it. It's because this is led by you and Alexis, both people who grew up here and are invested in the community, that the town threw its support behind you. They trust you, and in a town the size of Cranberry Harbor, that doesn't come easily."

Lizzie gets up and starts pacing. "I think this is exactly why I don't like big companies. They always think they know better, and they ignore the personal aspect of building something like Terra Marique, and miss so much. They miss what community building is all about. And I realize the Gazette has angel investors, but they trust what we're doing and don't try to control us."

"There's a reason you're the writer in the family," Jack says. "I could not have said it better, and if I need to submit something defending my leadership I sure hope you'll write it for me," he jokes.

"Of course, you know I'd be happy to," she says.

Jack walks over to her and they hug. "I'm so lucky to have you in my corner," he says, kissing her.

"We're both lucky," she says, kissing him back.

"What do you say we get out of here and go home?" he says, kissing her neck.

"Why, Mr. Cahoon, whatever do you have in mind?" Lizzie says playfully, gathering her things to leave.

"I think we need some time alone to further discuss how best to run our businesses, and you know, anything else that comes up," Jack says, taking her hand and leading her to the door.

They step outside, and Lizzie locks the door.

Before they walk to their cars Lizzie stops and looks at him.

"I really love you, and I'm so insanely grateful that I get to be married to you, live here, and run this paper, and you get to run Terra Marique. Who would have thought, huh? It all could have gone very differently had I liked writing for a Boston paper, and didn't get laid off—there is that—and if you'd liked the Silicon Valley life."

"Thank goodness we were both such quitters and came home," Jack says, laughing.

"Yes," Lizzie agrees. "Let's hear it for quitting!"

"So, I'll see you at home?" Jack says.

"I'm right behind you," she says.

CHAPTER 15

The Fourth of July was always the official beginning of the summer season on the Cape. People may have been coming and going for a few weeks, but this was it. It was full-on, all-hands-on-deck, summer on the Fourth.

Cranberry Harbor had been hosting both a parade and fireworks for many years. Lizzie couldn't remember a time they didn't have both, so it had been at least 30-plus years. It was always a bit crazy with so many people coming into town, but she still loved it.

Lizzie and Eric had each been covering different aspects of what was going to be happening to advance all the events - the parade, the theme this year? "Sea Life." She was definitely expecting a large number of sharks, seals and maybe some crabs, but you never know what some of the participants might come up with. The Cape was a place overflowing with creative people—from visual artists to musicians to actors to writers. It was what Lizzie and many others loved most about living here, along with the sense of community that was forged from all these creative people.

The morning of the parade Lizzie walked over to her parents' house to see what their plans were for viewing the parade. There was a long-held tradition of people the night before setting up their chairs all along Main Street to claim their spot. And just like with the seats at Sparrow Park, no one would ever dare move your chair, never mind take it. Her parents sometimes put chairs out, but mostly not, preferring a more come-what-may nonchalance to where they'd view the parade. She liked that and had followed suit for all her adult years.

"Hey, sweetie," her dad says, giving her a peck on the cheek when she walks into the kitchen. He's drinking coffee while also trying to get their dog Daisy to sit. This had been a losing battle since they'd adopted this sweet mutt five years ago, but Lizzie had to give her dad props for continuing to try. "One of these days..." he'd always say, ever the optimist.

"Hey Dad, and I see Miss Daisy is as stubborn as ever," Lizzie says, bending down to scratch her behind the ears. "Good girl," she says in a stage whisper. "You let him know who's boss!" she teases.

"Thanks a lot! Thwarted in my efforts in my own house," he says. He gives up and just gives the dog her treat. "So, when are you headed to the parade?" he asks, finishing his coffee and rinsing out his cup before putting it in the dishwasher.

"In just a few minutes. I wondered if you wanted to take one car? We can go the back way and leave it at the paper, if you don't have other plans, of course," she says, pilfering one of her mother's delicious gluten- and sugar-free raspberry scones off a platter on the counter. "Jack already left. Terra Marique has a float this year and he wanted to go do what he could to help."

"Morning, honey!" Gabby says, rushing in from upstairs. "I got waylaid upstairs, writing, thanks to you!" she teases.

"Really? Writing?" Lizzie asks.

"Yes," she says, pouring herself some coffee and breaking off a piece of scone.

"Your mother, per your suggestion, is working on a cookbook," Peter says, proudly putting his arm around her. "She wrote the most wonderful introduction about how eating healthy and eating well don't have to be mutually exclusive, and she has all these incredible studies she's citing, which is so inspiring, so people can actually see in black and white why eating a mostly plant-based, vegetarian diet is so beneficial, and... sorry honey, I'm stealing your thunder!"

Gabby laughs and gives him a squeeze. "No, I love it! I'm so glad it's resonating with you, and hopefully it will with others as well," she says.

"I'm so excited, Mom, and wow, you didn't waste any time getting on that!" Lizzie says. "I can't wait to read it, whenever you want me to."

"I will definitely be looking for editing help, and also, how understandable it is. I've never written professionally—well, other than as a doctor—so this is something wholly different," Gabby says. "I want to make sure the recipes are easy to follow, turn out well, and that it's also maybe informative and fun."

"That's a lot," Lizzie says, "but if anyone can pull that off it's you." She's quiet for a minute. "You know, I think there's a woman who summers here who works for a publisher in New York. Eric did a story about her last summer as I recall . I'll have to look that up. You know you don't have to write the whole thing, right? You can do a proposal. Maybe if you get that done this summer we could get it to her."

Gabby shakes her head. "I don't want to impose on someone when they're here on vacation."

"Don't worry, I won't impose. I promise.," She turns toward the door. "So, do you two want to come with me to the parade? I'd love to watch it with you!"

"For sure," Peter says. "Let me go grab my camera, not just a phone," he says smiling.

"The newspaper guy in him is always there, isn't it?" Lizzie says, smiling at her mom.

"Always!" Gabby agrees.

It is a good thing Lizzie knows all the back roads because by the time they get into town Main Street is blocked off, and there are people everywhere. Cranberry Harbor is definitely the place to be on the Fourth of July. There are kids on bikes, rollerblades, and running. The energy is contagious, and Lizzie, Peter and Gabby find themselves pointing and smiling at all the happy activity.

"Is it just me, or does it seem busier than usual?" Gabby asks as they pull into the Gazette parking lot and get out of the car.

Peter shakes his head. "Wow, yeah, I've covered a lot of these and I've never seen it like this," he says as they make their way down Main Street.

"Let's hope they all brought their good attitudes," Lizzie says, as they navigate the circus.

Those words are barely out of her mouth when a couple in their 40s, probably, pushes past them, whacking Peter on the back with one of their beach chairs they brought to watch the parade.

"Hey," he calls out, "an 'excuse me,' or 'sorry' would be nice!"

"Yeah, sorry," the woman says, waving him off.

"Are you okay?" Gabby asks, concerned about Peter. "I can't believe them!"

Peter rubs his lower back and shakes his head. "I guess I should be glad they weren't carrying anything heavier," he says. "Yes, I'm fine, thanks, sweetheart. I just can't believe how dismissive they were."

"This is exactly why I wanted to start the Kindness Project, Dad. There's way too much of that kind of attitude coming to town," Lizzie says. "You sure you're okay? Grrr, it makes me so mad when people act like others don't matter. The entitlement and selfishness is what gets to me."

They stop in front of Tall Tales and Sea Coast. Lizzie spies Anika standing outside the shop.

"I'll be right back," she says to her parents. "I just want to check in with Anika."

"Take your time, honey. I'm going to grab a few photos," Peter says.

"And I'm going to get us some iced chai. You want one, Lizzie?" her mom asks.

She shakes her head. "No thanks, I'm good."

"Hey! How are you?" Anika asks as Lizzie approaches.

"I'm good, but wow, this is crazy! I wonder why so many people came this year? This is a lot more than usual," Lizzie says, looking around, taking in the crowd. "I wonder what the draw is?"

"Well, I heard that the guy who hosts *Sharknation* is coming to town. Doing some sort of event down at the beach after the parade." She shrugs her shoulders. "I don't know, it's just what I heard."

"Oh man, I'm not crazy about him. It's a lot of chest thumping and fearmongering as far as I've seen," Lizzie says. "He gets everyone amped up and scared that it's inevitable if they come to Cape Cod they're going to get eaten by a shark. He even uses music from *Jaws.* I just can't stand how he's not a marine biologist or even from here and he is making tons of money off scaring people and creating so much misinformation."

"I know," Anika says. "I'm right there with you. We try to counter it with books that tell the truth about sharks, but we can't compete with a national TV personality. The one with the loudest voice is the most believed, unfortunately."

"Maybe sometime over the summer we can do a Q and A on the town green or something with some actual experts, get some scientists down here from Woods Hole to talk about what's really going on," Lizzie offers.

"That's a great idea! I love it," says Anika. "Fight misinformation with facts, and we could tie it in with some factual books."

"I love it. Let's talk about this soon." Lizzie pauses and looks around at the growing crowd. "So, are you all set for today?"

"Kind of," Anika says, scrunching her face a bit. "I'm never quite ready for the before and after the Fourth change. It's definitely like a switch gets turned on and suddenly everyone is here. It's an adjustment for sure. I know I haven't lived here that long, but I'm definitely in the rhythm of liking the quieter time of the off-season."

"I hear you," Lizzie says. "And if some of the behaviors I've seen are any indication of what's coming at us, well, we need this kindness project more than ever."

"Amen to that!" Anika says. "I should get back in the store and see what else I can do to get ready for the post-parade mayhem!"

"Good luck!" Lizzie calls after her. "Just remember, it's only eight weeks until Labor Day!" she says, laughing.

Anika laughs and gives her a thumbs-up.

When Lizzie finds her parents—a bit tricky given all the people—she quickly assesses that they're surrounded by former patients of her mom and big fans of Peter's from his days running the paper. She laughs to herself about being the daughter of two local celebrities and takes it in, loving how appreciated and beloved her parents are.

"Hi!" she says, popping into the small crowd they've gathered by the street.

"You all know our daughter, Lizzie, right?" Peter says, putting his arm around Lizzie's shoulder and giving her a kiss on the head. "She's doing the most amazing job with the Gazette. I can't believe how she's grown the readership, and that it's now being cited on CNN and other news outlets."

Lizzie feels like she's 12 again and her dad is bragging about her science research project on the life cycle of mussels. But inside, it does feel nice to have her dad proud of how she's running what he created and ran for decades.

"Truth be told, it was only one mention on CNN, and a few tags on social media from Boston news outlets," Lizzie says, wanting to set the record straight and feeling kind of embarrassed. "So... different topic, did anyone hear that the guy from *Sharknation* is in town and doing some event at Sea Meadow Beach?"

There's a collective groan.

"Yes, I saw his RV roll through town a couple of hours ago," says Stan, now-retired long-time reporter for the Gazette. "A part of me wants to go down there and heckle the guy," he says, shaking his head. "He's like a bad politician who preys on people's worst fears and spreads misinformation to make himself seem relevant."

"Anika Patel and I were just talking about offering some counter-programming this summer—get some scientists down here from WHOI, and get some truth out there," Lizzie says.

"That's a great idea," Peter says. "I still know a few folks down there if you want me to reach out, but I don't want to overstep," he says, looking concerned about being *that* dad.

"Not overstepping at all. That would be great, Dad, thanks," Lizzie says.

Suddenly they can hear the refrain from the high school band playing what sounds like *Born in the USA,* which makes Lizzie smile.

"Oh! It's coming!" she says, surprising herself with a little hop. No matter how many of these parades she's been to, and it is now over 30, she still gets excited. The town parade makes her feel like she's 5-years-old all over again.

"Do you know what the Terra Marique folks have planned?" Gabby asks Lizzie, who shakes her head.

"Jack had no idea. Alexis and various residents, artists, farmers and tech people were working on something. They wanted to surprise him." She shrugs. "They told him to just show up and to dress down, like he would to work in the garden. It's going to be a surprise to all."

Several floats go by, representing local businesses like Bradford's and Cranberry Harbor Hardware. There are dancing kids from Seaside Dance Studio, a gorgeous boat from Harborside Marine, completely covered with flowers. and then Lizzie sees it coming: a float with a banner blowing in the wind that says Terra Marique .

Even from a distance she can see a beautiful mural, depicting the community garden they had created there, and a small wind turbine, a replica of the one they had. As it gets closer she is gobsmacked by the robotic dog and children playing instruments surrounded by gorgeous plants. She can hear them playing and singing the Bob Marley song *One Love,* and there is Jack, plucking along, badly, on a ukulele, singing right along. The sight of him with those kids, singing, something he never, ever does in front of anyone else, makes her cheer and cry a bit at the same time.

"Yay, Terra Marique!" Lizzie cheers, as do her parents. Jack smiles at her, and shakes his head and laughs. She knows him so well, she can practically read his mind. She knows he also can't believe he's doing this.

"That float is the perfect representation of everything they do there," says Gabby. "They completely nailed it."

Lizzie waves as they pass and sighs. "Wow, that was amazing," she says. "And that song, when sung by kids? Whoa, it just destroys me! I love to imagine a world like that."

No sooner are those words out of her mouth than a man on a bike comes racing past them, so close he causes Lizzie to lose her balance and fall on her butt.

As Gabby helps her up, Peter is chasing after the guy, yelling at him.

"Are you okay, honey?" Gabby asks, concerned. She brushes off Lizzie's dress and is looking her over for any obvious wounds, but she looks okay.

"That was crazy. What was he doing? I'm glad if someone was

going to get knocked down it was me and not an older person who could have been really hurt." She's not hurt, but she's certainly shaken up.

Peter returns, winded, and shaking his head. "I caught up to the guy about a block from here. He'd stopped to drink some water, and I said, 'What the hell are you doing? You knocked down my daughter. You could have really hurt someone.' His big comeback? He shrugged his shoulders and said, 'Whatever,' and then he rode away. 'Whatever'?" He shakes his head, still furious.

In the meantime several people who saw the incident have gathered around, checking to see if Lizzie is okay. At this point she's more embarrassed than hurt, and angry as well.

"Seems like our kindness project may be coming along just in the nick of time," she says, rubbing her lower back a bit. "Do me a favor, though; let's not tell Jack what happened. I don't want to take away from what a great showing they had with their float."

"Whatever you say, honey," Peter says, pulling her close, "but if I ever see that guy again..."

"Thanks, Dad, for going after him. That was very protective of you. I appreciate it. And I agree, if I ever see him, I'll, I'll..." She shakes her head, not really knowing what she'd do. "Maybe if I'd been taking capoeira instead of yoga, like Alexis has sometimes suggested we do, I'd have had the skills to at least scare him a little bit. I don't think a standing tree pose would quite do it," she laughs.

"Okay, you're joking; now I can relax and know you're alright," Gabby says, giving her a kiss on the head.

Thankfully the rest of the parade is drama-free, culminating with the Salty Dogs, dressed in their uniforms, on a float, throwing out small boxes of Cracker Jacks to the crowd to lots of cheers.

Jack texts Lizzie that he is over at Sea Coast. He'd left the parade float before it headed back to Terra Marique.

Want to come meet me for an iced coffee? Ice cream? Both? XO

"Jack's over at Sea Coast. I think I'll head over there. You're welcome to come, or I can meet you back at the office to ride home in a little bit," Lizzie says.

Gabby and Peter look at each other.

"You want anything?" Peter asks her.

"Um, maybe in a little bit? I'm seeing a few people I want to say hi to—is that okay? Are you in a hurry, honey?" she says, looking at Lizzie.

She shakes her head. "No hurry, it's a holiday, and if I end up waiting for you for a little bit I can just use the time to update our socials. Take your time!"

She starts to walk toward Sea Coast, and her mom calls after her.

"You're sure you're feeling okay?" Gabby asks one last time.

Lizzie nods and gives her a thumbs-up, and turns to go meet her husband.

"Hey! That float was wonderful!" Lizzie says, running into Jack's arms, and he then twirls her around.

"Yeah? You think so? We were pretty happy with it, and we got a good response from the crowd," Jack says.

"Yes, it perfectly represented everything it's about. I loved it," she says, kissing him.

"Apparently I should be on parade floats more often if that's the response I get," he says, kissing her back.

"Hey you two, get a room!" they hear. As they turn around they see Alexis and Ian, followed by Ben, Sean and little Ollie. Lizzie can't help but notice Ollie's eyes are all red, like he's been crying.

"Everything okay?" she discreetly asks, looking at Sean and Ben.

"Yeah, the noise was a little much, and someone had some little bang snap noise makers they kept tossing near us and, well, he was not fond of them, and honestly, neither am I," Ben says. Ollie is now happily patting a golden retriever who was walking by with its owner.

"You'd think seeing it was making a little kid cry might have gotten them to stop," Sean says, shaking his head. "But nope, they thought it was great fun despite everyone asking them to please stop."

So much for kindness at the parade, thought Lizzie. First she gets mowed down, then people don't care that they're making a toddler cry? What is happening in Cranberry Harbor?

The family all returned home to take a bit of a breather before the fireworks. It felt good to get out of the fray for a little while and Lizzie and Jack were very happy to be in the quiet of their house, though even a couple of miles away from the center of town, in the middle of the day periodic snaps, crackles and pops could be heard. Lizzie always felt for animals on the Fourth. Every year the paper ran articles about how scary it was not just for domestic animals, but for birds and wild animals as well. She'd even run an editorial about how in many countries they'd switched to laser shows, equally majestic and brilliant, but with no debris falling into the ocean, and no noises terrorizing wildlife. But change was hard, and as Jack often said with a shrug, "People like blowing shit up." And he was right.

If it hadn't been part of her job to go to the fireworks, Lizzie would have been just as happy to stay home, grill something with her parents, and turn in early. But that's not the life she had, and as editor in chief of the town's weekly newspaper she had to be there.

"I can hear the enthusiasm in the sighs as you put on your shoes," Jack says empathetically. "Can't Eric cover it for you? He's going to be there anyway, right?"

"He is, but it's too much for one person. We need to cover different areas. If you're tired you don't have to come," she says. "No reason for both of us to have to go. I really don't mind; please just stay home and rest if you want."

"No way. It's the Fourth of July," he says, getting up off the couch. "Come here," he says, reaching out and embracing her. "I know we both have mixed feelings about the crowds, the noise, and the traffic, but it will be fun, I promise."

"You promise, huh?" she says, smiling at him. "Well, if you promise, I guess I have to go and see what possible fun times will ensue!"

CHAPTER 16

Lizzie and Jack lucked out. They'd had to park a fair distance from Sea Meadow Beach, but a police officer on her way there recognized them, told them to hop into her cruiser, and gave them a ride.

"Lily, thank you so, so much," Lizzie said as they exited the back of the car.

"No problem. I'm glad I spotted you two." She pauses and looks around. "I know I've only been here for three years, but does this crowd seem bigger than last year? I don't recall seeing this many people at the fireworks before." She looks a little intimidated.

Jack nods. "It does seem to have brought in the crowds, that's for sure." He's looking around, trying to see if he sees one familiar face. Not so far.

"Two other local towns canceled their displays due to budget constraints, so that may be why we're seeing more people than ever," Lizzie says, wondering what her plan of action should be. "Well, thank you again, Lily, and I hope it's a quiet and peaceful night for everyone."

As she and Jack start walking toward the beach from the parking lot, she pulls out her phone and starts taking some pictures.

"I was going to say you could go do your own thing if you like," she says, turning around and taking in the spectacle of it all, "but we might never find each other." She laughs.

"Yeah, I plan to stick with you. It should be starting pretty soon," he says, looking at the dusky sky. "It's going to be getting dark any minute."

The words are no sooner out of his mouth and the first fireworks go up, lighting up the skies, eliciting lots of oohs and ahhs from the crowd.

Jack has his phone out, too, taking pictures, knowing it's always better for Lizzie to have too many to choose from than not enough. It really is spectacular. They work their way down closer to the shore and closer to the action. The fireworks are being launched from a boat out in the bay and she wants to get a picture of that as well.

She is very happy to see the *Sharknation* guy has left, and from the small rumblings she'd heard, it was kind of a dud, which makes her feel very good about her community. Perhaps they weren't so easily scared and gullible about sea life.

Lizzie feels like a party pooper, but she is good after about 15 minutes of the action. Thankfully it ends in about 25 minutes. There are a few moans of disappointment, but most everyone seems ready to disperse and begin the long walk back to their cars parked up and down Sea Street.

"Hey, guys!" Lizzie and Jack hear as they're stepping off the beach.

"Hey!" Lizzie turns and sees Alexis and Ian, amazed to actually see some people they know. Lizzie gives Alexis a big hug, and Alexis squeezes her back.

"Where were you guys?" Jacks asks as they all start walking into the parking lot toward the road.

They look at each other with a look that definitely means something is up.

"Okay, friend, what's going on?" Lizzie says.

"Wow, I cannot hide anything from you, can I?" Alexis says.

"Hey, I've known you for most of my life, no, you cannot. Come on, spill," Lizzie says.

Alexis stops walking, so they all do, and she holds up her left hand, which is now sporting a beautiful vintage diamond ring, and she's beaming.

"What?! You proposed during the fireworks?" Lizzie says to Ian, admiring the ring, and then grabbing Alexis and hugging her.

"Hey, I'm a filmmaker; it seemed quite cinematic," he says, beaming and hugging Alexis into him tightly.

"Congratulations, man," Jack says, giving Ian a hug.

Lizzie finds herself welling up. She's so happy for her dearest friend.

"I'm so happy for you, for you both!" she says to Alexis, as the tears start to flow. The two friends embrace, and now they're both crying. And then laughing.

"Dear Lord, we're a mess," Alexis says, wiping her eyes and nose on the sleeve of her sweatshirt. "Look at me!" she says, laughing, "I'm a huge mess!"

"A beautiful, huge mess," Lizzie says, wiping her eyes too. "I am so happy for you both. You two are such a perfect fit, and I can't wait to get to be a part of the life you create together, which I certainly hope is here. You're not stealing my friend away, are you?" Lizzie says to Ian, hugging Alexis tightly.

"I wouldn't dare take her away from here," Ian says. "And I love the Cape too. My mom is here, and it seems like the perfect place to raise a family."

"Wait, you're not..." Lizzie asks, excited and wondering if there's more news to share.

Alexis emphatically shakes her head. "No, no, no, not yet, but hopefully, someday..."

"Well, is everyone ready to walk back to our cars?" Jack asks, very ready to head back.

"Yup, I want to go show Grandpa this beautiful ring," Alexis says, once again admiring the ring, which is glimmering in the starlit night.

"We have lots of planning to do," Lizzie says, taking Alexis by the arm.

"Yes, we do," Alexis says.

"I can't wait!" Lizzie says. "You know, the people here are very good at pulling off weddings without months and months of planning," she teases, referencing her own wedding that Alexis, Leah and her family pulled off in short order.

"To be continued," Alexis says, as she and Ian turn down a side street where they'd parked.

"Yes! And soon! Love you!" Lizzie calls after her.

"Love you too!" Alexis calls back, getting into Ian's car.

Before Lizzie knows it, it is Town Meeting day. She'd grown up going to town meetings in Cranberry Harbor. In eighth grade all students have to go to one town meeting and write a report on it. It was usually not the highlight of any student's middle school years, except the year Lizzie and Jack were at the special age, and her dad took them.

This particular meeting had become something of town lore. It had started off innocently enough. A group of people had gotten together who wanted to create a dog park, not far from where Terra Marique was now located. A few of them had gone to map out the property, take photos, and assess where they could have fences, some benches for people to sit, access to water for the dogs and such.

There were four people, three men and one woman, who were checking out the land that day. They were walking around with clipboards, measuring tapes, and cameras, when they stumbled, literally, upon a tryst happening between the married town manager, Evelyn Thompson, and the also-married fire chief, Fred Doyle. None of this would have ever become public information if the powers that be hadn't shot down the idea of the dog park without even hearing the benefits to humans and canines, what a positive draw it would be for Cranberry Harbor, and how they had raised enough funds to pay for it with private donations. No, a gavel went down, a unanimous, and unexplained "no" came out of Evelyn's lips, and then it was off to the races.

As forty Cranberry Harbor middle school students looked on, wide-eyed and confused, a barrage of expletives, accusations, and threats of punches to various people enveloped the room as details of the affair were bellowed to the very crowded high school gymnasium. A horrified moderator kept pounding their gavel, an hysterical Evelyn ran out of the building, her husband in quick pursuit after her, and then silence befell the room as Fred's wife stood up and yelled, "You have twenty-four hours to get all your things out of the house before I put them on the lawn and set fire to them!" And then she stormed out. At 13 Lizzie quickly recognized the irony and had to laugh a little at the idea of a fire on the fire chief's lawn. It was her first brush with realizing that adults don't have any more of an idea about what they're doing than kids do, and it sealed her desire to become a writer.

Needless to say, no other town meeting she'd ever gone to had lived up to that one. Even getting Terra Marique passed a few years ago, though it had some drama, couldn't come near that scandalous year. At least she hoped so.

Lizzie and Jack get to the meeting about fifteen minutes early, sign in, and take their seats. When she sees Connie arrive she goes over to talk to her.

"Hi, so we're still good for me to take a few minutes and talk about our kindness initiative?" Lizzie says.

Connie looks down at her notes. "Yes, I have you slated to speak quite early on, before people get restless, tired, mad or hungry," she says, smiling.

Lizzie laughs.

"Oh, you'd be surprised, or maybe not, how many people leave in a huff or just get tired. Heck, it's my job and believe me, there are many times I think I'd love to walk out."

Lizzie shakes her head. "I cannot imagine having to be here for the whole thing," she says. "In all honesty I've only made it through the whole meeting a couple of times, and probably then only because I came with my dad and needed a ride home."

"In many ways it's a wonderful example of democracy in real time," Connie says, "but in others it feels antiquated, and like a platform for those who like to hear themselves talk and hold people captive with their opinions. Sometimes it's wonderful. I've witnessed some incredible moments of humanity, and other times?" She shakes her head, "It leaves me wondering how we, as a species, have made it this far."

"Wow, well, now I'm a little nervous!" Lizzie says, a bit shaken.

"You'll be fine," Connie says, putting a comforting hand on her shoulder. "Just don't be surprised, as nice as what you're doing is, to have a few naysayers. It's what they do, so don't take it personally.

It's like a hobby for those folks. I think knitting or bird watching would be a better use of time, but," she shrugs her shoulders, "to each their own."

As Lizzie walks back to her seat by Jack she feels even more nervous, and Jack can see it on her face.

'What's the matter? You didn't get pushed off the docket, did you?" he asks.

"No, I'm scheduled to speak, but now, I don't know—what if people get mad? Or they think it's s stupid idea?" Lizzie says, feeling spooked.

"It's not a stupid idea," Jack says.

"Yeah? You love me. You thought when I wanted to get alpacas it wasn't stupid, even though we have no time—or enough land, really. I don't think I can trust you to vet my ideas," she says.

"Okay, alpacas were a dumb, albeit cute idea. This is not. Encouraging people to be kinder and look out for each other more is a big act of kindness and generosity in and of itself," Jack says. "And if anyone gives you a hard time..."

"Oh boy, it will be Evelyn and Fred all over again," she says, laughing and feeling a bit more calm.

"You're going to do great," he says, kissing her on the temple and squeezing her knee. "You've got this."

The meeting is called to order, a quorum is established, and the games are about to begin.

The first thing people have to vote on is the hiring of two extra lifeguards for the summer, and that easily passes. Voting had become much quicker since the town had invested in hand-held remotes, with the votes immediately recorded by Connie on a computer screen next to the moderator at the front of the room. In the days of yore—well, up until five years ago—each voter was given a card to hold up when they were voting, and several volunteers traversed the room counting those cards. The new system also makes some issues less nerve-wracking—like funding a new police station. One might feel self-conscious questioning the expense while several officers stood around the room. Now voting was kept private, allowing voters to remain anonymous.

After a second round of voting on replacing the dead hydrangea bushes on the town green passed easily, there was only one small amount of discussion. Someone brought up planting rhododendrons instead, but that was quickly revoked, and the hydrangeas won the day. Then it was time for Lizzie to speak.

Sharon MacKenzie, the moderator, read from the introduction Connie had given her.

"And now, Lizzie Martin, editor-in-chief of the Cranberry Cove Gazette, has a proposal she would like to bring before the town. Ms. Martin, the floor is yours."

Jack gives her a thumbs-up and she walks to the lectern and mic at the front of the room.

"Thank you, Ms. Moderator, and to all of you. I promise to not take much of your time," she says, then nervously clears her throat.

"By a show of hands, how many of you, while driving around Cranberry Harbor, have had someone cut you off, or slam on their horn, or give you a hand gesture we all know well, or fail to even raise their hand in thanks when you've let them into the street?" Lizzie looks out at a sea of raised hands. "How many of you have been that person not saying thank you to the checkout person at Bradford's, the person making and serving your morning coffee at Sea Coast, or even just smiling and saying hello to people in town?" She sees people looking at each other nervously, and raises her own hand. "We're all guilty of being in a hurry, having a bad day, and not being our best selves." She puts her hand down and takes the mic out of the stand and walks in front of the podium. A part of her doesn't recognize herself. She's never liked public speaking, but this feels good. It feels important, which takes precedence over her fear.

"I knew I wasn't alone in noticing an increase in the impatience, and at times incivility around Cranberry Harbor, especially during the height of the summer season. And I get it—life is hard, we're all busy, and it's not easy to remember to be kind." Lizzie is surprised to see how intently everyone is listening, many nodding in recognition. Maybe this isn't such a crazy idea after all. She begins walking slowly back and forth in front of the crowd. *Maybe this is what giving a TED Talk feels like,* she thinks.

"People honking more, being rude to sales staff in stores, and not treating servers at restaurants, coffee shops and ice cream stands well. Even little things, like waving thank you when someone lets you in traffic, or stops so you can cross the street, are in short supply, and it's making Cranberry Harbor feel different, less friendly, less who we've always been." She sees more people nodding their heads.

"So a few of us—me, Alexis Johnson, Leah Alden, and Eric Jackson—have been meeting to discuss the idea of making Cranberry Harbor a Kindness Zone." Lizzie hears someone sigh loudly and guffaw but refuses to let it throw her off. "Our idea is to make kindness, for lack of a better term, and in keeping with this present time, our brand." She stops for a few seconds, assessing the feel of the room. She doesn't think she's lost them, not yet anyway.

"We want to place some banners around town. Individual businesses can put up signs if they choose, and the library is on board as well. All we want to do is to remind all of us to just," she pauses for emphasis, "be kind." She picks up a sign Leah has made as a sample. It's a bumble bee, with the word KIND after it, a perhaps cuter way to say Be Kind.

"Kindness is contagious, in the best possible way," she says. "Our hope is that we can all be, I don't know, perhaps kindness ambassadors for the people who come here, and yes, for those of us who live here year round as well. All we're asking is for the okay of the town to put up some signs, a banner across Main Street, and maybe some items here and there, like a dispenser that will give people random acts of kindness they can perform, like putting someone's grocery cart back for them, treating the person behind you in line to their coffee, things like that."

She pauses as she's wrapping up. "I don't feel like it's a huge ask, but what I'm hoping is that there will be a huge benefit to all of us in so many ways. Does anyone have any questions?" She turns to Sharon, the moderator. "Is it okay to answer any questions?" Sharon nods, but also points to her watch. Lizzie nods back, getting the message to keep it short.

Lizzie's heart sinks when she sees the first person walking to the mic is Bud Mackelroy, fifth-generation Cranberry Harbor resident who never met a new idea he didn't need to complain about. As a matter of fact, he had chained himself to a tree at the Terra Marique property when that passed at town meeting, but he'd seemed to have had a real change of heart and had actually even taken a pottery class at Terra Marique, and frequently bought food from the vendors who used the commercial kitchen on site. Despite all that, Lizzie isn't sure how he is going to react to this idea.

He clears his throat and she braces herself for a barrage of negativity.

"I like it," he says. And that is it.

Lizzie looks over at Jack, who's looking at her wide-eyed as he shrugs and mouths, "Wow!"

"Thank you, Bud, I really appreciate that," she says.

"Anyone else?" Lizzie asks.

Right behind him is a very upset-looking Billy Taylor, his former cohort in all areas of disrupting positive progress in Cranberry Harbor.

Billy all but shoves Bud out of the way, grabbing the mic.

"Well, I never thought I'd see the day where we would pass rules for how we're supposed to behave. Isn't this America?" he says, looking around the room, seemingly expecting thunderous applause to come, which it does not. What does come is a collective moan and cries of "Sit down, Billy, no one wants to hear it!"

"So all you folks are okay with being told what to say, how to act?" he says.

Bud, who is still standing there, puts his hand on his apparently former friend's shoulder and says, "The lady is just saying we should be kinder to each other, Billy. That's a good thing."

"Ah, you've gone soft," Billy snaps. "Ever since you got that lady friend you've gone totally soft." He looks around the room. "If I want to give someone the finger I will, and if I want to blow my horn I will. Ain't none of you washashores gonna tell me otherwise! And Bud? I feel sorry for you," and then Billy shocks everyone by taking a swing at Bud. There's a collective gasp, and the police officers on duty come rushing over and grab Billy, who's squirming and yelling as they escort him out of the gymnasium.

"To hell with all of you!" he yells as the door swings shut behind them.

Lizzie takes a beat and catches her breath, and then sees her dad, Peter, get up, and she gets a lump in her throat.

"Wow, who knew kindness could be so controversial, huh?" he says. Leave it to Peter Martin to know how to bring everyone back and calm the situation. Lizzie smiles and shakes her head, feeling very proud to be his daughter.

"I promise I won't take long, or use this forum to gush about my brilliant daughter and her friends who want to do this, though I suppose I just did," he says, smiling. "Most of you long-timers know me. I've lived here my whole life. I started the Gazette in my twenties and ran it until last year, when my wonderful and talented daughter took it over." He pauses, looking pensive. "I love this town. I've never wanted to live anywhere else. But over time, lots of new people, new businesses, and more money, have come in and it's feeling different. I look at this as a way to bring back what we all love about Cranberry Harbor: that someone will stop to help you change a tire, bring you soup when you're sick, buy you lunch if you're a little down on your luck. That's what Cranberry Harbor is at its core. We're still that. But it's gotten a little fuzzy around the edges with social media and less interacting with each other face to face, heart to heart. We can be better, and we can do better by each other. I think this is a great idea, and I would even if Lizzie wasn't my daughter."

"Thank you, Dad," Lizzie says, holding back tears.

"If there's no more discussion, I think we're ready to take a vote," Sharon MacKenzie says from her moderator post. "The vote is a simple yes or no. You can use your remotes to vote yes, we are designating Cranberry Harbor to be a kindness zone, and while there is nothing legal or binding about said designation, we are committing to putting efforts into messaging throughout the town that we are a place where kindness matters. You can vote now," she says.

Within just a couple of minutes the results are on Connie's screen.

"We have 691 yes, and three no," Connie says. "The request passes."

Lizzie goes back to her seat, and Jack stands up to hug her.

"You did it! Congratulations," he says, kissing her.

"Well, it literally took a village. Wow, I did not see Billy trying to hit Bud happening," she says, looking at him as they both sit down.

"Yeah, me neither, I have a feeling there may have been some pre-town meeting imbibing involved," Jack says.

"Yeah, and unfortunately, years of displaced anger and resentment at everyone in town," Lizzie replies, to which Jack nods in agreement.

There are several more items on the warrant, but after speaking before everyone, and the drama of the attempted fight, she is finding it hard to concentrate or pay attention. She doesn't want to stay but knows it would be incredibly ungracious to leave before the final gavel is struck. And it seems to take forever. As always, there is controversy over a second dog park. Getting one had taken forever, and now a committee had formed to create another one, and several people were up in arms. You would have thought someone was proposing a strip club, not a place where local dogs could play with each other off-leash and their owners could socialize. Lizzie and Jack looked at each other and rolled their eyes, both more than ready to leave. That topic was tabled until there was more information about where the park in question would be located. The proposed site was deemed too close to Cranberry Harbor Elementary School, so a new site was to be explored. As annoying as it sometimes was, Lizzie did think how fortunate she was to live in a place where these were the problems. Of course there were bigger issues that they had dealt with over time, like the environment and preserving the Cape, affordable housing and jobs, but for today at least, it all felt very easy, and like these were pretty happy problems to have.

When that gavel finally does go down, signaling the end of the meeting, Alexis and Ian rush over, both of them hugging Lizzie.

Eric is there too, and has been taking notes to report on the meeting for the next edition of the Gazette.

"You did it!" Alexis says, jumping up and down. "You were awesome up there!"

"Thanks, friend. Yeah, I got a bit freaked out when Billy came up, wondering what kind of mayhem might ensue, but I did not see fists being thrown tonight," Lizzie says.

"Right? As your dad said, who knew kindness could be so controversial? That said, I have to say, who would have thought, after everything he put us all through over Terra Marique, that Bud Mackelroy would be the Zen Master of the town meeting?" Jack says. "I hope maybe Billy can get some help," he says. "That's not a fun way to go through life, for him, or the people around him."

"Very true," Lizzie says. "I'm just glad the drama didn't keep it from being approved, and I'll have to make sure to personally thank Bud for what he said."

"This was my first ever town meeting," Ian says. "Wow, it's amazing to see in real time people discussing the town, working as a community, and embracing this idea. You really could feel the energy of people taking in what you were saying. It was palpable." He's quiet for a minute and then turns to Lizzie. "Would you be okay if I added something about what happens to a small town when they decide to become more kind to the impact Terra Marique is having in this little piece I'm working on? I think it could be a really cool little case study."

Lizzie and Alexis and Jack all exchange looks, and Lizzie shrugs. "It's okay with me. What do you two think?" Jack and Alexis nod. "I mean this wouldn't be a big production, right? It would just be… you? Just you and a camera?"

"Yeah, just me. I'd just wander around town and—with permission, of course—talk to people, ask them about acts of kindness they've performed or witnessed, how it makes them feel to have someone do something nice, or even more so, to do something kind for someone else," Ian says, his creative wheels turning.

"I think that could be really good, and like I said, kindness is contagious. Maybe if other places see what we're doing here, they'll want to do the same thing too," Lizzie says. "Thanks for being interested in adding it to the film."

"Well, I don't know about all of you, but I could go for something to eat and to celebrate our victory," Eric says.

"Murphy's?" they all say at the same time.

"Murphy's it is," Eric says.

Lizzie has kept an eye on her parents, waiting for them to be free from the swarm of people surrounding them, and as she and Jack walk toward the door to leave, they are still surrounded. Between her dad having founded and run the town's paper for close to 40 years, and her mom having been the beloved family doctor in town for close to the same amount of time, Lizzie is used to the celebrity status they hold. And she loves that people appreciate the amazing people her parents are. Without saying a word, she walks up to her dad and hugs him, whispering in his ear, "Thanks, Dad, I love you."

He kisses her on the cheek and hugs her. "Love you too, sweetie," he says. She gives her mom a hug too.

"We're off to Murphy's if you want to join," she says.

They shake their heads. "We've got pickleball at 7 in the morning, so we've got to get to bed," Gabby says, smiling at them. "I'm glad you're going to go celebrate. You were so great!" she says, hugging Lizzie again. "Matt and Shannon apologize for not being here. Sophie came down with a cold and they didn't want to spread it around. They hated to miss it."

""I'm sorry Sophie's sick. I'll call them tomorrow. Thank you again for being here," she says, blowing a kiss as she walks to the door.

"Wouldn't have missed it for anything, not even pickleball," her dad jokes.

Lizzie smiles and walks out to the parking lot, feeling really good about what they've started.

CHAPTER 17

Their table at Murphy's also includes Leah and Jonanthan, who is becoming a bit of a staple in their gatherings. Lizzie is thrilled to see Leah happy in a relationship, though she does have passing thoughts about what is going to happen when the summer baseball season ends and it is time for Jonathan to leave. She wasn't a mother yet, but she sure could think like one.

Once they all get settled and have a beverage, Jack taps his beer mug with a spoon, and once everyone at the table has stopped talking, he raises his glass.

"To the next generation of movers and shakers in Cranberry Harbor," he says. "We have officially become the people who advocate for change, who work to make the town better, and who fight the good fight to make this town the best it can be," he says.

"This is sounding like an ad campaign," Alexis teases. "'Be all you can be in Cranberry Harbor!'" She raises her glass and they all clink.

Jack laughs. "Okay, all cliches aside, I'm really proud of all of you for how hard you've worked to make this happen. Most people don't bother, and you are all making things better, and you are the best."

"Well, right back at you," Leah says. "It is pretty amazing. I mean, look at this group. You started Terra Marique," she says to Jack. "You're running the town paper..." she says to Lizzie.

"You've taken over your family's business," Alexis says to Leah, who shrugs and looks down. "Don't be shy about it; that's a big deal!"

"You're right, I'm pretty proud of that," Leah says. "But what I want to get across is that, I don't know, it may sound hokey, but I think the future of Cranberry Harbor is in really good hands, and that the future doesn't look as bleak as I thought it was going to a few years ago."

"You thought it was bleak?" Lizzie asks.

"Well, yeah, when I came back after college to help my Grandma run Sea Coast, I thought it was going to turn into some rich person's town, with no more locals, no artists able to live here, no farming, no young families. But thanks to the people at this table, we're changing things, and we're making it better," Leah says.

"It's true," Ian says. "I know I'm an outsider, but I'm an outsider who loves the creative history of the Cape, and all the people who paved the way for people like me who want to create things, live near the beach, and not live a typical 9 to 5 life."

"It really does seem like a pretty magical place," Jonathan says. "Until I came here to work with the Salty Dogs I'd only come for a few vacations with my family, and all I saw was the beach, clam shacks, and ice cream shops," he jokes. "But all of you," he says, mostly looking at Leah, "have been so welcoming and let me in. It's been amazing to see more of the year-round community that makes this place unique. Thank you for letting me in."

"There's no getting out now," Jack jokes. "You're officially one of us."

Jonathan smiles and nods. "I appreciate that," he says, putting his arm around Leah. "It's going to be hard to leave at the end of the summer."

"You never know what might happen," Alexis says. "Cranberry Harbor can make some magical things happen."

"So, what do we do first?" Lizzie says, trying to get everyone organized.

Jack leans over and kisses Lizzie on the cheek. "This is what I love about my wife. She can have an amazing night, speak in front of almost 700 people, have them in the palm of her hand, completely supporting her idea, voting for it, and applauding her, but a half hour later, in her mind, it never happened and it's back to business as usual."

Lizzie laughs. "Wow, I really can't take a minute to bask, can I?"

"Nope, never have, and I'm not sure ever will," Alexis says. "But that's why we love you. And why we tease you!"

"Okay, for tonight let's celebrate, and tomorrow we plan," she says. "To kindness!" she says, raising her wine glass, and they all clink and smile.

They all had a wonderful evening out, but Jack finds himself awake in the middle of the night, trying to be quiet as he tiptoes downstairs where once again, at three in the morning he is sitting on the couch with his laptop. He is trying his best to not rain on Lizzie's kindness parade, but he'd had another call the day before with yet another VC, Sonia, a woman he'd known in his Silicon Valley days, and he was getting more and more nervous about being replaced as the director of Terra Marique. He'd analyzed his worry, wondering if it was just ego, that he didn't want anyone taking his place because it was his vision, his efforts—along with many others, of course—that had brought this amazing place to fruition. He felt pretty clean about that. Yes, there was some ego involved—he was human after all—but that wasn't what was keeping him up at night. It was more that no random person they would bring in from California, or anywhere else, would care as much as he did about Terra Marique. He'd seen this happen way too many times in his time out there. People who think only bottom line, who only see dollars and cents, and not the humans involved in whatever business they were invested in. Terra Marique isn't a commodity to him, to the people who live and work there, or to the town of Cranberry Harbor. It is a living, and breathing community, and he is determined to protect it from being taken over by the investors who had made it all possible, but somehow now, because some of the numbers they wanted to see weren't adding up, were getting nervous and wanted to plug in someone with more business experience than he had to run the place.

He knew he was getting way ahead of himself. That's what we all do in the middle of the night, that time when logic seems to go out the window and is replaced by the scariest, most negative thoughts we can have. He knew that no one had told him he was being replaced, but just having all these people asking questions was freaking him out.

Hours later, as Jack dozes with his laptop still open next to him, Lizzie comes down the stairs, and sees him, head down, lightly snoring. She glances at his screen, open to a page that lists, among other articles, *The Top 10 Rules For Running A Successful Company* and *How Do You Know You're About To Be Fired?*

Lizzie is stunned. She'd had no idea he was that concerned. Of course she knew about the meeting with the VC, but since he hadn't said too much more she'd hoped things had settled down. Then she started to think about how he'd been kind of withdrawn, even though he hadn't said anything. She suddenly feels awful that she'd been so focused on thinking about being kind to everyone in Cranberry Harbor that maybe she had ignored the most important person in her own life. He starts to stir. Lizzie doesn't want him to know she's seen what he was reading. She wants him to open up to her when he's ready, not force it on him. She quietly makes her way to the kitchen and starts making some coffee for them.

He walks in, stretching and yawning. "Good morning, babe, I guess I passed out while I was working on some stuff. Sorry I didn't come back to bed." He gives her a hug.

"I'm sorry you spent the night sleeping upright on the couch," she says, putting down the bag of coffee and hugging him back. "Everything okay? Anything I can help you with?" she asks, hoping he'll open up.

"No, thank you, though," he says, stretching some more, and reaching for a glass to have some water. "It's just some admin stuff I'm working on. It will be fine," he says, downing a tumbler of water.

"Okay, but remember, two heads are almost always better than one, okay? I'm always happy to support you, like I know you would me," she says, pouring boiling water from the gooseneck electric kettle into their pour-over coffee maker, already full with freshly ground Sea Coast coffee. This is a ritual that never ceases to make her feel like the biggest trend-following hipster around, but the coffee is so good she can deal with feeling a little cringey about it.

As she waits for the coffee she wishes Jack would talk to her about what's happening at Terra Marique. She knows he's worried, but about what she has no idea.

"So, what's on your agenda, Ms. Kindness Ambassador?" Jack says, starting to finally wake up a bit more. "I just have to say again, I'm so impressed by you deciding to do this and making it actually happen. You really are incredible," he says.

Lizzie walks over to him and gives him a big hug.

"That's very sweet. Thank you, honey, I appreciate it," she says, walking over to the coffee pot, where she takes out the coffee filter, puts it in the compost pot, and pours them each a lovely cup of the best coffee around. She takes a little cream; Jack drinks his black. It's become a nice little ritual with their ridiculously busy lives and she savors it.

"What about you? Anything other than the usual 8000 things you handle in a day on your calendar?" Lizzie asks, both of them now sitting at the kitchen table, looking out into the slightly neglected backyard. "Should we hire someone to mow for us?" she says, looking at how tall the grass is getting and how all the edges to the flower/weed beds are getting seriously ragged.

Jack sighs, "It really feels like the ultimate laziness, but neither of us seems to have the time, and I worry if we don't do it your dad will feel like he should help and then he ends up taking care of both yards, and that's not right." He lets out a sigh.

"Yeah, I've wondered the same thing," Lizzie says, pulling back the lace curtain and eying what could be a very sweet yard. "I suppose we could look at it as giving work to someone who needs it, and not being neglectful, lazy homeowners," she says, smiling at Jack. "Actually, there is a brother and sister in the neighborhood, the Millers' kids. I think Mom told me they came by. They were starting a lawn and gardening business for the neighborhood. Might be nice to throw some work to them. I'd feel less guilty not doing it ourselves if we were helping some local kids."

Jack, distractedly looking at his phone, clearly only caught a fraction of what Lizzie was saying. Nonetheless, he nods and says yes. Something involving local kids most likely deserves a yes.

"I know you didn't really hear me," she says, head tilted down, slightly smiling, "but I'm going to go ahead and reach out to those kids and ask them to come over and see what they could do."

"I'm sorry," he says, putting his phone down on the table. He reaches for her hand. "I did catch most of what you said, and if it means we don't have to mow the lawn I'm all in," he says, taking her hand and kissing it.

"Yeah, yeah, yeah, you think you can ignore me, and kiss my hand and it's all good," she says. She loves him so much. She knows there's something eating away at him so she's not going to bust him for breaking their cardinal rule about no phones when they're at the table together. But she is going to use the distraction to her advantage and get out of mowing the lawn herself.

Jack stands up and takes both of their cups, rinses them, and puts them in the dishwasher. "I am going to go take a shower. Did you want to use the outdoor shower?" he asks. "I don't want to nab it if you were going to use it."

"You go ahead. I can shower inside; it's no big deal." Before he walks out she calls to him, "Hey, I'm here, you know, for anything." She shrugs. "I've always got you."

"I know you do, and thank you," he says, hurrying off to grab a towel and head outside to the shower. He wants to get to work and see if he can prevent what he's worried is already in the works.

CHAPTER 18

Before going to the Gazette office, Lizzie has an idea that she wants to run by her mom. It was really nice to have a retired family practitioner in the family; she was always a font of information.

She knocked on the door as she opened it slightly and jokingly called to her mother, "Mom? You decent?" .

Her mother appeared, fully dressed and laughing, wearing a very cute Hello Kitty apron, clearly way ahead of Lizzie in getting things done.

"Yes, I'd say I'm quite decent," she says, curtseying and giving a little twirl.

"Very nice. Gee, it's only 8:45 and you're already cooking? And wearing a pretty awesome apron, I might add," Lizzie says, looking over the assemblage of ingredients on the counter. "What are you making? Looks like lasagna, perhaps?"

"Yes, once a month I make four medium-sized trays of lasagna to bring to the Cranberry Harbor Senior Center for them to give out to people in need of some hot meals," she says. "And this very cute apron was a gift from Sophie, who decided I did not have enough Hello Kitty in the house, and as she says, 'Hello Kitty is life,' so I had to have this. I thought it was very sweet of her."

"It was very sweet of her; she's the best." Lizzie pulls up a stool and sits down.

"I just heated up some water for tea. Do you want some?" her mom asks, already taking a mug off the shelf. "What kind?"

Lizzie loves her mom so much. Without being controlling or intrusive she makes everyone feel cared for and loved. Lizzie is well aware it's a gift not many people have, but Gabby has it in spades.

"I'd love some. How about that lemon ginger one to your left?" she says, stealing a small chunk of mozzarella while her mom's back is turned.

"Here you go. I even put in one squeeze of honey, just how you like it," Gabby says, returning to her lasagna assembly line. "So what's up, buttercup?" she asks.

"Well, I had an idea this morning about the kindness project, and it made me think of you," she says, pausing to take a sip of tea.

"And what might that be?" her mom asks, looking up from her work.

"There's so much research out there about happiness and stress, and how studies have shown that doing things for others is a great way to increase your own happiness," Lizzie says.

"That's all very true," Gabby says, pausing her lasagna-making to think. "I just read a study the other day in a medical journal about how performing acts of kindness boosts your own confidence, makes you happier, and encourages others to pass it on and do kind things for others. People erroneously think that happiness comes from getting, but more and more science shows real, deep feelings of happiness and gratitude come from giving. It's exactly what you're doing in Cranberry Harbor."

"Would you ever let Eric interview you, as a retired doctor, about the physical and mental health benefits of kindness? I think it's better for him to do it than me," Lizzie asks, knowing her mother hates the spotlight.

"You think anyone would care what I have to say? I'm retired, I spend my days making lasagnas, driving people to their doctor appointments, babysitting for Sophie..."

"And are you happy?" Lizzie asks.

Gabby smiles. "Very."

"Bingo," Lizzie says. "But you can also speak to the balance of it all with self-care. Like you and Dad play pickleball, you practice mindfulness, go for walks and do yoga. You may be retired, but you're also super active."

"Happiness and well-being are very much connected to taking care of your body—eating well, moving, and community," Gabby says. "Sure, tell Eric to call me. I guess I do know a thing or two."

Lizzie gets up, rinses out her mug and puts it in the dishwasher. "You think?" she laughs as she hugs her mom. "Almost 40 years of practicing medicine seems to have taught you a thing or two, huh? I have to scoot, but I'll have Eric call you in the next couple of days. I think a piece about the trickle-down health effects of being kind to others could be really good. Thank you for being willing to help!"

"Always willing to help you, sweetie," she says, giving Lizzie a hug.

"Love you," Lizzie says. "See you later."

"Love you too, have a great day," Gabby says, continuing to assemble her lasagnas.

Lizzie has one more stop to make before hitting the office, Tall Tale Books. She'd been so busy planning for Town Meeting that she hadn't had a chance to see Anika and Jay to see what they might like to do for the kindness project. If she knew them, they were probably already way ahead of her.

The bell on the door frame jingles when she walks in, but she doesn't see Jay or Anika anywhere.

"Hello?" she calls out. "It's Lizzie," she says, as she eyes the new arrivals. She always wishes she had more time to read and vows right then and there that this fall she will finally join the monthly Tall Tales Book Club.

"Hi!" Anika says, coming out from the back of the store. She gives Lizzie a hug. "I hope you haven't been out there long. We were unpacking a shipment in the back and had that back and forth conversation we seem to have 100 times a day: 'Was that the door?' 'Did you hear someone?' It's never ending! So, what's up?"

"I feel terrible I haven't been in before to talk to you about the kindness project. It's not for lack of interest in having Tall Tales be a part of it, that's for sure," Lizzie says.

"No worries! Jay went to Town Meeting last night—the kids had a Salty Dogs game—and said despite a little drama, all went well and the town agreed to the idea," she says, straightening some books on the table near the entrance that were askew. "Sorry," she says, "force of habit."

"You and Jay are always so great about participating in the many Cranberry Harbor town activities, and I wondered if you had anything you'd like to do or are already doing, and what we could do through the Gazette to help promote it, but no pressure," Lizzie says, suddenly worried that the last thing Anika needs in the midst of Cape Cod summer busyness is one more thing to add to her plate.

"We have been thinking of a few things. One is well, we usually suspend the monthly Story Slam during the summer because it's just too much with how busy we are, but we thought we might do one, only do it outside on the town green so more people could come," she says.

"That sounds fun!" Lizzie says. "Do you have a theme?"

"Yes, we were thinking, and let me know if this sounds silly," she clears her throat, "'Tall Tales presents: Tales of Kindness: Something Someone Did For You That You'll Never Forget.'" Anika scrunches up her nose. "Too cutesy?"

"No! I love it!" Lizzie says. "And maybe we could get the folks from the Seaside Scoops to bring their ice cream truck there for the event? If there's not a Salty Dog's game that night."

"Oh, good idea, no problem. We'll make sure to schedule it when there's not a home game, which would be a good idea anyway. That's a very good reminder," she says, grabbing a piece of paper to make herself a note.

"I really do love that—thank you so much!" Lizzie says.

"We also want to have a pay-it-forward program, so people can buy a book for someone else, like how people pay for a coffee for someone, but with a book. I'm thinking especially children's books," Anika says. "Oh, and have a display of books about kindness, children's, novels, nonfiction, and offering 10 percent off any books about kindness."

"Wow! You've really given this a lot of thought, and I can't believe your generosity—well, actually I can. You and Jay are always so generous in giving to the town," Lizzie says.

"Did I hear my name?" Jay says, coming out from the back of the store.

"Yes, you did. I was just thanking Anika for all of the amazing kindness project ideas," Lizzie says. "Hi Jay, how are you?" she says, giving him a hug.

"Good." He takes a deep breath. "This is I think our fourth summer owning the store?" he says, looking at Anika for confirmation, and she nods. "But it still hits like a tsunami. I'm never quite ready for the added traffic, in town and in here, and the increased hours. It's a lot, but I should not complain. We have a pretty sweet life here," he says.

"But still, it's a lot, even for those of us who have been here for our whole lives. I laugh at how you'd think after over 30 years I would be used to the influx of people, but every year it's like it's a surprise," Lizzie says, rolling her eyes. "I think you seem to handle it very well. Have you found summer help yet? I know that can be hard."

Anika nods. "Yeah, we have two local kids, one going off to college in late August and one who's going to be a senior, so he might be able to work part-time even once school starts, which would be great," she says.

"Oh good. Well, you know this was my first job, along with Sea Coast, when I was in high school and college," Lizzie says.

"We're happy to hire you, you know, on a trial basis, to see how you work out," Jay teases, "if you're ever looking."

Lizzie laughs. "Oh my gosh, the idea of a job that I could do and then go home and not think about sounds delightful," she says.

Anika nods in agreement. "Oh boy, do I hear you. The idea of owning your own business sounds like total freedom, until you do it and then realize you are completely tethered to your work 24/7. I love it, and I wouldn't trade doing this for anything, but some days, I'm with you. I'd love a job I can forget about and relax."

"Something tells me none of us would be happy for long. We'd find ways to add to that job and end up being the manager of the shop, or organizing the workers into a union...we'd find some way to make it more than just a job we go to," says Lizzie.

"Yes, hence the woman who runs the newspaper starting a kindness project in town, because clearly you don't have enough on your plate," Jay says, cocking his head.

Lizzie nods in agreement and shakes her head. "Oh, believe me, I know. I wonder what the heck I'm doing when I'm trying to manage a few new freelancers, we only have Eric and me full time, and we are smack in the middle of our busiest season."

"Well, you know what they say," Ankia says. "If you want something done, ask a busy person."

"So true," Lizzie says. "Well, speaking of busy, I had better get to the paper and see what's happening there, but I think first I will grab myself an iced coffee next door to fuel myself for a few more hours." She starts to walk to the door and turns around. "Thank you both so much for all you do. Honestly, you make life so much better for all of us here in town. Thank you."

"We consider it a privilege to get to do it," Jay says.

"What he said," Anika says, "and take care of you, okay? Don't burn yourself out. Delegate and keep going to yoga; it's good for you."

"Yes ma'am, I will! See you soon!" Lizzie says, closing the door behind her.

Lizzie walks over to Sea Coast and hesitates for a moment when she sees a line of about 15 people ahead of her. Ah, summer in Cranberry Harbor. She ponders leaving, but there's no iced coffee at the paper, and now that she's thought of having some, she can't get it out of her head. She pulls out her phone and figures she can at least check her email while waiting.

A very well-dressed man and woman come in and get in line behind her. They're notable because you don't usually see fancy business attire in Cranberry Harbor, especially during the summer. Mostly it's comfortable clothes, with the occasional business casual outfit. As she checks her inbox they begin to talk, and she can't help but overhear. She likes to think of herself as a journalist, not a nosy person, as she eavesdrops.

"Are you sure it's a good idea to just show up like this? I don't think he's going to be happy to see us," says the guy.

Lizzie can practically hear the young woman shake her head

and dismiss him as she lets out a sigh. "We have a large stake in this business, and have every right to do a surprise visit, whether the current CEO likes it or not," she says as the line very slowly moves along.

"It's not really a business, though, right? It's a nonprofit, and it's doing very well by all our metrics: sustainability, lack of employee turnover, the population is at a stable place, it's not losing money, it's actually sustaining itself," the guy defends.

Lizzie tells herself she's merely being a good journalist as she continues to listen while the line slowly moves forward.

"He may think he's a born CEO and that Terra Marique is thriving, but the numbers could be better, and I'm not so sure some tech bro running it is the best idea," she says. "And besides, I've always wondered what it would be like to live on Cape Cod," she adds, sounding, Lizzie thinks, a bit like a Disney villain.

A chill goes through her because now she knows exactly what and who they're talking about. They're talking about her husband and it takes every bit of restraint to not turn around and give this arrogant woman a piece of her mind. "Be kind, be kind," she says in her head over and over. She finally gets to the counter, feeling stunned and scared for Jack. "Um, a large iced coffee, please?" she says to the young man behind the counter. She mindlessly thanks him, pays, leaves a tip in the jar, and walks to her car with her coffee.

When she gets in she's so confused. Jack has been stressed out, but she didn't think it was that serious. Does he have any idea what and who he's dealing with? She pulls her phone out and calls him.

"Hey, honey, how's your morning going?" he asks.

"It was going great until I ran into a woman at Sea Coast who I think is after your job," she says. "What's going on? Is everything okay?"

"Shit, so she's here?" he says.

"Yes, she is, and apparently she'd love to live on the Cape."

CHAPTER 19

Being a journalist does give one some very handy research skills, and as soon as Lizzie gets to the Gazette office she begins searching for the woman she'd seen at Sea Coast. Over the last year various venture capitalists had come and gone, apparently not unusual for the industry, so she wasn't sure at this point who the main investors were. The lists she is seeing are mostly male, something she finds annoying, and then deciding that isn't the point, she keeps scrolling.

Finally, after about 20 minutes she finds the woman she'd seen in line at Sea Coast. Her name is Amanda Solomon, and she is a senior associate at Bragg, Anderson and Miller in Boston. She graduated with an MBA from Harvard two years ago and appears to be on track to become a partner at her firm. What Lizzie doesn't get is why she would want to come to Cape Cod and run Terra Marique. It doesn't make any sense. She shuts her computer and begins pacing around the office, wondering what is happening at Terra Marique and how Jack is. She knows better than to call him, and that he will call when he can, but it is driving her crazy. Thankfully, Eric comes in and provides a much-needed distraction.

"Hey," he says, getting himself situated at his desk. "So..."

"Yes?" Lizzie says, wondering what's coming.

"It's only been a day or so, but I think people are pretty psyched about the kindness project," he says.

This is the perfect, much-needed distraction from worrying. "Really? Do tell!" she says, sitting down across from him at their desk.

"I went down to Sea Meadow beach to grab a few photos of the crowded beach for social media—you know, just see what's going on—and the Seaside Scoops ice cream truck was there, and they were giving out popsicles to any kid who wanted one," he says.

"That's really nice, but maybe they were just doing a promotion?" Lizzie says, not so sure this is at all related to their initiative.

"Oh no, they had a sign on the truck that said 'Cranberry Harbor: Bee Kind.' It was so great to see!" Eric says.

"Wow, really? That's so amazing! Already? It's only been a couple of days," Lizzie says. "Were people excited?"

"Yeah! All the kids were smiling, waving their popsicles around. It was a fun scene. I got some good pictures and quotes from both the ice cream truck guy, Marco, and some of the parents and kids. I'll write it up and get it up online as fast as I can," he says.

"Did Marco say why he was doing it?" Lizzie asks.

"Yeah, I asked, of course, and he said that he was really touched by what you said at town meeting the other night and that he wanted to do something to help spread some kindness and happiness around Cranberry Harbor," he says.

"Wow! I hoped for things like this to happen around town, but I don't know, I wasn't so sure they would." She pauses for a minute and looks out the window at Main Street. "The world just seems so cynical sometimes, and like everything is measured by how cool it is, or if it's going viral," she gets a little choked up, probably partly because she's worried about Jack, "but here someone is feeling good, and doing good by giving popsicles away. It's not a huge thing, it's not creating world peace or solving the climate crisis, but it's humans being kind to humans, and it's easy to forget how powerful that is."

"For sure." Eric is multi-tasking, uploading photos, referring to his notebook and typing. "Sorry, just give me five minutes. This is just a quick hit piece. I'll be right with you."

Lizzie shakes her head. "No, do your work. I should be leaving you alone. Thank you for being on the spot and capturing that." She opens her computer and sees the photos Eric has sent to her.

There's one of a little girl beaming at Marco in his ice cream truck with his handmade 'Bee Kind' banner under the Seaside Scoops name, as he hands her a popsicle.

"This one," she says, turning her screen to Eric. "This is the cover of the Gazette this week. "Brilliant. It's so great, Eric. Thank you for capturing this amazing moment. This," she says, looking at the photo, "this is what the kindness project is all about. Right here in this one exchange."

"I know, right? I agree, I got lucky on that one, because as soon as she had that in her hand she took off," he says laughing. "But I did get permission from her mom to use it," he says.

"You're always thinking, thank you," Lizzie says. "I think this one could win us a New England Press Award. It says absolutely everything without any words."

"Well said," Eric says, smiling and continuing to type away. "Okay, and it's off to you for a final edit and final approval," he says, pushing his chair back and putting his hands behind his head. "I really like this," he says.

"What? Writing for the Gazette? Because I like you writing for the Gazette too," she says, smiling back.

"No—well, yes, but I mean I like this project. It feels so good to go out hoping to capture people being nice to one another, you know?" He leans forward, elbows on the desk. "I mean, I know it's not exactly a hotbed of crime and action around here, but we do our fair share of reporting about crummy things. This just feels like, I don't know, like we're getting to be on summer vacation in a way, and getting to have fun seeing people hopefully being their best selves, and it's pretty nice."

"I hear you," Lizzie says. "I'm really glad we're doing this in the summer, not in the off-season, partly because hopefully we can help the people working in businesses in town deal with less grumpy people, but maybe because it's the height of the summer season it will get some regional, if not national, attention and maybe we can help kindness go viral!" Lizzie laughs at herself. Even though she's only in her mid-30s, she has moments of worrying she's trying too hard to be relevant and make things happen. When she says things like that she often pictures a teenager rolling her eyes at her, thinking, *as if*, though that is a saying that is probably so dated she has further dated herself, and surely a teen would just shrug their shoulders and sigh.

Eric, who's a few years younger, laughs. "The idea of you and me doing anything that goes viral seems next to impossible, but we millennials can dream," and they both laugh.

Lizzie gives Eric's piece a read, and as usual finds no errors. *How the heck does he turn in such clean copy every.single.time?* she wonders. "This is perfect, as usual. I'm posting it now, and," she glances at the clock, "we're right under the wire in getting it to the printer for the print edition tomorrow. Well done, sir."

"Okay, so that's done, now what to do..." She swivels her chair around and starts thinking about Jack again.

"You okay? You seem worried," Eric says. "This edition is great, for a change," he jokes, trying to get her to smile.

She turns her chair back around. "Very funny," she says. "I don't know what it is, but there's something going on with Terra Marique and the current investment group, and I'm worried about Jack. He's not saying much of anything but I know he's worried and he's not letting me in."

"I'm sorry. That's got to be hard," he says. "So this isn't the original investors?" he asks.

"No, he's been through a few firms. It seems like it's kind of like student loans, where your loans get sold off to other people, and while you had a relationship with one group, new people come in, and they're not invested in the project. Well, they are financially, but they're not emotionally invested in what you're doing. It's a numbers game, and I'm not happy that it's gone this way," she says.

"Wow, that's got to be tough. I didn't realize that was going on," Eric says. "What's your worry?"

"My concern?" She takes a deep breath. "That even though this was his idea, that he shepherded it through all the town's red tape, got it through town meeting, got it built—ahead of schedule, no less—and has it running beautifully, that they'll want to replace him with someone with more leadership experience. His background is in tech, and I'm worried as numbers people they won't think he adds up."

Eric takes a deep breath and sighs. "And you don't think you're just projecting? Worrying for no reason? Not that you ever do that," he says, smiling at her.

"Me? Worry for no reason? Nah, I never do that," she says, laughing, well aware of her penchant for worry. "Normally I would say it's just me, well, being me, but I've caught some calls he's been on. Granted, I'm only hearing his side, but I see his body language and demeanor, and he seems worried. He's not sleeping, and then today..." She stops and shakes her head. "And then today at Sea Coast, there was this man and woman behind me in line, and they seem to be from this new-ish VC company, and she was talking about the current leadership, how he was a 'tech bro,'" she says using air quotes and rolling her eyes, "and that she's always wanted to live on the Cape...I called Jack and he knew who I was talking about and then she walked in."

"Damn. I can see where that would be troubling, for sure," Eric says.

"I don't want to intrude in his business dealings, but I'm so worried and want to know what's going on, and wonder if he could use a good Hail Mary pass," she says.

"Heck, I can go over. I can just happen to stop by for a quote for a story," he says.

Lizzie isn't so sure this is a good idea. "I don't know," she says, scrunching up her face. "Jack is a very smart guy who also happens to know me very well. I think he would immediately connect the dots and not be too thrilled that his wife was sending in a surveillance team. But thank you."

"Then why don't you just happen to drop by with some coffee or a smoothie or something? That's not out of the norm; you do that a lot. It could be a needed break for him. Sometimes an unexpected and unwelcome meeting could use a good interruption," he says.

Lizzie ponders the idea. True, she does do that a few times a week, and she's sure Amanda Solomon didn't notice her in the long line to get their coffee.

"I see those wheels turning," Eric says. He shrugs. "Just go over. Like I said, he might be very happy for the break."

She's still thinking, overthinking probably, as is her way. And then she just stands up. This is her husband, darn it, and she wants to make sure he's okay, protocols be damned.

"You're right. I don't know why I'm so nervous about it. I talk to people all the time, but for some reason this situation has me spooked." She picks up her pocketbook and keys and heads to the door, then turns around. "Thanks for the nudge. I appreciate it."

Eric smiles at her. "Any time, and feel free to nudge me if you think I need it sometime too," he says. "And hey, make sure to let me know what's going on. I'm invested now."

"Will do." She takes a deep breath. "Wish me luck!"

"Luck!" he calls out as the door closes, and he turns back to his work.

Within five minutes Lizzie is pulling up to Terra Marique. There is a very fancy electric car parked next to Jack's older hybrid. She picks up the iced coffee she bought for Jack out of the cup holder and walks toward the main building where Jack and Alexis's offices are.

She walks to his office and the door is wide open, but no one is there.

"Huh," she says out loud and puts the coffee down on his desk. She takes her phone out of her pocket to text him, but then sees his phone sitting on the desk.

"Hey you," she hears behind her. It's Alexis.

"Hey back. I was just out and thought I'd drop off some coffee for Jack, but he's not here." She's the worst liar on the planet and assumes that Alexis can see right through her, but she doesn't seem to.

"Oh, that's so sweet of you," she says, walking in and putting a stack of files on Jack's desk. "He's around here somewhere. They were here just a minute ago."

"They?" Lizzie asks, feigning ignorance. Well, it's not really a stretch; she really is in the dark about what's going on. "He's with other people?"

"Yeah, this pair from Boston," Alexis says. She shrugs. "I'm not sure what's going on. I mean, people from various VC organizations show up. Usually it's for a photo op at the nonprofit they're helping fund, or something like that."

"Was that the feeling you got? That it's just a cursory visit? Nothing serious?" Lizzie asks.

"I don't think so," Alexis says, now showing some concern herself.

Lizzie kicks herself. Now she's gotten Alexis worried. She just shouldn't have come.

"Well, he's busy, clearly, so I'll just take off. You can tell him I came by and..."

"Lizzie, I know you, You know something, I can tell," Alexis says, looking toward the door. "Tell me fast—what do you know?"

"Nothing, really, I know nothing." She thinks of the woman, Amanda, saying in line at Sea Coast that she'd love to live on the Cape and doesn't think that's nothing, but she doesn't want to incite panic. "I'm sure it's all fine," she says unconvincingly.

"I don't believe you," Alexis says, and then Jack and the others return.

"Hey, honey, what brings you here?" Jack asks, giving her a kiss on the cheek and whispering, "Thank you!" in her ear.

"Oh, I'd gone to get myself an afternoon coffee and thought I'd bring you one," she says very stiffly. She looks at the man and woman and clears her throat.

"Oh, I'm sorry," he says, turning to his guests. "Amanda Solomon and Trevor Park, this is my wife, Lizzie Martin. She's the publisher and editor of our local paper, the Cranberry Harbor Gazette."

"Hello," Lizzie says, shaking their hands. "It's very nice to meet you. What brings you to Cranberry Harbor?"

Amanda shifts her weight from one foot to another, clearly a little uncomfortable. "Oh, you know, just checking on our investment here, and its fearless leader," she says, giving a very forced and fake smile.

She's an even worse liar than Lizzie, who is hard to top.

"Well, I hope you can find a little bit of time to check out the beach, or grab an ice cream before you head back to Boston. You must try Seaside Scoops, which got their start here in the business incubator my husband started for local young entrepreneurs," Lizzie says. Telling someone they should stop for ice cream on their way out is the Cranberry Harbor version of the classic Southern *bless your heart.*

"Maybe another time," Amanda says, looking insufferably smug to Lizzie.

"Yes, next time," Lizzie says, not cowering to Amanda's power pose. Two can play this game. She's not sure how she's feeling and if acting fits in with her kindness project, but sometimes you have to stand up for yourself, or in this case, your husband.

Amanda clears her throat and extends her hand to shake Jack's. "Jack, we'll be in touch. Liz, it was very nice to meet you," she says, clearly not happy to have met Lizzie. She doesn't shake her hand and barely looks at Lizzie.

Trevor, whose body language declares he's an underling, dragged along to be a bit player in Amanda's scheme, smiles, gives a half-hearted wave, and dutifully follows her out the door. Lizzie can hear the *Wizard of Oz* Wicked Witch of the West music in her head as she watches them go to their car through the wall of windows in Jack's office, Amanda gesturing angrily.

"Well, she seems fun," Lizzie says, smiling, once the coast is clear.

Jack laughs. "Oh my God, that was the most tense hour I think I've ever spent in my life. Thank you for showing up and helping end that... I can't even call it a meeting. It was more like an ambush. Talk about a serendipitous moment, thank you." He walks over and hugs her, hard. "Wow." Lizzie feels his whole body let go as he hugs her.

"What did they want?" she asks. Jack pulls away, shakes his head, and runs his hands through his hair.

"I don't really know," he says, pacing slowly around his office, like he's trying to regain some kind of equanimity. He shakes his head again and sits down with a deep sigh. "She was claiming to be here on behalf of the VCs, but it didn't feel like that. It felt like she was scoping out the place for herself somehow. I don't know, I'm probably completely off, but for the most part things have been good since this team took over. There's always some jockeying for power with these folks, but I haven't felt any concerns over how things are being done here, our progress, nothing, not until she came on board."

Lizzie sits down beside him and rubs his back. "Well, I'm very glad I decided to stop by." She looks over at his iced coffee, which now looks more like watered-down coffee. "What do you say we get out of here and go get you a new coffee, or hey, an ice cream?" she says, giving him a kiss.

"Really? I can have an ice cream before dinner?" he says, jumping up off the couch. "Any kind I want?" he says, laughing.

"Any kind you want. My treat," Lizzie says.

"God, I love you," he says, hugging her.

"I've always got your back, honey, always," she says, taking his hand and walking out of the office.

Jack puts his arm around her. "We're a formidable team, you and me," he says, kissing her head.

"Yup, no one messes with you, even if I have to be not so kind. I will make an exception," she says.

CHAPTER 20

They are delighted when they pull up to the Seaside Scoops truck parked at Sea Meadow Beach to see Ben, Sean and Ollie there as well. They are all decked out in their finest beachwear, and have obviously been enjoying a gorgeous Cape Cod summer day.

"Hey guys," Ben calls out, waving them over. "Come join us in some extremely bad parenting as we give our son ice cream before his dinner."

Lizzie looks over at Ollie thoroughly enjoying his little cone.

She squats down. "What kind of ice cream do you have there, Ollie?" she asks.

"'Nilla," he says, extremely focused on the task at hand, namely eating that ice cream before it melts in the July heat.

"It looks delicious," she says, giving him a kiss on the head as she turns her attention to the flavor offerings on the chalkboard menu.

"How are you?" Sean asks, as they all exchange hugs. "I feel once summer starts we never see anyone. It's so nice to see you!" he says, thanking the server in the truck as she hands him a very big and delicious-looking cone.

"That looks yummy, what kind is that?" Lizzie asks, unable to decide what flavor she should ruin her dinner with.

"It's a cantaloupe sorbet," he says. "Want a taste? It's amazing."

Lizzie takes a small bite. "Wow, that's like frozen sunshine," she says. "I may have to consider that one."

"So how's everything at the Marshside?" Jack asks, looking like he's relaxing a little bit after his surprise meeting/attack at Terra Marique.

"Good. Crazy busy, but good," Ben says. "The inn is booked solid for the next six weeks, right?" he asks Sean, who, while devouring his cone, nods yes.

"Wow, that's great, but tiring, I'm sure," Jack says. "Honey, do you know what you want?" he asks Lizzie as he gets to the front of the line.

"Yes, I'm going to have a medium salted caramel cone," she pauses. "Or a medium cranberry orange sorbet in a dish…ugh, I can't decide! They're all so good! Okay, salted caramel it is, final decision."

Jack laughs. "You're sure? Because, you know, we can never come here again. This is your one and only chance to get ice cream for the entire rest of the season," he teases.

"Very funny. Yes, I'm sure," she says. "What are you getting?"

"I'm going to go old school with a twist and have two scoops - one scoop of Oreo cookie, with a scoop of coconut ice cream," Jack says.

"Ohhh, nice combo," Ben says. "I like it."

"Well, that means a lot coming from a chef," Jack says.

A line is starting to form behind them and they get their cones and step aside.

"So how's everything at the Gazette? At Terra Marique?" Sean asks, gently wiping Ollie's mouth.

"The paper is good, busy, and with the kindness project now officially underway, we're going to be busy covering what I hope are lots of acts of kindness around town. Please let me know if anyone does anything extra, especially nice at the Marshview," Lizzie says. "We want to have lots of acts of kindness from cover to cover, and on our social media."

"Will do," Ben says. "In the land of opposites we had two people try to book two rooms right before we came over here. Super intense woman from Boston, I think she said. She was not happy that we were totally booked, having ignored the No Vacancy sign outside." He shakes his head.

Jack and Lizzie look at each other.

"Wow, she sounds like a lot," Jack says, taking a big bite of his ice cream.

"It's par for the course," Sean says. "Most people are cool, but we get some who come pretty close to uttering 'don't you know who I am?' which always makes me want to laugh. Like I'm going to say, 'Oh no! I did not! Let me throw someone out of their room so you can have it!'"

"I'd say entitlement is my least favorite attribute that we sometimes see around here," Lizzie says.

"I'm with you. There are a lot of things I can look past, but that isn't one of them," says Sean. "Hey, we're all set up on the beach. We have plenty of room on our blanket. Come sit down for a little bit."

Jack and Lizzie look at each other, and shrug. "Sure," they both say at the same time, and they follow the guys across the parking lot to their spot.

Lizzie feels a tad overdressed in her skirt and tank top, but it's poor Jack in long pants and a Terra Marique polo shirt who is definitely not beach-ready either. But there's a nice breeze, and it's headed toward five o'clock, so it's not too, too hot.

"Do you realize other than a couple of drive-bys and maybe one walk, and that picnic with Leah and Jonathan, this is only the second time we've actually sat down on the beach this summer?" Lizzie says. "How is that possible? There's something very wrong when two people, native Cranberry Harborites, not washashores, haven't been to the beach all summer."

"I think you're probably well within normal stats for people who grew up here and live here now. You know locals don't go to the beach, at least much, in July and August," Ben says.

Ollie has finished his ice cream and has moved on to a major excavation and building project at the front of the blanket, and he's taking it very seriously.

"Wizzie, look what I made!" he says, proudly showing her a road with a large hill of sand at the end. "That's the school where all the big kids go," he says, making an engine noise as he deftly moves the school bus he's taken out of his bag of toys and safely delivers all the imaginary kids to their destination.

"I love it, Ollie," she says. "This is an awesome road."

"How're things at Terra Marique?" Sean asks, opening their

cooler and revealing enough snacks and drinks for many people. "Ben packed this, not me," he says, laughing. "He always over-packs."

"And aren't you glad I do, because now we can offer our friends here something to drink to wash down their ice cream," Ben says. "We've got plenty of water," he says, handing them each one.

Lizzie looks at the metal bottle. "I love these, and they're recyclable, right? So much better than plastic. Thank you!" she says, opening it up and taking a sip.

"Yeah, these are so much better for the planet, and for us. That study that came out talking about all the microplastics they found in water bottles was really terrifying," Sean says.

"Yeah, it's part of the mission at Terra Marique to keep it as plastic free as possible," Jack says. "It's something that's really important to me, to the mission."

Lizzie sees him get a little wistful. "You have so many good initiatives there, honey, it really should be studied. Oh wait, it is!" she smiles.

"What?" Ben asks.

Jack, in his usual humble way, tries to dismiss it, brush it off, but Lizzie won't let him.

"It's true, not only has Ian been making a film about it, but he knows lots of folks at MIT and Harvard and they're studying what Jack's been doing and," she turns to Jack, "is it okay for me to tell them?"

He nods, looking embarrassed. "They're going to be sending some interns and teaching a class on what he's created," Lizzie says, beaming.

"It's really no big deal," Jack says. "It may not even happen. But it's been fun to talk to them and get even more sustainability ideas from them."

"But don't tell anyone yet," Lizzie says. "This is just beach blanket talk for now."

"Our lips are sealed," Sean says. "You must be so excited, though, to even get this notice. It's amazing. I'm excited, and I'm not even a part of it!"

"Yes, you are," says Jack. "You both helped us create the foundation for the daycare center. Your input was invaluable, and your painting classes, Sean, have a waiting list, so I'd say you're both more than a little involved."

Sean concedes, "Okay, I'll let myself take some credit for that, and as long as we're talking about it, Ben's plant-based cooking classes are really popular too. You know, as long as we're taking credit for the awesome success of Terra Marique," he says, laughing.

"What I love so much is that the tendrils of what's happening there reach so many people. People who live there, work there, take classes, buy or create products made there, from food to art. It really is the future I think, though I know, of course, I'm a little biased," Lizzie says, reaching out to take Jack's hand.

"Okay, so I'm feeling really uncomfortable. This is sounding like my eulogy," he says, and everyone laughs. "Hey, new topic: we have to get together to play some baseball. When's that going to happen? We need to do it at least once before the summer is over. We just have to!"

"You're so right. I'm sorry we dropped the ball, no pun intended," Ben says. "You're right, we said we were going to do it and we need to."

Suddenly Lizzie's wheels begin turning.

"Hey, what if we..." she says.

"Uh oh, guys, I know that look. This is about to turn from just a few of us getting together to play some baseball for fun into a fundraiser, a whole town event, or something much more than a few friends getting together to play ball," Jack says, shaking his head but smiling at his wife.

Lizzie laughs. "Wow, I really am a killjoy, aren't I?"

"No, you're just earnest and determined," says Ben.

"With lots of goals and plans," echoes Sean.

"Yeah, a killjoy." Lizzie shakes her head.

"Okay, so yes, Ms. Killjoy, what are you thinking that will take our casual game and turn it into something...earnest?" Jack asks.

"Well, now I just feel weird," she says.

"Spill it," says Ben, peeling a clementine for Ollie.

"Fine. Okay, so what if we had a townie game and people could sign up to play? We could make it a fundraiser for something in town, and we wrap it around the kindness project," she says.

"Like what? Giving hugs to refs instead of yelling at them?" Jack quips.

Lizzie laughs. "No, just like make the whole afternoon or evening, whenever it is, about being kind to others and having fun, just regular folks playing and having a good time. We could have food, music…" She starts to doubt herself. "Eh, it's probably a dumb idea and we'd have to time it around the Salty Dogs schedule, and it's going to be August before we know it. It would be a lot to put together on short notice, right?"

The three men all shrug. "I don't know, it doesn't seem like that big a deal. Get some local band, get people to sign up to play, maybe a couple of food trucks," Ben says. "Kind Fest!"

"Oh, I like it!" says Lizzie. "Jack? I didn't mean to hijack your game with your friends, it's just…"

He grabs her face and kisses her. "It's just this is who you are, and I love that about you. Let's do it!"

CHAPTER 21

When you know (almost) everyone in town, it's amazing how quickly you can put together a small-ish town festival. It also helps if you happen to be in charge of the local newspaper to get the word out, and that you've promised a very fun event for the whole family.

So it is not surprising, that four weeks—okay, four weeks and one day—later, the ground is set for *Kind Fest.* They even managed to get t-shirts and hats to sell, featuring a bumble bee next to the word Kind on them. This was all thanks to yet another small business that had gotten its start at the Terra Marique business incubator. Printworks! was started by a fantastic young couple who had come to Cranberry Harbor as J1 students from Brazil to work at Sea Coast, had worked several summers, decided they wanted to make Cranberry Harbor their permanent home, immigrated here, and started their own screen printing and embroidery business. Business was booming, and as a way to give back to the community they donated their design team and the first 100 shirts. It was incredibly kind and generous.

Ian had some friends visiting from California who happened to be musicians, and they'd volunteered to play, and so this up-and-coming group, Surfside, who'd had a top-twenty record last year, agreed to donate a set to the cause, so it all came together quite easily. Lizzie hoped that it wasn't one of those events that it seemed to all work out too easily, and then there was a big mishap the day of.

Not a fan of public speaking, Lizzie had enlisted two rising seniors to co-host. Grace Eldridge and Ethan Hallet were both theater kids and had started a chapter of *We Dine Together,* a national club that ensures no student ever sits alone at lunch. Lizzie had met them when she went to the high school in April and wrote a story about the club for the Gazette. She immediately loved them and knew they'd be perfect kindness ambassadors for the event.

So they are all set to go. All they need is no rain, and for people to turn out. Neither of those things ends up being an issue. Lizzie and Jack are both stunned as people begin pouring into the parking lot and taking their places on the grass surrounding the Salty Dogs field.

As they stand near the dugout Jack puts his arm around Lizzie.

"Look at this! Look what you made happen!" he says, kissing her.

She shakes her head. "No, this wasn't just me. This took you, all our friends, our family—it took..." She chokes up and Jack hugs her harder. "It literally took a village. We definitely have the best town in the world, right?" she says, wiping her eyes. "I can't believe this."

All around the field are handmade signs saying things like "Kindness Matters," "Be Kind," "Be A Buddy Not a Bully," and several "Spread Kindness Like Confetti."

"But this was your idea, sweetie. You are the one who started this whole thing. I'm so proud of you!" he says as they embrace, and Jack gets teary too.

"Well, sis, you really make it hard to be your little brother and feel like you do anything that matters around here," her brother Matt says, giving her a quick hug as he arrives.

"Well, you do know that's always my end goal when I do anything in life," she says, putting her arm around her brother. "Where are Shannon and Sophie?" she asks, looking around for her sister-in-law and niece.

"Sophie insisted on dressing up, so they're a few minutes behind me," he says. He pauses and looks around. "You've drawn a playoff-level crowd," he says. "This is incredible." He looks over at Jack. "So this is your idea of just a few of us getting together to play some baseball, huh?" he says. "I'm not feeling very confident about playing ball in front of all these people, how about you?"

Jack shakes his head. "Man, I haven't even thrown a ball, let alone swung a bat in about four years. I'm thinking a little practice might have been a good idea."

"You think?" Matt says, looking a bit panicked.

They're soon joined by Sean, Ben, Ian, half the staff from Murphy's, including owner Sean Murphy himself, some high school players, and some other guys Lizzie doesn't know. A quick head count of 20 guys lets her know they have enough players to make this happen.

When the band had signed on it was decided to make this an abbreviated game. They were only going to play five innings so there would be time for music, food, and the outdoor games that had been a last-minute add-on. It seemed everyone wanted to be part of Kind Fest, and Lizzie couldn't believe it.

She is further shocked when she looks out past the crowds and sees that three Boston news vans have arrived as well.

"Holy shit," she says.

"Aunt Wiz, you said a bad word," says Sophie, who'd suddenly appeared at her side.

"You're so right, Sophie, I'm sorry. I was just surprised to see news trucks here covering this," she says.

"Holy shit," says Matt, walking over to his sister and seeing the satellite trucks.

"Daddy!" Sophie admonishes. "You owe me a dollar now. You too, Aunt Wiz," she says, putting out her hand.

"I got you," he says to Lizzie, handing his daughter two one dollar bills. "Sorry, sweetie, I'll try to do better."

"Okay," she says, putting the bills in her pocket. "That's all I can ask for, Daddy, that you try to do better."

"Thank you for understanding," he says, leaning down and kissing his little girl.

"I know you're nervous and these things happen," she says, patting his hand that's on her shoulder.

Matt and Lizzie exchange a look and smile.

"That's a very smart little girl you have there, bro," she says.

"Oh, keeping up is extremely challenging," he says, widening his eyes and shaking his head.

"Okay," Jack says, trying to get the attention of all the players. "While they get everything all set, do some introductions and get this thing going, let's all go over to the dugout and figure out who's doing what." There had been some phone calls, texts and emails between all the players, so he did know who was playing for who, and roughly what positions they were playing. Both dates when they'd planned to practice had been rained out, and that was concerning him.

While they all walk off, Lizzie, clipboard in hand, prepares to do her very short introduction to the event and Grace and Ethan.

The person in charge of sound and music for the Salty Dogs had volunteered to work the festival and came over to Lizzie with a mic.

"Whenever you're ready," he says, handing it to her.

"Thank you," she says, looking down at her watch and seeing it's 4:02. The event is scheduled to begin at 4, so it looks like it's showtime.

Nervously, Lizzie walks out to the pitcher's mound, mic and her notes in hand.

"Hello, Cranberry Harbor!" she calls out. "Welcome to our first ever Kind Fest!"

There are cheers and applause from the crowd.

"I'm Lizzie Martin, and I am so happy and honestly, blown away, to see how many of you have turned out today. Thank you so much for supporting our mission to bring more kindness to Cranberry Harbor."

There's more cheers and applause, and a few loud "THANK YOUs" from the crowd.

"Without further ado, I want to introduce our hosts for Kind Fest, Grace Eldridge and Ethan Hallet, both recent Seaward Regional High School graduates and co-founders of the local chapter of *We Dine Together,* a national organization started at a high school in Florida that makes sure no one at their school sits alone at lunch. Please give a big Cranberry Harbor welcome to Grace and Ethan."

The crowd stands up and Lizzie is moved to tears. This town really is something.

"Thank you, everyone," they both say, having been given their own mics.

"We started our *We Dine Together* chapter during our sophomore year," says Ethan, looking far more comfortable out there than Lizzie felt. She's amazed watching their poise.

"We were both born and raised here," Grace says, "but we saw how often new kids looked so uncomfortable and nervous and we wanted to do something to help, and well…"

"Yeah, and being just two people we couldn't exactly do it ourselves, and we'd heard about this group and formed a club here," Ethan says. "And now we have 48 members, and so many friendships have been made, and yeah, no one ever eats alone at our school. Unless they want to," he says, laughing, while the crowd erupts into cheers and applause.

"We thank Ms. Martin for asking us to come here today. It's a real honor to be part of this," says Grace. "What we've come to see is if someone takes the chance to do something, like we did, or the town is doing, it sort of takes off and builds and builds, and you can't even remember that it was just like an idea you had, because it's become this big thing. That's what this is. It's the idea of people being kinder to each other turning into a big thing."

"So with that in mind, several people from the high school are going to be coming around selling raffle tickets for various prize packages donated by local businesses, and the money raised is going to go to the new playground fund, which will also include new basketball courts," says Ethan. "So give generously!"

"Alright, so it seems we've done all we're supposed to do for now, right, Ethan?" Grace says, and Ethan nods. "So let's get out of the way and start the game! Thank you!"

Ethan takes off his hat and waves it to the crowd. "Thank you for coming, everyone, and remember 'Be kind!'" he calls as they jog off the field and the players run on.

"You two were great. Thank you so much for doing that," Lizzie says as they run up to her. "I'm so grateful to you both."

"Thank you!" Ethan says. "That was really fun!"

"Scary, but fun," Grace says. "I've never been in front of that many people in my life," she exclaims, shaking her head.

"It's good practice for when you run for office," Lizzie says, only sort of kidding. She can see both of them having great futures being community leaders.

"Ha!" Ethan says. "Yeah, I'm not so sure I'd want to do that, but you never know."

"What you two are doing at the school with the *We Dine Together* program shows incredible leadership, empathy and kindness," Lizzie says. "I will not be the least bit surprised if at some point I find myself voting for, if not both of you, at least one of you."

"Thank you, Ms. Martin, that's really nice of you," says Grace.. "I'm going to school in Boston next year, and I'm still not sure exactly what my major's going to be."

"Don't let her be all humble here, Ms. Martin. She's going to Harvard," Ethan says, smiling at Grace.

"Fine, well, you're going to Brown, so there," she teases back.

"Wow, two Cranberry Harbor Ivy League-bound kids—this town has a lot to be proud of," Lizzie says. "Congratulations! I'd love to do a follow-up piece on you both once you get settled into school, if you'd be interested. No pressure."

"Sure!" they both say at the same time.

"I'd love that," Grace says.

"Me too," says Ethan.

"Well, I should let you two go find your spots to watch the game," Lizzie says, hearing the announcer starting to introduce the players and get ready for the game to start.

Since both teams were playing for Cranberry Harbor and there was no time to get shirts for everyone, they were each wearing their own team colors from their own closets. Jack's team sports blue t-shirts, and the other team, green. It wasn't fancy, and it didn't need to be. It was just for fun and to raise awareness about the Kindness Project. But mostly to have fun. Hence they were referred to as the Blues and the Greens.

Lizzie spots her parents, Shannon, and Sophie on a blanket near right field, and leaves her post to go sit with them for a little bit. She hasn't seen Alexis or Leah yet and scans the crowd as she gets close to her family.

"Hi everyone," she says, sitting down quickly to not obscure anyone's view.

"Hi, Aunt Wiz, look what I made!" Sophie says, showing off her new friendship bracelet which spells out "Be Kind."

"I love that, Sophie, you are so clever! I've never made a bracelet," Lizzie says, holding Sophie's wrist and admiring her handiwork.

"I'll teach you if you want," Sophie says. "Mommy taught me and the other kids at the library, so I can show you."

"Shannon, this is great. You are something else," Lizzie says. "How are you doing? You feeling okay?"

"Very, well, thank you. I had my 24-week checkup today and everything is looking good!" Shannon says. "Your mom went with me and asked all the important questions," she says, smiling.

Lizzie looks over at her mom, who shrugs. "A retired doctor can be an asset or a pain in the..." she says, laughing. "I try to be the former."

"And that you are," Shannon says.

"Look, Aunt Wiz, Uncle Jack has the bat," Sophie says, getting them all to actually look at the game.

"First up at bat for the Blues is Jack Cahoon, CEO of Terra Marique. Pitching for the Greens is Sean Murphy, owner of Murphy's on the corner of Main and Cove," says the announcer.

"Where's Daddy?" Sophie asks.

"He's over there," Lizzie says, pointing out her brother, Matt, warming up, taking some swings with a bat near the dugout.

"And here comes the ball, and ohhh, it's a swing and a miss for Cahoon," the announcer says. "Good effort, but he's got to connect with the ball."

"Strike one!" the umpire calls out.

"Come on, Jack, just relax into it. You've got this," Lizzie says, trying to will him a good hit.

The next pitch comes and *bam!* He hits it. It's a ground ball to the shortstop. Jack throws down the bat and runs as fast as he can to first, where the first baseman is waiting for the shortstop to get the ball to him, which he does, but not before Jack has run over the base and is safe on an infield single! Lizzie and her whole family jump up and are screaming.

"Go Jack!!" she yells.

"Go Uncle Jack," Sophie says adorably, mimicking her aunt.

Next up is Matt. He'd been a really good player in high school and played all four years, but gave it up in college, instead devoting all his time to school and Shannon. He is a natural athlete, which comes in handy since he spends his days climbing roofs for his solar panel company, though he is more often relegated to the design and selling side of things now that the business has really taken off. Still, it's fun for his parents and sister to see him up at bat once again.

And after two swinging strikes, which Lizzie can see is frustrating him, he hits the next ball that comes over the plate, and it goes flying. And it's gone! He hit a home run to deep left center. He crushed it, and the entire park erupts into applause and cheers.

"Yay Daddy!!!" Sophie is jumping up and down, and Shannon has to explain to her that she'll have to wait to give him a hug until after the game. She is quite bummed about that. Five-year-olds don't really get the concept that when Daddy is playing a game you can't just run into the middle of it.

Jack trots around the bases, with Matt not far behind him, and they high-five, both beaming, after they've gotten home.

At the end of the first inning of this abbreviated game it was Blues 3 and Greens 1. There was also the music, games, and food to get to. And by the time they got to the end of that fifth inning, with the Blues winning 6-4, Lizzie could tell they were just as glad to not have to play a full nine innings. They looked beat.

As soon as the players jog off the field, the Surfside crew begins loading in their equipment, and they are miraculously ready to go in about 10 minutes. Since they are Ian's friends he introduces them, and they do a tight half-hour of California-inspired surf tunes, along with a couple of ballads. A few folks, including Leah and Jonathan, get up and dance too. It's really sweet.

The biggest surprise of the day, however, was when Bud Mackelroy approached the grounds crew after the music and asked for a moment on the field.

Lizzie holds her breath. She has no idea what to expect from him. He could be a bit of a loose cannon, though at town meeting he'd seemed completely on board with the Kindness Project. Hopefully his old pal Billy hadn't gotten to him.

"Hello everyone. Most of you locals know me. You summer folks will not, but I have something I want to say," he says.

Jack and Matt have joined the family and they all look at each other, collectively hoping it's all going to be okay. Three thousand people have gone absolutely silent.

"I love Cranberry Harbor, never lived anywhere else, never want to live anywhere else," he says. "Last year I was lucky enough to meet a lovely lady who had moved here from New Hampshire because she loved the ocean and wanted to live near it. I met her at the beach when her pup had broken off his leash, and I helped her get him back."

"Where is this going?" Jack whispers to Lizzie, who shrugs her shoulders.

"That lady, Miss Millicent Smithson, became my sweetheart. The first one I've had since high school. Millie, darlin', will you come down here?"

"Oh wow, now I see what's happening," Lizzie says. "Bud is one brave man," she says, smiling and clapping along with everyone else as they watch a very embarrassed but smiling Millie walk onto the field. Ever the journalist, she takes out her phone and begins taking pictures—which, of course, she will ask for permission to run in the paper.

"Well, this is sure taking the excitement away from my home run," Matt teases, and the whole family laughs.

When she gets there, Bud takes her hands, and then gets down on one knee. When he does that the crowd goes wild. Everyone is standing and cheering.

Bud puts down the mic he's been holding, but you don't need to hear the words to know what's happening. Millie's little hop and emphatic nodding tells everyone her answer is yes.

"Wow, I did not see that happening at our little Kind Fest," Lizzie says, as Jack puts his arm around her and she snuggles into him. "You never know what's going to happen, do you?"

"Who would have thought Bud of all people would propose in

front of the entire town?" Gabby says. "I've known him his whole life, and wow, what a change!"

"Love can make a guy do crazy things," Peter says, kissing Gabby on the head.

Lizzie, standing with her family, takes it all in. She looks around the park and she can't believe what she's seeing. It's not easy, but she's trying to capture it with photos and video. Thousands of people, many of them crying, so moved by this man's pledge of love. She's crying too, so grateful to call this place home and to be surrounded by so much love.

CHAPTER 22

Real life seemed pretty dull after all the energy of Kind Fest. Having worked in media for most of her life, Lizzie wasn't surprised to see how much coverage it got in the Boston news circles, but even she was a bit stunned when Bud's proposal went viral and was in the top ten shared videos on TikTok.

"Who would have ever thought Bud Mackelroy would become a hit on social media?" Lizzie asks Eric, as they're sitting at work. "Do you think the guy even has a Facebook account? I don't think so."

Eric laughs. "Yeah, he doesn't exactly scream 'wants to be even more connected to people and the world.' I mean, he did have a brief moment of fame when he chained himself to a tree at the Terra Marique property to protest it, so I would have thought any other viral activity would not have been for something so…sweet?"

"Yes, 'sweet' is not exactly a word anyone who's lived in Cranberry Harbor would ever have used to describe Bud." She's quiet for a minute and is thinking. "It's pretty cool to see how people can change. They really can evolve, right? It makes me think about what we're doing with the kindness project here in town. I wonder if it will have any lasting effects on people? On the town?"

"And how does one measure that?" Eric asks.

"Good point. It's not like there's some metric to measure kindness," Lizzie ponders.

Eric laughs. "It reminds me of the gauge Santa has in his sleigh in *Elf*," he says. "Remember? When more people start believing in him the meter registers it and then his sleigh can fly."

"I love that movie so much," Lizzie says, wistfully. "Yeah, hmmm, I wonder what we can do? How can we see if this project is having any effect on people, businesses?"

"Well, we could ask them. We are journalists, after all," he says.

Lizzie laughs. "That's a novel idea, actually asking people something rather than speculating." She shakes her head at her moment of cluelessness.

"Yeah, there are way too many media outlets doing that these days, that's for sure," he says, shaking his head as well.

"Maybe we should take to the streets and ask people for some stories. Things they've witnessed or done themselves while the Kindness Project has been going on," Lizzie says.

"Sure, maybe go to a few different places, like Sea Coast of course, and maybe the town green, places where people congregate?"

"Good idea. I also want to follow up with my mom. Eric interviewed her for that piece where she talked about how being kind is good for your health, but maybe ask her some questions about how to keep this project going in your own life," Lizzie says.

"I like that idea," Eric says. He's busy writing in his notebook, and then stands up. "I'm going to head out and maybe go to Bradford's and the town green. You want to take Sea Coast and what else?"

"Sure, okay, yeah, I'll go to Sea Coast, and then…" She's thinking. "Oh, maybe the library, the bookstore, and Toy Works?"

"Sounds good, and I'll swing by the Marshview, talk to Ben and Sean, and then Terra Marique? Or would you rather do that?" he asks.

"No, that's perfect, better you than me—you know, professional boundaries, I think," she says. "This is a lot. We're not going to get to all these places today. Let's aim for a few stories by the end of the day tomorrow."

"That sounds good," Eric says, picking up his notebook, a couple of pens, and his baseball hat—a Salty Dogs hat, of course. "I will see you later," he says, tapping the brim of his hat and giving a nod.

"How very *Newsies*," Lizzie says, laughing, referencing the 1992

Disney movie. "Good luck out there in the wilds of Cranberry Harbor."

Eric went to Bradford's Market first. Like Sea Coast Coffee, Bradford's was a local hub for getting the local take on what was happening, running into your neighbor, a friend you went to elementary school with, and yes, lots of summer folks too. There was a big chain supermarket on the edge of town, but Bradford's was where just about everyone stopped for that bottle of wine, some good fresh produce, and the occasional lottery ticket. It was especially popular with older folks who didn't want to have to navigate a football field-sized grocery store. It was a much more manageable size.

Having now lived in Cranberry Harbor for over three years, Eric is considered a local, especially since he writes for the Gazette. He'd picked a good time to stop by. It was during one of their unscheduled lulls, so he was able to approach a few people working in the store. The first person he found was Daniel, a young guy from Jamaica who Eric thought had been working there for at least a couple of years. They often chatted while Eric picked out his produce.

"Hey, Daniel, how are you doing today?" Eric asks, notebook in hand.

"Good, you?" he says, continuing to neatly unpack a large box of bananas.

"I'm good. Hey, I wondered if I could ask you a couple of questions for the paper?" Eric asks. "It's about the Kindness Project that's been going on."

"Sure, what do you need?" he says.

"We're just wondering if people around town have noticed any difference in how people are acting—if they're being more kind? Seem happier?" Eric asks.

"Huh, I hadn't really thought about it," he says, pausing, a bunch of bananas in hand. "For the most part people are pretty nice when they come in here. I mean, once in a while someone can be in a bad mood or something, but mostly people here are pretty nice."

"That's good to hear. So nothing significant that you've noticed so far?" Eric asks.

"Huh, well, now that I'm thinking about it, yeah, I do notice more people saying thank you to me for what I'm doing, which is nice," he says, smiling as he thinks about it. "Yeah, they seem like, I don't know, that they notice me, like I'm not just a piece of furniture to work around as they pick their fruit and vegetables. So that's pretty nice. Feeling appreciated is very nice," he says.

"I like that, feeling appreciated is very nice for sure. Thanks, Daniel," Eric says. "Have a great rest of your day."

Eric spots the store owner, Tim Bradford, over by the service desk and walks over.

"Tim, nice to see you. Eric Jackson from the Gazette," Eric says, seeing that Tim doesn't seem to know who he is..

"Of course, I remember you. Sorry, I see so many people every day," Tim says.

"No apology needed. I can't imagine how many people you see and talk to in a day. I won't keep you. I know how busy you are, but we're doing a story about the ongoing kindness project and I wondered if you'd seen any acts of kindness that might be inspiring to share with our readers," Eric says.

Tim lights up. "Yes, we're seeing a definite uptick in people offering to take someone's grocery cart back, helping older people load their bags into their cars, and just generally being kind, but one of the kindest things I've seen came from one of our own. Here, come with me," he says to Eric, motioning him to follow. He stops at the second register they come to. "Eric, this is Jessie. She's worked here for, what is it now, Jessie? Ten years?"

"Nice to meet you, Eric," she says, and nods at Tim. "Yes, it will be ten years next month."

"Eric writes for the Gazette and was asking me about kindnesses I've observed since the town has been doing the Kindness Project, and I thought he had to meet you," Tim says. "Jessie is the most thoughtful and kind person. Could you tell him what you did?"

Jessie blushes and looks embarrassed and waves him off. "Oh my goodness, it wasn't that big a deal," she says, humbly.

"Indulge me, and tell him," Tim says, "and let him decide if it's a story worth sharing." Eric opens his notebook and gets ready to write.

She shakes her head and takes a deep breath. "Okay. Well, last week a man came in, did his shopping, and came to my checkout. He had diapers, baby food, milk, bread, all the staples, but also a small bouquet of flowers, some sushi, and a bottle of wine from the sale rack. I rang it all up and it was about $50. He reached into his pocket, and I could see by the look on his face that he didn't have his money. He said, 'Oh my God, I left my wallet at home. It's my anniversary, and I ran out to get something for dinner for my wife and me while the baby is sleeping. She's kind of colicky so we don't get many breaks.' I asked him where he lived, and he said about 15 minutes away. I realized that by the time he went there, came back and went home again he and his wife wouldn't be able to celebrate. So I paid for his things and told him to come back the next day." She shrugged, like it was no big deal.

Eric was stunned. "Wow, was he someone you knew from here?"

Jessie shook her head. "Not really, I just wanted to be kind," she says and points to one of the *Bee Kind* posters in the store. "If he didn't come back, it wasn't like I'd be out $100. It was only $50." She shrugs. "I wouldn't be out that much money."

"Yeah, but that's still a decent amount of money to risk on a stranger," Eric says. "So did he come back?"

She smiles. "Yes, he did. He came back the next day, paid me back, and gave me a gift card to Tall Tales Book Shop for $100." She smiles and pats the book next to her register. "We'd had a brief exchange about another book I had here, and I told him I sometimes read a little when it's slow and how much I love books. He remembered that. A very nice man."

Eric is blown away by the story. "Wow, that's incredible." He's actually choked up. "Thank you so much for sharing that with me. And thank you for being such a kind person. We're lucky to have you here."

Eric leaves Bradford's feeling first, that there's no way to top that story, and second, he is so glad he gets to call this town home.

On her excursion into town, Lizzie was finding similar heartwarming stories. She decides to drive by the local playground near the middle school where young parents often congregate and is thrilled to see the place full of parents and kids as she gets closer. She's a little surprised, though. There aren't usually so many people there, so she decides to get out of her car and check it out.

It had been a while since she'd brought Sophie here. *Note to self,* she thinks. *I need to schedule an afternoon date with my niece.* She's surprised by the sight of a whole lot of new equipment and toys. There's even a three-sided shed with shelves of balls, jump ropes, wiffle balls and bats, and a few folded up doll strollers. She'ss confused. It hadn't been that long since she'd been here, and she hadn't reported on any measures taken by the selectboard to allocate funds for improvements. It wasn't like it was a terrible playground before, but it was definitely in need of some love and upgrades. It was often thought of as the land of misfit toys—castoffs from grandparents whose grandkids were now teens, things like that. But now, looking around, it is hardly recognizable.

She spots a woman sitting on what looks like a new bench and sits down beside her.

"Hi, I haven't been here in a while. Did the town recently implement all these improvements? Buy new toys and equipment? This is incredible—what a huge difference!"

The lady smiles and shakes her head. "Isn't it incredible? No one knows who did it. It must have happened in the middle of the night last night. Several of us meet here a couple of times a week with our kids, and we pulled up this morning, as usual, and the place was completely renovated. I'd been here yesterday with my daughter and her friend, and it wasn't like this. Someone came in during the night and did it. Crazy, right?" she says, shaking her head as she looks around.

"Really crazy, and no one knows who's responsible?" Lizzie asks.

"Nope," she says, shaking her head.

"I'm Lizzie Martin. Sorry, I should have said that in the beginning," she says.

"Oh right, from the Gazette and town meeting," she says. "I'm

Ellie Rodriquez, nice to meet you." She waves to two little boys having the time of their lives with the fleet of new trucks.

Lizzie sits back and takes it all in. New climbing equipment, new swings, new Little Tykes cars—there was always only one that was pretty worn out, but all the kids still vied for it. Even the sandbox area, which had been full of old plastic buckets and faded shovels, was cleaned up, beautifully stocked with brand new toys. The broken structure that had at one time provided a roof over the area to provide some cover from the sun was also new.

"Wow, so someone came in during the night and did all this? And nobody knows who?" Lizzie asks, taking out her notebook.

"Nope," Ellie says, shaking her head. "It's a mystery," she says, widening her eyes. "There's a note over there," she says, pointing to a new beautiful little gazebo, a structure surrounded with freshly planted flowers. The old water fountain, probably from Lizzie's parents' childhood era, has been replaced with a gorgeous state-of-the-art bottle filling station.

Lizzie gets up. "Be right back," she says, walking over. There's a framed note that's beautifully illustrated that says, *Do Your Little Bits Of Good Where You Are; It's Those Little Bits Of Good Put Together That Overwhelm The World. Archbishop Desmond Tutu.* As she steps inside she sees another sign, reading, *No Act Of Kindness, No Matter How Small, Is Ever Wasted. Aesop.*

Lizzie's eyes fill with tears. This transformation is so incredibly kind and generous. And for someone to do this completely anonymously, during the night, not looking for any accolades, is unusual to say the least, and an outstanding act of random kindness.

She goes back to Ellie and sits down. "Wow" is about all she can get out.

"Right?" Ellie says. "I'm curious, of course, about who did this, but there's a part of me that thinks it's way cooler and more exciting to not know."

"I agree," Lizzie says, noticing more and more new toys, and how beautiful the grass looks. They'd even brought in new sod. "Obviously they had to have permission from the town, and the police have to have been looped in, but as much as the reporter in me knows I should go ask them about it, I really think I don't want to," she says, feeling filled with so much joy.

"Oh yeah, keeping it a mystery is much better," Ellie says. "I've had fun listening to the rumors this morning. Everyone has a theory."

Lizzie turns toward her. "Really? I'm curious—like what?"

"Well, one person said maybe it was Ben Affleck. His mom has a house on the Cape. Someone else said Harry Connick Jr. He lives nearby, and I also heard the Obamas," Ellie says, smiling and nodding.

"Really? People think the former president had a crew come in and re-do our local playground in Cranberry Harbor?" Lizzie laughs, shaking her head.

"Hey, I didn't say these things, I'm just saying what I heard on the parents hotline," Ellie says, laughing. "You're the writer; what's your theory?"

Lizzie sits back, looks around, and thinks for a moment. "My gut tells me it's someone local, not necessarily really rich, but who had some money they wanted to do something with and didn't want a fuss made about it or them, so they decided to do it this way," she says. "But hey, maybe in his retirement President Obama is renovating one playground at a time across America. That story is a bit more enthralling, for sure."

"But yours is a lot sweeter, and I think you're right," Ellie says. "But it is fun to speculate."

"For sure!" Lizzie says. Just then Ellie's boys, who appear to be twins, come running over. They look to be about three and are adorable.

"Mama, can we have a snack?" one of them says.

"Of course," Ellie says. "What's the magic word?" she asks.

"Please!" they both yell. And with the magic word spoken Ellie takes out an assortment of sliced fruit and some reusable bottles with water and sits them down.

As they chow down on the apples, oranges and grapes, Lizzie asks them, "So what do you think of the new playground?"

"It's awesome!" they both call out with a level of enthusiasm Lizzie wishes she had for anything in her life.

"Is it okay to ask them about it?" she asks their mom.

"Of course, ask away!" Ellie says.

"It's very nice to meet you both. I'm Lizzie. So what's your favorite new thing? Or more than one thing," she asks.

"I like all the cars we can drive. When there was only one we had to wait a long time to have one to use. Now there's enough for everyone!" one says.

"Yeah, that, and all the toys like balls, Frisbees, and stuff over there," the other says, pointing to the shed.

"Oh, by the way, this is Phineas," Ellie says, pointing to the little boy on her left, wearing a Pokemon t-shirt, "and this is Jesse," she says to the one on her right, wearing a Beatles *Hard Day's Night* one.

"Nice to meet you, Phineas and Jesse. I'm a Beatles fan too, Jesse, nice shirt, and I love Pokemon too, Phineas." She writes down their names. "Would you be okay if I took their picture for the paper? I understand completely if you don't want to do that," she says.

"No, it's fine," Ellie says. "We love the Gazette, and it will be a fun keepsake for them to look back at. Where would you like them?" she asks.

"Hmmm, where would you like your picture taken, guys?" Lizzie asks.

"On the swings!" they both say, getting up and running over to the new swings.

"Swings it is!" Lizzie says, following behind them.

She gets that shot, and then asks the other parents if it's okay to take some photos at a distance, just wanting to give a sense of what a transformation has taken place at the playground. The more she looks around, the more incredible it seems that someone, or a group of someones, made this happen. This kindness thing is really making an impact on the town.

She thanks Ellie, Jesse and Phineas before she leaves, and feeling like the day could not possibly get any better, she heads over to Sea Coast to see what is happening over there.

CHAPTER 23

She should have known that she'd end up bumping into Eric there. The place is packed, but everyone seems really happy, and smiling, not a grumpy person in sight.

"Mind if I join you?" she asks Eric.

"Please do!" he says. "How's it going?"

"Amazing! You?" she asks.

"Yeah, it's crazy, everywhere I go I keep hearing about these wonderful things happening! If I wasn't here I'd be convinced that it was some fabricated story that someone had made up, but I'm seeing incredible things, over and over." He shakes his head. "Right before you got here some guy came in—don't know who he was, but he treated everyone in here to whatever they wanted, and apparently left his credit card open for the next half hour for anyone who comes in."

"Wow! Did you get his name or anything?" Lizzie asks, ever the reporter.

"I followed him out and tried to get him on record. He was wearing a baseball cap and sunglasses, clearly didn't want to be seen, but I called after him and asked him why he'd done that, and he turned around, shrugged, and said, 'Just paying it forward with kindness. There was a time when buying a coffee for myself would have been out of the question, but now I have more than I need, so why not share it?' and he got in his car and drove away."

"It wasn't President Obama was it?" she says, laughing. "Sorry, a joke from earlier. That's incredible. It really is amazing what's been going on."

"It is, but that's not the most amazing thing I heard," Eric says.

"Okay, do tell!" Lizzie says, leaning on her elbows and getting closer.

"There was a young teacher—second grade, I believe—who was going to have to leave Cranberry Harbor because her apartment is getting turned into a short-term rental, and when the PTA heard about it, they all scrambled to help her find a place, and your husband jumped in and is helping her, with some grants, a GoFundMe the parents started, and a first-time home buyer mortgage, and she's going to buy one of the tiny houses at Terra Marique. So she's staying," he says.

Lizzie smiles, "That Jack, he's a pretty good guy."

"He sure is, and she in turn is adopting a cat from someone there who has discovered they're allergic, so it's a total win/win/win," he says.

Lizzie sits back in her chair and looks around at the very happy summer crowd in the coffee shop. She spies Leah behind the counter and waves to her, so she hurries over to the table to say hi, taking a seat.

"Hi guys," she says, "how's everything going?"

"Good. Eric was just telling me about the amazing guy who was just in here. That's so great!" Lizzie says.

"Right? And on top of treating everyone he included huge tips for all the staff. I've never seen anything like it," Leah says.

"And you have no idea who it was?" Eric asks, still trying to get the scoop.

"No, but one of the girls working mentioned that there's a movie filming in Wellfleet, and she was thinking it was maybe an actor from that? She thought he looked familiar," Leah says. "I think it's more fun leaving it a mystery. It's refreshing to have someone do something nice and not take pictures for Instagram, or make it about themselves somehow, you know?"

"Agreed," Eric says. "It's heartwarming to see something generous done without fanfare."

"How's everything else going?" Lizzie asks Leah, who knows that means, "how are things with Jonathan?'

"Pretend I'm not here," Eric says, going through his notebook, checking his notes, and looking quite occupied.

Leah shrugs. "Good, really good, but the season is winding down, playoffs will be starting before we know it, and they've had a pretty rocky season, so chances are they won't make it, so he'll be leaving. Which stinks."

"It totally stinks," says Lizzie. "I'm so sorry. Where will he be heading? It sounds like he's been moving around a lot the last few years."

"He has, and he's really tired of it," she says. "He doesn't have anything official lined up yet, but he'd really like to maybe try to stay here," she says, wistfully.

"Good luck with that," Eric says, then catches himself. "Sorry! Not listening, I'm not listening."

Leah and Lizzie laugh. "Of course you are," they say. "Any thoughts from a guy's point of view?" Lizzie asks.

"I have not had a relationship in about three years, so I'm probably not the best person to ask," he says, shaking his head.

"No opportunity or no interest?" Leah asks.

"Huh, probably both," he says. "I mean, you know, Cranberry Harbor is an awesome place if you're already settled down, but it's not exactly a hotbed of social activity for singles."

"Oh, I hear you," says Leah, "It's next to impossible to find someone under 40, heck, under 50, or who isn't divorced with kids—not that there's anything wrong with that, but I'm only 27. I want to have a clean slate and someone my age. Doesn't seem like it's too much to ask."

"Sadly, it is in Cranberry Harbor," Eric says.

"I refuse to believe you two can't have the happy endings you're looking for," Lizzie says, sitting up and clearing her throat. "Leah, if this town can make it work for a second grade teacher to find a place to live, damn it, we can find a place for a great assistant coach... um, without a job. Yeah, that might be rough. Let's put a pin in that one for a moment, and move to Eric here."

Eric looks worried. He's a pretty private guy and it's clear he's not sure he wants his boss and her friend meddling in his social life.

He shakes his head. "I'm good, don't worry. I can take care of myself, thank you very much though."

"Did you ever go to any of the Book Lovers events at Tall Tales?" Lizzie asks, ignoring his statement. "Oh! Speaking of singles events, when I was checking around town for things that are happening, I saw that they were going to be doing their first speed dating night at Murphy's. Would you ever do something like that?"

Eric's eyes get big and he shakes his head emphatically.

"So that's a yes?" Leah teases.

"Oh, come on. Hey, it could be a good first person story for the paper," Lizzie says, winking at him. She knows Eric is shy, but when he's working he can talk to anyone. Lots of reporters are like that. She sort of is too.

"Are you assigning me to write this? So I have no choice?" Eric says, smiling slightly.

"You know you can always say no to an assignment," Lizzie says. "But it could be a fun story. They've never done it before."

Eric lets out a loud sigh. He knows there will be no living it down if he doesn't go, whether he's writing about it or not. "Fine, I'll do it," he says. "But you owe me. I'm going to goad you into having to go write a story the next time they do an autopsy on a shark and are cutting it open…"

"Eww!" she exclaims. "He knows my tendency to get both upset and nauseous at bloody nature events."

"It's why I am always the one to go cover anything that sounds death or dismemberment related," Eric says.

"Well, when you put it that way, I wouldn't want to go either!" Leah says, scrunching up her face. "On that disgusting note, I have to go bake some oatmeal and dried cranberry cookies," she says, standing up and pushing her chair in. "In the meantime, if you hear about anything that might be suitable for Jonathan, let me know. Oh, he's also a certified middle and high school math teacher, which is what he'd really like to do. And thank you both for all the kindness spreading. It really has been a nicer summer because of it."

"Happy to do it," Lizzie says. "See you later. Hey," she says, and Leah turns around. "We need to do a beach yoga class some time. It can't just be summer people who get to go!" Leah gives her a thumbs-up, and disappears into the kitchen.

"I should get going, move on to the next thing, which is I guess writing up my stories and uploading all the photos and writing cutlines," Lizzie says.

"Hey, you never even got anything. You want me to grab you an iced coffee to go?" Eric says.

"That's sweet, but I'm good. I think I'm going to leave my car here for now and walk back to the office. Take in a little bit of the kindness circling around downtown," she says.

"As you wish," Eric says. "I'll see you back at the office in a little bit."

All too often she's in such a hurry during the summer, Lizzie doesn't take the time to walk the stretch of Main Street between Sea Coast and the Gazette office. This time of year it is abuzz with kids with ice cream, babies in strollers and people enjoying their vacations. She feels like she is in a commercial as she takes in the summer scene.

When she gets to the town green with its lovely gazebo, the little free library box, and the newly added Kindness Mailbox that someone had donated, she feels really good about what they've all created.

"'Scuse me," a little voice says to her, bringing her back to the present moment.

Lizzie looked down and there was a very sweet little boy holding a flower. She crouched down.

"Hi," she said. "What have you got there?"

"It's a…" he looks over at his mom and dad.

"Zinnia," they both say, smiling at him.

"It's a zina, and it's for you," he says, handing her the flower.

Lizzie, resisting bursting into tears, takes the flower. "Wow, thank you so much. This is beautiful! My name is Lizzie, and this is the nicest thing to happen to me today. Thank you."

"You're welcome," he says, running back to his parents, who are holding a basket full of more flowers.

She stands up and walks over to them.

"Thank you, this is really sweet," she says. "I'm Lizzie Martin. Are you visiting the Cape?"

"We actually moved here last year. I work at Terra Marique with a few other tech people who are working on a renewable energy project. Oh, I'm sorry," the mother says, shaking her head. "I'm Molly, and this is my husband Josh, and our son Walter."

"It's so nice to meet you all," Lizzie says. "Terra Marique has grown so much I realize I don't know everyone anymore."

"When Walter heard about the town doing kind things for each other he wanted to pick flowers from our garden and bring them here to give away," Josh says. "We absolutely had to say yes to that."

Lizzie crouches down again. "That was a wonderful and thoughtful and very kind idea, Walter. You are going to make a lot of people very happy today," she says.

"Jack says it was you and a few others who came up with this idea. Thank you. We all need more kindness, that's for sure," Molly says.

"It's been an absolute joy. We've been blown away by all the big and little things we're seeing. Have you been to the playground since someone made all these improvements?" Lizzie asks.

"We haven't," Josh says. "Maybe we can bring the kids there some flowers, Walter? Want to go check out the new playground?"

Walter nods emphatically, jostling some of the flowers out of the basket onto the grass. They all bend down to retrieve them.

"Well, I should let you all get on with your day, and I need to go put this beautiful flower in some water. Walter, thank you again!" Lizzie says. "It was so nice to meet you all."

"Likewise, I hope we see you again," Molly says. "Thank you again, not just for the kindness project, but for the Gazette too. It really helps keep us looped into what's happening here."

"That's so nice to hear. You're so welcome. We love getting to share the stories of Cranberry Harbor with everyone!" Lizzie says. "I hope to see you again soon!" she says, turning to walk away.

As she walks to the paper she feels like she's living in a very sweet movie starring Jimmy Stewart or Donna Reed. But it's not a movie. This is her hometown, and she's feeling so very fortunate that she is indeed having a very wonderful life.

CHAPTER 24

"So you really think this is a good idea?" Eric asks, looking incredibly uncomfortable as he pleads his case to Lizzie.

"I love a great first-person story," she says, smiling at Eric. "Do you know the number of things I've done that have scared the hell out of me that I was assigned to write about?"

He stops pacing and sits down. "Like what?"

"Okay, so I've been sent to Newport to ride a polo pony, I've gone fly fishing, climbed a very high rock wall at a gym, sang karaoke in front of a huge roomful of people, done improv, competed in a trivia contest, modeled evening gowns, gone to beach yoga..."

"Okay, hold on, that doesn't count; you love to go to beach yoga," Eric protests.

"True, point taken, that was a fun one to do, but taking part in a New Year's Day polar plunge? I'm allowed a beach yoga class for all the things I didn't want to do, or was scared to do," she says.

"I'm not scared," he kind of pouts.

"You sure? Because you seem scared. What do you have to lose?" Lizzie asks.

"Speed dating just seems so weird. Like an overly caffeinated job interview. You have five minutes to talk to someone and see if they might be a fit for the role of your girlfriend or boyfriend," he protests.

"Or see if they're someone who might be interesting to have a cup of coffee with," she posits, shrugging her shoulders. "No one is proposing marriage here. It's just a fun event at Murphy's, and I thought it could be a fun angle if you wrote it in first-person." She takes a breath. "Don't you think it could make the story more interesting? Like what does it feel like to go to something like this, the thoughts going through your head before, and then while you're talking to someone you've never met and are seeing if they're someone who would be fun to spend more than five minutes with. Don't you think you kind of know pretty quickly when you meet people? Not just for dating, but in life. I'm betting you've got a pretty well-honed radar." She pauses and sits back in her desk chair. "But you know, I would never force you to do any assignment, so if you absolutely don't want to do this, I will not make you. But I may tease you for a good, long time about not at least trying it."

"You really went to Newport and rode a polo pony?" he asks.

Lizzie nods. "Yup, a magazine paid me to go and take a lesson. Want to know the hardest part? Well, besides being pretty scared to get on the horse. Pony is an extremely misleading name by the way; those horses are huge."

"So what was the hardest part?" he asks, now curious.

"You hold the polo mallet with your right hand and the reins with your left," she says.

Eric nods. "And you're left-handed."

"Yup, I'm *really* left handed, could not hit that ball with my mallet in my right hand to save my life, which felt in peril as I, an incredibly inexperienced rider, tried to stay on the horse, swing my mallet, and not end up being trampled. See? I'm betting speed dating doesn't sound so bad right about now." She smiles at him, hoping she can wear him down.

He lets out a deep sigh.

"Look, I'm mostly giving you a hard time at this point. I really don't want you to do anything that feels weird, or out of your comfort zone. I can just go and cover it as a standard story, or we can just do a story to advance the event and that will be that. Don't stress out about it, okay? I just thought it could be a fun angle, that's all. And since I'm married and Alexis is engaged, you're the person I thought of," Lizzie says.

Eric takes a deep breath. "Truth be told, I haven't been on a date, speed or otherwise, in over a year, and I guess this brought up some stuff for me," he says.

"I'm so sorry. Forget I said anything. It's no big deal. I was just trying to think of something different from what we usually do and did not mean to make you feel weird. Forget all about it. It's all good. I'll just get some quotes from Sean Murphy and we can run the details of the date and time, and it will be all good, it's not a prob-"

"I'll do it," he blurts out, interrupting Lizzie.

"Really? You're sure you want to? You don't have to," she says.

"No, I mean yeah, I don't like letting fear or feeling uncomfortable stop me from doing things. I should do this," he says, looking not quite convinced.

"Sleep on it, and we'll talk about it tomorrow, okay?" Lizzie says.

"Okay, but my answer will still be yes," he says, his shoulders looking a bit less taut.

"So I have to ask, why the flip?" Lizzie asks.

Eric shrugs. "I don't like not doing things because I'm afraid to. That's not a good reason."

"I'm not so sure. I don't want to jump out of an airplane, and so far that's a choice that has served me well," Lizzie says.

"Well, hopefully speed dating will be a lot less dangerous than skydiving. At least I hope so," Eric says, smiling.

Lizzie raises her eyebrows. "I don't know, falling in love can feel a bit scary..."

"No one said anything about falling in love," he says. "I'm going to write a story and talk about what it's like to go to one of these things. That's it," he says.

Lizzie nods, but deep down inside she thinks he's just put out a big dare to the universe and she can't wait to hear what happens.

Speed Dating 101

By Eric Jackson

So this is a different kind of reporting for me, writing about dating—speed dating, to be specific. But we journalists put ourselves into the fray of stories, and while I know this is not on par with being embedded with troops in a dangerous area of conflict, I am pretty conflicted as I get ready to put myself out there, not just personally, but publicly for all of you to see. In keeping with the theme of the summer, be kind.

And so begins Eric's piece about his sojourn in the world of speed dating. Lizzie had gone to Murphy's as well, knowing Eric couldn't be participating in an event like this and be taking photos. After securing permission from the participants and promising to take photos with backs to the camera and such, wanting to respect everyone's privacy, anyone interviewed before or after had complete control over their names being used and could certainly say no to all of it.

Lizzie can tell by Eric's body language that he's nervous and it makes her feel bad. Maybe she never should have suggested he do this. Had she been a jerky boss? She hopes not.

The concern had been that there would be many more women than men, but it seems fairly evenly matched. When participants come in and register they're asked if they want to be matched with men or women, and there seems to be a good mix of straight, gay, lesbian and trans folks. Lizzie is very pleased to see that, and pleased that she lives in a town where everyone is not just welcome, but cared about and respected.

The restaurant has been set up with a few different sections, and Lizzie can see Eric heading to where he'd been directed. He looks over at her and gives a nod, but he isn't smiling. He is, however, writing furiously in his notebook.

With almost anything you're feeling anxious about, anticipation is always worse than the actual doing. It's funny how we can move through life feeling like we're good at our jobs, we've got solid friendships, and we are a decent person, but the idea of basically being interviewed for the job of "boyfriend" lays bare any insecurities you may have.

"Welcome, everyone. My name is Sienna Miller—no, I am not that Sienna Miller—and I'm here tonight to facilitate this very fun event," she says. "Maybe you'll meet your soulmate, or maybe a new friend, or maybe you'll just go home and think you had a fun night out and talked to some interesting people. No matter what, it's supposed to be enjoyable," she says, looking around at everyone, "so don't put too much pressure on yourself. Just be yourself and have fun. So is everyone ready for round one?" There are a few hoots and hollers. Eric, no surprise, is not one of the ones hooting or hollering. "So you will have five minutes with each date. If you are someone who doesn't particularly like small talk, please see the basket on each table with some questions to ask. Things like, 'Best book you ever read?' 'What's your favorite way to spend a rainy day?' And in keeping with Cranberry Harbor's kindness theme, we've added questions like, 'What's something you're grateful for in your life?' and 'what is a random act of kindness you've either performed or witnessed?' Okay, so, those of you who have been assigned to stay seated, stay right where you are, and the movers will start at their first tables right now." And with that Sienna rings a chime, and the first five minutes begins.

My first date came over, sat down, and asked if I lived in Cranberry Harbor or was visiting. I said I live here. She seemed disappointed by that information. I was also aware, and I perhaps should have mentioned this earlier, that I am one of only a handful of people of color, which is never a surprise here, but I'm suddenly wondering if any of these women have dated a Black man, or considered dating one.

"What do you do? Like in the winter?" she asked.

"My work keeps me pretty busy. I'm a journalist, and I'm working on a book as well. What do you do?" I don't want this to be a monologue and I feel the pressure of the ticking clock.

She said she worked in marketing in New York, and I got the feeling I was not what she was looking for. I saw her gaze wandering around the room, which is to be expected. This is like a dressing room at a department store. Not everyone is going to be a fit...

Lizzie tries hard to not be the biggest snoop ever and watch Eric, but it's difficult to not look at him at all. It isn't a huge space, and he is one of her best friends and a colleague. When she sees his first date sit down she can tell right away from both their body language and awkward pauses in conversation that they are not a match. A part of her feels so sad. She wants him to meet someone, but then realizes it is none of her business, and the odds are not great that at one speed dating event he'd meet the love of his life. It is just that with Alexis and Ian engaged, and things going well for Leah and Jonathan, well, she wants her last single friend to find love too. That wasn't too much to ask, was it? For all her friends to be happily coupled? She realizes by thinking this she's assuming everyone *wants* to be coupled, which is not always the case. *Stand down,* she thinks to herself as the bell rings and everyone changes partners. It's like a very low-energy do-se-do.

The next woman who came and sat with me was very quiet and didn't seem too into the idea of doing this. I could relate. I have not been on a traditional date in a while, so this is way out of my comfort zone.

I'm finding the fact that I'm a journalist is met with a certain amount of... not really derision, but perhaps curiosity? It's a feeling of late that journalists are about on par with how people feel about lawyers. You know all those jokes, like "Why don't sharks bite lawyers? Professional courtesy." I do not necessarily agree with that assessment—any lawyers reading this please note that—but I've begun to feel journalists are being similarly viewed, and it's very strange.

Wanting to see if we can get away from the focus on work, I take one of the questions out of the basket on the table and read it. "Here's a good question," I said. "What does your perfect day look like?" I thought this could be a good conversation starter. Ended up, not really because she just shrugged and said, "I don't know."

I won't bore you with how dates three, four and five went. Suffice it to say, not well. I was starting to wonder if I'd forgotten to wear deodorant, or if my breath was bad. Maybe what I was wearing wasn't good? I should have asked some friends to help me choose an outfit. So now you're witnessing something I'm not proud to share, dear readers—a self-confidence spiral that I was quickly descending. My internal dialog was, however, interrupted by date number six, someone I immediately recognized and was very happy to see.

Hold the presses. Is that an actual smile I see on Eric's face? Lizzie thinks his latest date looks familiar. He looks positively delighted for the first time in what feels like an hours-long event but, in reality, has only been 45 minutes at best, she sees, eying the clock on the wall. She smiles too, thinking maybe number six is the charm. Within a few seconds she realizes where she knows her from. She's Jessie, the young woman who works at Bradford's, the very one who paid for the young dad's groceries when he'd forgotten his wallet. The man who came back the next day and didn't just pay her back, but gave her a gift certificate for $100 to Tall Tales.

Just when I was ready to throw in the towel for the night, a woman came over and sat down. In the interest of full disclosure we had met once before, and I was really happy to see her. To protect her privacy I will not reveal her name, but I was delighted to get a chance to talk with her again. So delighted in fact, that we both decided to turn in our Speed Dating log sheets and go get some ice cream.

So all in all I'm feeling pretty good about speed dating...maybe you should give it a try the next time Murphy's offers it. And don't give up if your first, second, even fourth and fifth dates aren't a match. You may, like me, find a spark on date six.

"So, would you fire me if I left now?" Eric asks Lizzie, while Jessie waits for him, looking as delighted as Eric.

"Oh, you're totally fired," she teases. "No, you've more than done your duty. I'm so happy you met someone! I see her all the time at Bradford's and she's always so nice. What are the odds that she'd come to this and you'd meet up again?!" Lizzie is thrilled for her friend.

"I don't know. I'm starting to think there's something in the water in Cranberry Harbor that makes people fall in love, or at least, like. She's amazing. She's studying for her Master's in creative writing and writing a novel while working full time at Bradford's, and she's so kind, like what she did for that dad," he says.

"That's incredible. I had no idea she was a writer. Hey, see if she'd like to freelance a little, you know, in her spare time," Lizzie jokes. "You go. Don't keep her waiting, and I will see you at the office tomorrow. Have fun!" She waves to Jessie, and then they're out the door.

From what Sienna tells her after the event, it is a pretty successful evening. Lots of people had given permission for their contact information to be shared with at least one of their dates, which made her happy.

Ever the journalist, Lizzie asks her a question for the story they'll be running.

"I'm curious. Do you think that people are shying away from dating apps and that events like speed dating will have a resurgence?" she asks Sienna.

"Yes, younger people in particular are wanting to get off their phones and meet people in real life," Sienna says. "I'm even seeing more and more Gen Z young adults trading in their smartphones for flip phones. They want to meet people in person and have actual conversations with them. Not text, not email, but meet in person and see what they think."

"There may be hope for humanity yet," Lizzie says. "Thank you for allowing us to cover this, and let us know if you do any other events locally you'd like to promote in the paper."

"Will do," Sienna says. "Okay, that's a wrap," she says to her team.

And it's a wrap for Lizzie too, who is feeling even more grateful than usual to have Jack to go home to.

CHAPTER 25

When Lizzie gets home Jack is on the couch with his laptop, looking very serious.

"Hey," she says, snuggling up next to him. "Please promise me I will never have to be out there again," she says, putting her arms around him.

"Aw, you're quoting Carrie Fisher, spouting Nora Ephron," he says, kissing her.

She sits up. "You don't know how happy it makes me that you know that. I feel like my work as a romcom loving woman is complete," she says, hugging him tightly.

"What have you done to me," he says, dramatically throwing his head back and laughing. "I used to know lines like, 'Look at the big brain on Brad…'"

Lizzie nods. "Tarantino, *Pulp Fiction,* said by Samuel L. Jackson," she says, smiling.

"Well done," he says.

"Hey, you can like romantic comedies *and* Quentin Tarantino," she says. "Knowing a Nora Ephron line won't kill your street cred, I promise."

Jack closes his laptop. "So how was it—lots of love matches?"

"Hard to tell. Oh! But Eric met someone. They left together to go get ice cream!" Lizzie excitedly shares. "She's so nice. It's Jessie, from Bradford's. I hope it works out."

"Well, even if it's just ice cream, that's very nice," he says, tempering Lizzie's enthusiasm a bit. "Not every date has to end at the altar, you know."

"You're right. Jeez, when did I turn into a mama bear wanting all my friends to be engaged or married? I am getting old!" she jokes.

"Nah, you just want everyone to be happy, which is very sweet, but it will be what it will be, right?" Jack says.

"Yes," she says, looking at Jack and then giving him a very romantic kiss.

"To what do I owe that, Ms. Martin?" he says, enjoying the attention.

"To my gratitude for being married to you, for not looking for that proverbial needle in a haystack, and for being so happy," she says, kissing him again. "What do you say we put all our work aside for the night and take this party upstairs?"

Jack puts his laptop on the table, stands up, and offers his hand to Lizzie. "I think that is a stellar idea, my love. Let's go."

Lizzie stands up, and Jack leads her upstairs. She laughs to herself for feeling a little shy and giggly. Maybe being around all those people meeting for the first time rubbed off on her, and she finds herself blushing as they get upstairs and Jack closes the door behind them. She's glad that her husband still has this effect on her, that she still gets butterflies, and she can still feel like the luckiest woman on the planet to get to be married to him, and she hopes that feeling never goes away.

Lizzie wakes up before Jack the next morning, and not wanting to disturb him by checking her phone for emails—a terrible habit, she knows—she slithers out of bed and slips on her robe that is hanging on the bathroom door.

She's finishing up her first cup of coffee when Jack slowly makes his way downstairs. He sleepily smiles at her as he kisses her on the head and sighs.

"Boy, I really conked out last night. I haven't slept that well in, well, weeks," he says, making his way over to the Chemex coffee pot and pouring himself a cup.

"That should still be pretty hot. I just made it like 10 minutes ago," she says. "I'm very glad you slept well. I've noticed you've been tossing and turning a lot lately."

"I'm so sorry if I've been keeping you awake," he says.

"No, it's fine. I've just noticed it; it's fine. Well, not fine. I've been worried about you. Is everything okay at Terra Marique? Are the VCs still giving you a hard time?" she asks, looking for a way to stop saying fine.

"Kind of. I don't know; it's hard to say. Some of them are really happy with how everything's going, but then there are a couple—well one, Amanda," he says, not exactly rolling his eyes, but on the verge.

"Oh yes, Amanda. She was a lot," Lizzie says. "She gave me pause."

"Yeah?"

"Yeah, remember what I heard her say to the guy she was with when I saw her at Sea Coast, about thinking it would be nice to live on the Cape? It just felt like she had ulterior motives for coming here to see you," Lizzie says.

"Right, I'd forgotten about that in the midst of everything else," he says. "The thing that gives me pause is how many great executive directors of nonprofits I've known who've been booted out because rather than ever looking at the board, if things aren't going well, they blame the director, get rid of them, and the cycle continues."

Lizzie is suddenly feeling very worried. "Do you think they're trying to get rid of you? I will have to give several people a piece of my mind if they try to oust you from the nonprofit you created and built!" She sits bolt upright and her heart is racing. "How dare they?!"

Jack rubs her back. "Honey, no one is telling me to pack my things and get out. I'm just preparing myself in case something comes up. I get the feeling she's gunning for me, saying I'm not bringing in enough new revenue and that occupancy isn't at 100 percent yet. Things like that. I'm just trying to make sure I've got all the documentation and facts I need."

"You haven't even been open for two years," she says. "I think what you've done is incredible! I know I'm more than a little biased, but all of the businesses that are working out of there, the community interaction with classes, events...it's phenomenal."

Jack sits back and thinks. "You're right. I sometimes lose sight of how short a time it's really been, but it is pretty incredible how much we've done, isn't it?"

"Yes! I know what you mean, because sometimes it feels like it's always been there, but it's still a relatively new endeavor, and it's already a vital part of our community," Lizzie says.

Jack sighs. "I'm going to try to keep thinking the best, preparing for the worst—well, not the worst, but for some pushback—and keep doing my job the way I've been doing it, and see what happens."

"You are the person who should be running Terra Marique, Jack. Not only was it your idea, but you grew up here and you care about this community in a way no random candidate from a headhunter's search would ever be able to replicate. Running Terra Marique isn't a job to you, it's a passion and a commitment to the people of Cranberry Harbor, the Cape, and the planet that sets you apart," Lizzie says.

"Anyone ever told you that you are really good with all the words?" Jack teases. "You should do something with that skill." He laughs.

"Gee, that's a good idea. Maybe I'll run for office!" she says.

"Yes, add being on the selectboard to your already overflowing plate," Jack says. He leans over and hugs Lizzie. "Thank you for talking me down from the ledge. I could feel I was on the verge of really spinning out of control with worry."

"I understand, but I know all too well that worrying doesn't help," she says. "I heard a great quote from that *10 Percent Happier* guy, Dan Harris. He said, 'When you find yourself going down a rabbit hole of worry, ask yourself, is this useful?' I have to ask myself that a lot."

"You needlessly worry? I find that very hard to believe," Jack teases, smiling at her. "I had a very nice time last night, by the way," he says, tenderly kissing her neck. "So nice that I wish we both didn't have to get out of here. I'm deeply resenting that."

Lizzie smiles and hugs him back. "Yes, there are times that being responsible adults really does stink. I did not appreciate being a carefree—well, sort of carefree—college student nearly enough."

Jack laughs. "You've never been a carefree person, Lizzie. You were born responsible. And reliable, and..."

"Ugh, boring! I was born boring," she says, only half-kidding.

"You are far from boring," Jack says, getting up from the table and stretching. "You are very curious, smart and kind, and none of those qualities are the least bit boring." He brings the coffee pot over to Lizzie, who shakes her head no, and he pours the remaining coffee into his cup.

"Thank you. I'll have my second cup at Sea Coast," she says. "So predictable," she smiles at him.

"I love our life, even if it's a bit crazy and over-committed sometimes. I wouldn't trade it for anything else," Jack says, downing the rest of his coffee, rinsing his cup and putting it in the dishwasher. "I'm off to take a shower," he says, leaving Lizzie to her thoughts. And worries. Always with the worries. She sighs, gets up and puts her cup in the dishwasher as well.

"Is this useful?" she says out loud as she goes upstairs. "Hardly," she replies, making herself giggle a little. "You're a work in progress," she says as a way to comfort herself. Maybe someday she'll stop being such a worrier, but until then, she'll just embrace it, and keep reminding herself to ask, 'Is this useful?'

CHAPTER 26

It didn't take very many weeks after the Fourth of July for many locals to begin to wonder, *Is it almost over?* It's the yin and yang of living in a tourist town. It's so quiet, sometimes too quiet, in the off-season, but then in the height of summer where it feels like every person on vacation in the world has decided to take theirs on Cape Cod, it feels overwhelming. Augustitis—it is is for real, and it happens to locals every year.

"I feel like Goldilocks," Lizzie says to Eric, who's already hard at work when she plops into her office chair opposite him.

Eric stops typing, sits back and smiles. "And why is that, Ms. Martin?" he asks.

"Because I feel like there's about three days a year where the weather is just right and it's not too crowded here, but also not too empty, that feel just right," she shrugs her shoulders. "Goldilocks."

"Ah, I get it, and I really do get it." Eric leans forward and takes a sip of his coffee. "I've lived in New York, L.A. and Boston. I even spent a few months in Montana, but this place is a totally different animal. I've never been anywhere that has such a huge swing in population. What did I just read in the Cranberry Harbor annual report?" He fishes under some papers and other detritus on his desk for the report. "Yeah, the year-round population is something like 6400, and in the summer it swells to about 20,000. That's a huge difference for a little town."

"Yeah, it is," Lizzie says. "No wonder I get whiny and weary," she laughs.

"And created a kindness project," he reminds her.

"For sure!" she says. "Speaking of which, any new stories or stats coming in? I haven't checked our social media yet today," she says, opening up her laptop. She's quiet for a moment or two as she scrolls the page she created called "Kind Acts in Cranberry Harbor."

"Oh wow," she says, putting her hand on her chest. "Here's a story about a beloved lost stuffed bunny that a little girl dropped while riding in a trailer attached to her mom's bike on the bike trail." She continues to read. "Ohhh, the mom posted a photo of the little girl and the bunny, 312 people shared it, and it was found within an hour and a half and returned to the little girl. I love that."

"That is really sweet," Eric says. "Hey, maybe we should have a little weekly column where we share stories like that? 'Kindness Counts,' or something? We could make that a regular column, even after the summer. You know, to keep this going?"

"I love that," Lizzie says, opening a new document. "It would be wonderful for people to see all the kind acts that add up over a week." She keeps looking online to see what else pops up. "Oh! Here's another one. Wow, a summer resident, who had purchased a second home to use as a short-term rental property, has decided to instead rent it year-round, affordably, to two young Cranberry Harbor firefighters and a teacher from the high school. It was posted by the teacher, who said she wanted to share this incredible act of kindness. Wow, isn't that fantastic?"

Eric is now intrigued and starts looking at the Kind Acts page too. "Here's another keeper. Listen to this. A couple went to Safe Harbor daycare center and asked that their names not be used, but they wanted to cover the childcare costs for a year for two families in need. That's a lot of money. Childcare is crazy expensive. I know from my sister it's thousands of dollars a year. That's incredible!"

"Amazing!" Lizzie is still reading too. "Oh, and here's a story of a little boy who, when he found out his friend couldn't afford a bike, offered him his, and when the local bike shop heard about it, they gave them both new bikes, refurbished the old one, and gave that to someone else."

"That's amazing," Eric says. "Kindness really is contagious, isn't it?"

"Right?" Lizzie says, taken aback by all she's seeing. "I mean, I thought this was a nice idea that might catch on a bit, but I had no idea how this would explode. I think people really needed this, right? It's hard by yourself to start something, but if you feel there's a community effort behind a project or mission, it makes it a lot easier to jump in. It's definitely contagious in all the best ways," she says, having completely forgotten all about feeling grumpy about the traffic and long lines at Sea Coast.

The two of them stop talking as they begin writing their respective pieces. The silence is short-lived, however, as outside the office window music starts playing from the sidewalk.

Lizzie's the first to get up and look out the window, but she is quickly joined by Eric. They're both stunned to see a group of about 10 or 15 high school-aged kids with guitars, tambourines, and even a ukulele, smiling, singing and waving a big handwritten sign that reads, "Thank You for The Kindness Project!"

"Can you believe this?" Lizzie says, feeling choked up. "Wow!"

"This is a testament to you, Lizzie. You made this happen. We have to go down there," Eric says, grabbing his phone to make sure he can take some photos.

"I feel so self-conscious," she says, shaking her head, and putting her face in her hands. "I didn't do this alone, not by a long shot."

Eric takes her hand and begins to pull her toward the door. "But you started this. This was your idea. Come on, let them say thank you to you, if not for you, for them. You know better than anyone that doing for someone else is really what it's all about."

"You're right. I just don't want this to be about me, but you're right."

When they walk around the corner to the front of the building all the kids start cheering and jumping up and down.

"You are all so sweet," Lizzie says, "I can't believe this! Thank you! But it's not just me, it's everyone!" She's feeling so emotional it's hard to not just burst into tears, which she's thinking might freak out all these very happy kids.

"But it was your idea!" one boy says, coming forward and handing her the sweetest hand-picked bouquet of wildflowers.

Then one of the girls calls out to everyone, "Okay, are you ready for the main event?"

"Yeah!" they all shout.

"I wonder what they've got up their sleeves to top all this?" Eric whispers to Lizzie. Clearly he's feeling emotional too.

And then, from behind all the big kids, comes a little boy, about four or five, just beaming, "Hi!" he says, and Lizzie's heart melts.

"Hi!" she and Eric both say.

"I'm going to sing you my favorite song that my sister and I sing, okay?" he says.

"Very okay," Lizzie says, barely holding it together.

His big sister, ukulele in hand, comes over and says, "Okay Robbie, you ready?"

"I was born ready!" he says, clearly having been taught that by his sweet sister.

Then she begins strumming and Robbie, with a smile that could light up a room, begins sweetly singing.

"Don't worry about a thing, 'cause every little thing's gonna be alright..."

Robbie goes on to sing all four verses of the Bob Marley classic and by the end—heck in the middle—Lizzie and Eric are both crying tears of total joy and when Robbie is done, he runs up and gives Lizzie a huge hug, and she hugs him right back so hard.

"Are all of you okay if I share the photos and the video of Robbie singing on our social media?" Eric asks. "I feel like the rest of the town has to see this. It's too beautiful not to share."

All the kids nod emphatically and say yes. Robbie and Amanda's mom and dad have come out of somewhere. Lizzie was so enthralled by the song that she hadn't noticed them.

"Hi, we're their parents," the dad says. "I'm Will, and this is my wife, Laura, and we wanted to thank you as well for this wonderful project. Robbie has been going to the programs at the library, and the project inspired all these kids to start finding ways to bring kindness to people in their lives, and strangers too."

"You've gotten them to put down their phones, a miracle in itself," says Laura, "and they're out every day trying to see how many random acts of kindness they can perform in a day. It's become a bit competitive, but in a very good way."

"Yeah, until they knock someone down vying for who gets to help them cross the street," Will laughs.

"Kindness as a competitive sport is not something we've thought of," Lizzie says, smiling. "I am just so blown away by this," she says, taking it all in. "That they took the time and made the effort to come down here is just remarkable. I feel like I'd love to do something to thank them, like treat everyone to ice cream or something?"

"That is incredibly thoughtful and generous, but I think we'd like to keep this to them doing for someone else just for doing it, not for getting something out of it," Laura says. "I hope you aren't offended. It's very sweet of you."

"Oh, I totally get that, and it's a very good point. But maybe down the road a bit I will surprise them back with something."

"I'm betting seeing their pictures in the paper will be a huge thrill for them," Will says. "We should get all these kids back home. We were the parents who volunteered since we have the littlest one," he says, picking up Robbie.

"Robbie, thank you again for singing me that beautiful song. You made this the best day ever," Lizzie says.

"You've got a real future ahead of you, sir," Eric says, giving him a fist bump.

Robbie laughs and buries his head in his dad's chest.

"Thank you again!" Lizzie calls out to the kids as they begin to walk away. "Stay kind!" she says, to which they all raise their fists and march on.

"Well, how are we supposed to go back to work now?" Lizzie asks. "That was incredible!"

"I say we take a little break and go get some iced coffee," Eric says. "My treat!"

"Well, if you're paying, how can I say no?" Lizzie says as they start walking toward Sea Coast. "So with all this excitement, I haven't had a chance to ask you about the rest of your evening last night—you know, with Jessie," she says, playfully nudging him and taking his arm.

"Oh no, I'm not going to kiss and tell," Eric says, visibly beaming.

"Oh! So there was kissing?!" she teases.

"My lips are sealed," he says, looking happier than she's seen him look in a long time.

"I'll get it out of you, Eric. I will ply you with cookies…" she says as they continue to walk.

"I will only say I had a wonderful time and am looking forward to seeing her again," he says, still smiling ear to ear.

"Fine. We'll leave it at that. For now," she says, opening the door to the coffee shop and holding it for him. "I'll just say I'm really happy for you."

Eric nods "And I'm happy for me too," he says, smiling and looking quite wistful, Lizzie notes. She can't wait to see what happens next in this newest Cranberry Harbor love story.

CHAPTER 27

Speaking of Cranberry Harbor love stories, the newly engaged Alexis and Ian are already in line when Lizzie and Eric walk in, along with a lot of other people.

"Hey you guys," Alexis says, looking like this line is moving way too slow for her today. "There seems to be a bit of a holdup with the line. Tell me what you two want and I'll order it. No sense in all of us waiting here."

"Yes, please, don't feel you need to stand here too. It could be a while," Ian says, looking up from texting.

Lizzie looks at Eric. "If you insist…Iced coffee? Anything else?"

"Nope, I'm good. I brought my lunch today and I'm trying very hard to emulate your mom and eat healthier," he says.

"Gabby will be very proud," Lizzie says. She reaches into her pocket for some cash and hands Alexis enough to cover the coffees and a tip. "Here you go, two large iced coffees, please, and thank you very much." She looks around at the lack of seating. "Why don't we go snag some seats outside on the deck for us all?"

"Sounds good.You both take your coffee with a little bit of cream, right?" Alexis asks.

"Um, if it's not a pain, some almond milk would be great," Eric says, looking a little self-conscious, not wanting to be like all the memes about vegans he sees all the time.

"Not a problem, I prefer it too," Alexis says. "We will eventually join you outside. I think," she says, sighing at the long line.

Among her many improvements to Sea Coast, Leah built a deck last year that has become a popular spot to hang out. Lizzie chides herself for not taking advantage of it more often, but once the weather turned nicer, the crowds arrived, and she tended to not hang out quite as much as she did in the off-season.

Thankfully they were able to snag a table and grabbed a fourth chair when they asked the couple sitting next to them if they were using it.

"I should do this more often," Lizzie says, taking a deep breath and admiring the beautiful plants Leah had placed around the perimeter. "This time of year I kind of turn more inward and avoid the crowds, and as the editor of the Gazette I really should make more of an effort to be out and experiencing what's happening in town."

Eric shakes his head and smiles.

"What? What's that about?" Lizzie asks.

"You will always, always, always, find a way to make yourself wrong no matter how much you do and how well you do it," he says.

Lizzie thinks for a few seconds. "Ugh, yikes, I really do, don't I? That is not good." She sits back. "Add that to the list of things I need to work on."

Eric laughs. "Yup, classic Lizzie, even being nicer to yourself is another thing to put on your to-do list. Just chill a little bit, be in the moment, which I know is hard when your whole life is deadlines, but even for just a few minutes a day find a way to just... be."

"When did you get all Zen and everything?" Lizzie asks. "It's not like you're not exceptionally driven too," she says.

"You're right, which is why I decided to start doing some meditating, try to eat better, and maybe make my away-from-work life a little bit more of a priority," he says.

"And just in time to have met someone, huh?" Lizzie says, still wishing Eric would share what he's feeling. But she understands. This isn't Alexis, her best friend, who's going to spill all her feelings.

"Perhaps," he says, and right on cue, a rescue arrives in the form of Alexis and Ian bearing iced coffees.

"Wow, thank you for taking one for the team and waiting in that line," Lizzie says, accepting her cup from Ian.

"So how was speed dating last night, Eric?" Alexis abruptly asks, taking a sip of her coffee.

"Oh, you two planned this, didn't you?" he laughs, looking at the two of them.

Alexis is confused. "What? I think I missed something here."

Lizzie laughs. "I've been pumping him for details about the date *after* the speed dating he went out with Jessie--"

"Oh, that really nice woman from Bradford's? I love her! We talk about books all the time when I get in her line," Alexis says.

Eric and Lizzie start to laugh.

"Yes, that's her," Eric says.

"Don't let them bully you into talking about it," Ian says. "They will try to wear you down and get you to reveal feelings, and you don't have to do that," he teases. "You two, leave the poor guy alone and let him sort out his own affairs." He catches himself. "Well, not affairs. Jeez, now you've got me all flustered too!"

Lizzie and Alexis start to laugh.

"Wow, honey, I didn't realize this was such a hot-button issue for you," Alexis says, kidding with him.

"New topic," Lizzie says, saving the day. "What are you working on, Ian? The film about Terra Marique is done, right?"

He nods, having just taken a bite of a scone. "I'm just tweaking some of the sound, but it's really good. I'm finally ready to show it to Jack, I think. I was afraid he might think I focused too much on him and what he's done, but that's the narrative. Without him this never would have happened, and it wouldn't be happening. But he's so humble, he kept saying anytime I was filming him to not make him the focus."

"Yeah, that sounds like Jack," Lizzie says. "He does not like being the center of attention anytime, and most especially when it comes to Terra Marique, because he believes it's all such a team effort." She pauses. "I get that and respect it, but I worry sometimes that because he's so humble the people behind the scenes with the money don't know how much he does."

Alexis nods emphatically. "Oh for sure, especially that Amanda person. She keeps calling and asking for more statistics, and she's never very pleasant about it," she grumbles.

"I'm planning on having a screening at Beachfront Cinema at the end of the summer, not sure if before or after Labor Day, but he's going to have to suck it up and let the footage show just what he's done," Ian says, smiling, but determined.

Lizzie raises her iced coffee, "Here's to Jack, his hard work, his dedication, and to being comfortable for...how long is the movie?"

"88 minutes," Ian says.

Lizzie nods. "For being comfortable in the limelight for 88 minutes." They all clink their coffees.

"Speaking of people not always taking enough credit, how's the kindness project going?" Ian asks Lizzie.

Lizzie laughs and nods. "Okay, I hear you." She points to herself. "Pot, meet kettle...but I'm not as bad as he is!" she says, laughing.

"Yes, you are," the trio says in unison.

"Fine, I'll work on it." She clears her throat. "It's actually been pretty amazing, right Eric? The posts we're seeing on our social media about things people are doing, or see others doing, around kindness are pretty incredible."

"It really is," Eric agrees. "I really do feel like it's changed the vibe around town this summer."

"I didn't even think about it until now, but even standing in the long line inside waiting to get our coffees, I didn't hear one person complain, get mad or be demanding," Alexis says. "That's pretty incredible, especially in August on Cape Cod."

"It probably helps that Leah put that big sign over the ordering counter that says 'Be Kind!'" Lizzie says.

"And I love over all the doors as you're leaving there are other signs that say, 'Stay Kind,'" Eric adds.

"As we head into Labor Day do you think there's anything we should be planning to do? I know we had the baseball game and everything at the beginning, but should we close out the summer with something for everyone to participate in, maybe on the Town Green?" Lizzie asks.

"Yeah, that's a good idea," Alexis says, thinking. "Maybe some live, local music, and maybe ask some people, especially kids, to share what it's meant to them to focus on finding ways to be kind? Like a story slam of kindness stories?"

"Yeah, I like that," Eric says. "Maybe we could get Jay and Anika from Tall Tales to run that part of it, since they have story slams at the store every month? I bet they'd love to do that."

Lizzie takes her phone out of her pocket and begins to jot down some notes so she doesn't forget. "These are all great ideas. I love them. I think recognition and a bit of ceremony are important steps to cement new behaviors. Not to sound all psychology-y or anything, but if we want to see these changes continue, we need to have some rewards woven in, I think."

"That's a really good point," Ian says. "I vote for having the ice cream truck there as well, you know, if we're talking treats," he smiles.

"Oh yeah, ice cream is definitely a very Pavlovian approach to changing behaviors for the better," Alexis says.

"So before or after Labor Day? Do we want to make this more focused on locals, or include summer visitors as well?" Lizzie asks.

"Hmmm, good question," Eric says, thinking. "Maybe before? To bookend it being a summer-long project, and maybe they'll feel inspired to take the message home to their own hometowns?"

"Oh, and maybe in the fall we can continue to spread the message and keep the momentum going into the holidays?" Alexis says. "We do have the big Turnip Festival in Eastham every year. Maybe we can have some activities there. They're always looking for ideas."

Eric laughs. "I will never stop smiling that I now live in a place that every year chooses to celebrate turnips."

"Hey, don't you go knocking our turnips, pal," Lizzie says, teasing him. "Eastham turnips are the best, right, Alexis?"

"Uh, yeah, sure..." she says, wrinkling her nose. "I have to say, Eastham or California. I'm not a big turnip fan," she says. "Sorry. But the festival is a blast!"

"Why, how dare you!" Lizzie says in feigned disgust. "Yeah, not my favorite vegetable either, but in solidarity we have to at least pretend to like them, right?"

"Yes, here's to turnips!" They again all toast.

"Well, Eric, we have a paper to get out. You ready to head back to the office?" Lizzie asks.

"Yes." He pushes back his chair and stands up. "This has been wonderful. I'm so glad we ran into you two."

"Me too," Alexis says. "And I can't wait to hear more about your next date with Jessie!" she adds, laughing, loving giving him a hard time.

"I'm seeing her tonight, so you won't have to wait too long. This is a very small town. I'm sure whatever we do will be all over by tomorrow," Eric says, shaking his head and smiling.

"We will wheedle all the details out of you," Lizzie says, as they all start walking to their respective workplaces.

"Oh, I have no doubt. I know you people," he says.

"Best of luck keeping anything private," Ian says. "You have my sympathies and support."

"I appreciate that, sir," Eric says. "Solidarity, bro," he says, as they both laugh at the lack of possibility that either Lizzie nor Alexis will let it go.

CHAPTER 28

After work, when she arrives home, Lizzie decides to take her after work drink—some iced herbal tea—across the yard to visit her mom. You'd think living in clear view of each other that they'd see each other all the time, but days often go by when there is only a wave between them as they each get into their cars or are watering some plants outside.

She knocks as she opens the French door by the deck a bit, not wanting to disturb Gabby, and calls out, "Mom? You around?"

Her mother comes out of the pantry, carrying an armful of food, and smiles. "What a lovely surprise!" she says, putting all her ingredients on the counter and giving Lizzie a big hug.

"Sit! Sit!" she says, pointing to the stools at the counter. "To what do I owe the honor of seeing you after a long work day?" she says, organizing what looks like the makings for some kind of brown rice dish.

"I just haven't seen you in a few days, and I miss you if I don't see you!" Lizzie says, taking a sip of her tea. "How are you? And what do you have going on here?"

"I'm great, and well, per your and your father's suggestion, a very passionate suggestion, I've been working on some recipes for a cookbook," she says, looking slightly self-conscious about this very new endeavor.

"Really? I think that's wonderful;!" Lizzie says. "I really think you're onto something, Mom, with your medical background, your love of food, and your obvious talent for creating healthy and delicious recipes. It's a great idea. How far into this are you?"

"So I've been doing some research, and because it's nonfiction I don't need to write the whole thing, so I'm working on a proposal, a bio, some case studies including your dad—an overview, who the market would be for this type of book, a marketing plan, and of course," she says, gesturing at the food on the counter, "some sample recipes."

"You really have done your homework. I'm very impressed," Lizzie says. "This is so exciting, Mom! Are you having fun?"

"I am! I'm kind of surprised by that. Maybe living with and being surrounded by you writers has rubbed off on me, but I'm finding it's just kind of flowing. And I've had fun doing all the research about the impact of not eating highly processed food, eating more plants and eating no or way less sugar, meat and dairy has on overall health. It's pretty miraculous," Gabby says.

"You're exactly on-trend, that's for sure. I'm always reading about healthier eating, and you have been way ahead of the curve for a while. You've sure influenced Jack and me and how we eat," Lizzie says. "We're not quite as good as you and Dad, but we're getting there, though I've been a little tired lately and not so on top of it. I think it's a combination of summer busyness, the kindness project, the paper, and just life on Cape Cod in the summer. It can be draining."

"I'm sure you're right, but if you keep feeling tired or rundown, check in with Dr. Butler. She can check you out," Gabby says. "No other symptoms?"

"No, not really." Lizzie plucks a banana from the bunch on the counter. "Mind if I steal one? I'm starving."

"Help yourself." Gabby stops to think. "So the biggest challenge in doing this is having to measure and be precise with measurements. You know me; I cook by the seat of my pants! It's a good exercise though, and even if no one wants to publish this I'll have at least written down my best recipes for posterity!" she says, laughing.

"I have no doubt someone is going to want to publish this," Lizzie says, taking the last bite of her banana. "People love good food, and they seem to really like, if what I'm hearing on podcasts and seeing online is any indication, well-sourced and science-backed reasons for making better choices. They don't want anecdotes from celebrities, they want people like you, doctors with the science to back up what they're saying. I think this will get snapped up by a publisher very quickly."

"Me too!" exclaims Peter, coming through the door. "Hi sweetie," he says, giving Lizzie a hug. "And hello my other sweetie." He gives Gabby a kiss as well.

"Hi Dad, what have you been up to?" Lizzie asks, finishing her tea.

"I was visiting with a summer friend. He's a great guy, Gerald Brooks—maybe you've heard of him?" Peter asks, sitting down next to her.

"Gerald Brooks from NPR? The host of *Brooks on Books?* Oh my God, yes, I listen to his podcast every week. I didn't know he summers here. We should do a story about him--" Lizzie is beside herself, but her dad quickly interrupts her.

Peter shakes his head. "Yeah, no, there's a reason you didn't know he spends summers here."

Lizzie nods. "Okay, got it, but wow, how did you meet him? And how did I not know you were friends?"

"Pickleball," Peter says, smiling at her. "See? Great things can come from playing pickleball."

"Yeah, I need to look into that. I may be missing meeting Oprah or Taylor Swift by not playing pickleball." She still can't get past her dad knowing one of her favorite podcasters. "Is he as funny and charming as he seems on air? And dear Lord, he's so well read!"

"Yes, he's all those things, and his husband is just as wonderful," he says.

"Wow, I'm so jealous," Lizzie says.

"Well, we will have them over for dinner sometime and you can meet them, okay?"

"Yes, please!" she says, clapping her hands.

"You should tell her the news, honey," Gabby says, grinning.

"News? What news?" Lizzie asks.

"Gerald mentioned me to his agent, who then mentioned me to his publisher..."

"Oh my God! Do you have a book deal?!" Lizzie exclaims.

He holds up his hand. "Pending their acceptance of my book proposal, but Gerald is helping me with that, and it's looking good."

Lizzie can hardly believe it. "I think I need to move back in here and absorb these book writing vibes. We've got cookbooks, and… and, what's your book, Dad?"

"It's part memoir, writing about starting the Gazette and running it for all those years, and also about what's happening to newspapers across the country and how we need to start a campaign to save journalism, especially small town independent newspapers," Peter says.

"I love it. I am so proud of you, Dad, and you too, Mom. Boy, I'd better get going on a book…wait, Matt's not writing a book about solar energy is he? 'Cause if so, I'm definitely going to be the black sheep of the family," she jokes.

"Not yet, but you never know," Gabby jokes.

"Great, no pressure," Lizzie laughs, shaking her head. "All joking aside, Dad, I'm really impressed with that message, and with someone like Gerald Brooks behind you this could get real, like, national attention. Wow, I'll be lucky if I can get an interview with you for the Gazette!"

"Ah, my heart will always be with where it all started," Peter says. "I am also certainly going to write about the next generation taking the lead and how vital it is to have young journalists like you and Eric carrying the movement forward. It can't be left to die as we older journalists retire."

"I cannot wait to read what you're doing, Dad. If you need a first reader, I'm right here," Lizzie says.

"I'm glad you offered, because I didn't want to burden you with anything more to do," Peter says. "Thank you. I can't think of anyone I'd rather have reading and editing as I go."

A sudden wave of nausea comes over Lizzie. She pops up and hurries into the bathroom. "Be right back," she says.

A few minutes later she comes out, looking a little pale.

"Honey, you don't look so good. Sit back down," Gabby says, helping her to the stool.

"I just threw up. I've never thrown up from a banana. Maybe I've got a bug or something," she says.

Gabby and Peter look at each other. "Or maybe…"

Lizzie's eyes widen. "No, it couldn't be that," she says. "Besides, it's not even morning."

"Honey, morning sickness doesn't always happen in the morning, and you said you'd been feeling tired…" Gabby looks at her, doctor's hat now on. "Have you had nausea at other times? When was your last period?"

Peter has always been a very cool dad, and having been married to a doctor for decades he is not *that* guy, but he doesn't want Lizzie to feel uncomfortable. "I'm going to go get some notes I printed out in the study to show you," he says, excusing himself.

Gabby and Lizzie laugh when he leaves. "He's such a good guy," Lizzie says. She takes out her phone. "Let me see, I keep track on my phone." She starts scrolling. "Huh, this can't be right. According to this I'm three weeks late," she says, stunned at her forgetfulness. "How did I not notice that?!"

"Um, working 50 or so hours a week, starting the kindness project, summer in Cranberry Harbor… there's been a lot going on," Gabby says.

"You really think I might be, that I could be…pregnant?" Lizzie says, not sure how she feels. There's never a perfect time to have a baby, but this *really* feels like not a good time with all of Jack's stress at Terra Marique and how much she needs to work keeping the paper going. It's a lot.

"I think it's a very distinct possibility," Gabby says, tempering her excitement, sensing Lizzie's surprise and overwhelm. "The only way to know for sure is to take a test, and believe it or not, I have a couple here from when Shannon was trying to get pregnant and I got a deal on some at the pharmacy."

"Wow," Lizzie says, shaking her head. "Do I feel dumb. It never even occurred to me." She takes a deep sigh. "Well, there's no time like the present. Let's take a test."

Just as Lizzie and Gabby start to go upstairs to get the test, Jack comes bursting in.

"The board just called a meeting. The VCs might be pulling their funding.It looks like Amanda has made her move and wants me out," he says, looking completely overwhelmed. "She wants me out and wants to be the interim director until they decide what to do."

Lizzie rushes over to him and hugs him. "It's going to be okay. We've got this, alright?" She hugs him again and thinks this is *really* not a good time to talk about maybe being pregnant. That conversation is just going to have to wait.

CHAPTER 29

A glass and a half of wine—for Jack, not Lizzie, just in case—later, Jack had caught his breath, and the four of them began to strategize what to do next.

"I'm just so stunned, Jack," Gabby says. "You *are* Terra Marique. You created the concept, got the town to back you in the use of the land, got nonprofit status, and got it all built, and it's now a huge part of the community, and home to lots of residents. I almost can't remember what it was like before we had it. Everyone uses it. And that's all because of you." She shakes her head.

"I agree," says Peter. "This is ridiculous. You get rid of the person who created the project, and replace them with who? A person who's never lived here, has probably only visited, and doesn't know anyone or anything about Cranberry Harbor." He sits up and shakes his head, pulls his notebook in front of him and starts writing. "We're not going to just accept this. The land belongs to the town, so whoever they decide to lead this project has to be approved by the town. It's that simple."

"You really think so, Peter?" Jack asks, not looking like he believes that.

"Yes, as part of the lease the town maintains that bit of control; that was to make sure that no bad actors—no corporations or developers —would try to come in and undo all the good you've done."

"And that means the town would have to vote on it, right?" Lizzie asks, making her own lists. She knows she's in a precarious position with running the only paper in town, and her husband being the executive director of Terra Marique, but she and Eric have navigated this territory before, and they will again. "So that would mean there would have to be a special Town Meeting, right Dad?" she asks, not looking up from her notebook.

"Yes, the investors, and this woman, Amanda, would have to essentially pitch the town on why you shouldn't be the director, and why she should. It feels like a no-brainer to me. The town is one hundred percent behind you."

"But what if they've got numbers, or some other information someone has been collecting that I don't know about?" Jack asks, looking concerned.

"That's why you have a lawyer, and you've got a great one in Adam Lowell. He specializes in nonprofits, so he'll be able to guide you," Peter says.

"Can we start a campaign? Maybe not the right word, but can we start letting people know what's going on, or is that against the rules?" Gabby asks.

"Question number one for Adam, huh?" Jack says, writing it down.

"If it is okay to get the word out and let people know, I think I've got a good idea..." Lizzie says, smiling.

Gabby, Peter and Jack are all waiting for this big idea.

"Let's show Ian's film all about Terra Marique to the town! Maybe we could do it right on the Town Green? We invite everyone to come, and let them see from the inside how this project came to be, how it was built, how it's going now, and who's responsible for that," she says, pointing to Jack.

"You really think so? It sort of feels like a cheesy political campaign move to get people feeling all sentimental about Terra Marique and, I don't know, about me."

The other three all nod, and Lizzie says, "Um, yeah! That's the point. People vote with two things, their pocketbooks and their hearts. Terra Marique has both going for it. So many businesses are flourishing who get to use the facilities there, there's affordable housing there, so more people can actually live and work here. This has been such a win for this town, and if people don't know that already, I have a feeling they will after seeing Ian's film."

"I think that's a fantastic idea, Lizzie!" says Peter. "None of this hiding your light under a bushel, Jack, you have to fight back, and fight back with all the tools you can muster."

"We don't even know what the angle of the film is. I mean, I know he's supportive of the project," Jack says, "but maybe I don't come across as a super effective or competent director."

Lizzie shakes her head. "Are you kidding me? He was telling me today that he was worried you're going to not like it because a lot of it is about you and all you've done to create this amazing place and to make sure it stayed true to its mission and thrived. I think it could be the most surprising card we have up our sleeve, should they decide to move forward with their ridiculous plan. What I want to know is why are other people going along with her? You've always had complete financial transparency and the other investors have been thrilled."

"I wondered the same thing," Peter says. "Putting on my reporter's hat, I can't help but wonder what else is going on here. Something smells rotten about this."

"I know Amanda comes from a lot of money, and apparently her dad is the one who controls the purse strings, even though she's the face of their group. And I get the feeling that she's always gotten what she wants, and she thinks it would be 'fun'--the word someone told me—to live on the Cape and run a nonprofit. She thinks it could be really good for her 'brand,'" Jack says, rolling his eyes.

"Ah, so this is a chance for her to grow her own profile, to hell with what's good for Terra Marique, or Cranberry Harbor," Gabby says. "Wow, well, I guess that's the world we live in now, huh?"

"It's not going to be our world, not if I have anything to say about it," Lizzie says. "So I'd say the first thing we do is reach out to Adam, see where we stand legally, and where you stand contractually, Jack, and then we take it from there. If he says we're good to go showing Ian's film, then we contact him, see if he's cool with that, and get the ball rolling. When were they talking about having this meeting?"

"Soon, I'd say, very soon," Jack says, his face looking concerned.

"We've got you," Gabby says. "And these folks don't know Cranberry Harbor. We're loyal, and we don't mess around when one of our own is being attacked."

"Gabby's right, Jack, this whole town is going to back you, I know it. These Boston folks aren't going to know what hit them when we all come together to defend one of our own," Peter says.

Lizzie laughs. "Wow, I wouldn't want to mess with you people," she says. "I'm waiting to hear someone say 'go ahead, make my day,'" she teases. "I'm glad I'm on Team Cranberry Harbor, that's for sure!"

"Being on the side of what's right is always the best side to be on," Peter says. "We're going to win this battle, I don't have any doubt."

"Well, I certainly married into the right family," Jack says, a little choked up. "Thank you. I am feeling a lot less scared than when I walked in here."

Lizzie leans over and hugs him. "You're not alone; we're all in this together," she says, leaning her head on his shoulder. "Like Mom said, we've got you. And we've got this."

"Thank you, everyone," Jack says, standing up, still looking somewhat worried, but not as panicked as when he walked in. "Okay, so I'm going to go home, take an outdoor shower, and try to let go of all this angst. You coming?" he says to Lizzie.

"You go ahead. I'll be right behind you," Lizzie says.

After he's left Lizzie says to her mom, "I decided that this is not the right time to hit him with 'oh! And guess what! Not only do you have to worry about losing your job, we're going to have a baby and possibly be down one income!' Yeah, I think I'm not going to bring this up right now, but I will take you up on that test," Lizzie says.

"Follow me," Gabby says, walking to the stairs.

"I'll let you two do this, but I'm right here if you need anything," Peter says.

Lizzie follows Gabby into her bathroom, where she takes a pregnancy test box out of the linen closet.

"I have to say, I always think of you as having anything anyone might need, but this goes above and beyond, Mom," Lizzie says, taking it from her.

"What can I say, I was a good Girl Scout, always prepared," she smiles. "I will leave you to pee on your stick, and we can wait for the results together," Gabby says, leaving Lizzie alone.

Lizzie opens the package. It has two tests in it. Maybe if you don't like the results, positive or negative, you can have a re-do.

She follows the directions perfectly, her hands shaking a little. She's not sure what she's hoping for. She's always assumed they would very rationally make a decision when it was time to have a baby, go through a few months of trying, and then hopefully, without too much fanfare, she'd be pregnant. As she finishes up she finds herself thinking back to a few weeks ago when she'd flirtatiously lured Jack upstairs and is thinking that may have been the night. But who knows? She washes her hands, opens the door, and sits next to her mom on the end of the bed.

"These newer tests are pretty quick," Gabby says. "You feeling okay?" She puts her arm around Lizzie.

Lizzie nods, but she's still not quite sure how she is.

In under five minutes, the answer is right there in her hand. The test announces it quite clearly to her and her mom: *Pregnant.*

Out of the blue Lizzie bursts into tears.

Her mom holds her. "Are those happy or sad tears?" Gabby asks, stroking her hair.

"I don't know!" Lizzie wails. "I don't know why I'm crying!"

"Because you came over here to say hi and two hours later you're finding out you're pregnant. I don't think that was on your to-do list for today," Gabby says.

Lizzie shakes her head, unable to say anything.

"You're going to be okay. Everything is going to be okay," she says in that way mothers can say things that even as adults, their kids need to hear.

"Yeah? You really think so?" Lizzie says, her nose and eyes both running.

Gabby leans over and grabs a tissue. "Here, honey, take this."

Lizzie sits up and blows her nose. "Would I be a terrible spouse if I didn't tell Jack right now about this? I think he has more than he can handle on his plate, and I know him; he'll pretend to not flip out, but inside he will be worrying about how we're going to make this work, what if he loses his job, et cetera, et cetera...so my thought, until we have a better idea of how things are going to play out with Terra Marique, is to just keep this between you, Dad and me."

"I think that is a very generous and thoughtful thing to do, and like he said, the meeting is going to be pretty soon. It's not going to be months or anything, just a couple of weeks. You certainly know we won't say anything to anyone," Gabby says.

"Thank you. I'm so grateful to have you and Dad, so I'm not all alone in this. That would be really hard," Lizzie says. "And I'm okay to not see a doctor quite yet?"

"I can keep an eye on you. I can even prescribe your prenatal vitamins. Just keep them in your nightstand for now. Or here, and just come over to take them every day," Gabby says.

Lizzie lies back on the bed and Gabby joins her.

"Wow, I'm going to be a mom, Mom," Lizzie says. "I'm still not quite believing it."

"Yup, and you're going to be excited, scared, tired, thrilled and everything in between. It is the best and scariest ride you'll ever go on," Gabby says.

"You really think I can do this?" Lizzie asks, staring at the ceiling.

"I know you can do this, and you and Jack are going to be great parents," Gabby says.

"I'm going to hold you to that," Lizzie says.

"No problem, it's a sure bet as far as I'm concerned," Gabby says, hiding her excitement a little bit, not wanting to overwhelm Lizzie. But deep down? She's turning cartwheels she's so excited.

CHAPTER 30

"Okay, you can do this. You're going to keep this all to yourself for a little bit so Jack can focus on keeping Terra Marique together," she says to herself, as she takes deep breaths while walking back to their house from her parents.

"I'm back!" she calls out, not seeing Jack right away. "You here?" She doesn't see Jack anywhere. "Jack?" Walking into the kitchen she sees a note on the counter.

Went for a run; needed to clear my head. Won't be too long. J xo

"Okay." She walks back into the living room and plops down on the couch. Not only is she dying to tell Jack she's pregnant, she wants to tell Alexis, and Leah and Anika. She especially wants to ask Anika how she felt when she first found out she was having a baby. Was she scared? Terrified? Overwhelmed?

She always knew she wanted to have kids—well, at least one—but the *idea* of a baby was much different than the reality. She'd only known for about an hour, so chances were as time went on it would feel less...overwhelming, right? But she wasn't so sure. How was she going to handle having a baby and running a newspaper? Would the Gazette fall apart? Would she? What if the quality went down so much that people stopped subscribing and then her investors would think it was a losing endeavor and pull their funding, and she would have killed the newspaper her father started from scratch and had run for over 30 years?

"Okay, you are spinning," she says to herself. "None of that is going to happen. You are catastrophizing and telling yourself a story that hasn't happened and will not because you will make sure it doesn't." She shakes her head. "You are becoming an internet meme," she says.

She gets up and literally shakes her body. "It's okay, it's okay, let it go," which then makes her think of *Frozen*, and she finds herself thinking of the song "Let it Go." Her mind is racing and she's seeing the humor in it at least, and Jack walks in from his run just as she's laughing.

"Well, I want what you're having," he says. "What's so funny? Please share it with me, because I'm in desperate need of a good laugh." He takes off his running shoes and goes into the kitchen to get some water. Lizzie follows.

"Oh, I was just doing my usual—you know, jumping to all the worst-case-scenarios, and I made myself laugh because I'm so good at that," she says, determined to not give Jack one more thing to feel stressed about. She walks over to him and goes to give him a hug.

"Oh, you don't want to hug me now. I'm a sticky, sweaty, smelly mess, but I appreciate the thought," he says, drinking his water.

"I don't care, I love you even when you're smelly, sweaty and sticky," she says, hugging him.

He hugs her back tightly and sighs. "Yeah, I really needed that," he says.

"Me too," she says, sitting down at the table. "Did the run help at all?"

He shrugs. "A little, but it's hard to shake this off." He sits down, joining her, but jumps back up immediately. "Sorry, it's hard to sit still." He runs his hands roughly through his hair. "I just can't believe it's come to this, you know? That one person, with their own agenda, can decide they think I'm not doing a good job and call a meeting to vote on whether or not to lay me off and try 'someone else' in charge? Namely her? The rest of the board seems to feel good about where we are fiscally, with our mission…" He sits down again. "And the thing that gets me—I mean, of course I've got skin in this game and my ego is a bit hurt, and I certainly don't want to lose my job, but even more than any of that, I don't want anything to happen to Terra

Marique, to all the people who call it home, who run businesses from there, who take classes or come to workshops that we have. Amanda doesn't give a damn about Cranberry Harbor or the people here, she just thinks putting 'ran a nonprofit' on her resume will make her look good. It's self-serving and shallow, but I'm not sure I can say that without looking bad myself, you know?"

Lizzie feels so terrible seeing Jack reeling like this. He's always the calm, cool and together one and the one calming her down. This change of roles is making her very glad she decided that now is not the time to share any baby news.

She scoots forward on her chair, sitting on the front edge, and takes his hands. "Listen to me. You are going to find there's so much support for you, you are not going anywhere, and when you are no longer running Terra Marique, it's going to be because you chose not to, not because some power-hungry venture capitalist decided to take over."

Jack takes a deep breath. "You almost sound convincing, if I could get rid of this awful, nagging voice in the back of my head saying I'm not qualified to run it, and second-guessing all my decisions in the last few weeks."

"Well, just tell that voice to shut it, and tune it out. We have a plan, and we're going to fight back. Amanda has no idea how Cranberry Harbor fights for our own, and not only are you one of our own, so is Terra Marique." She takes a deep breath. "Remember when you had to sell the town on the idea of it? Getting up at Town Meeting and making that pitch to the whole town? You did it, and you have shown them that they were correct to back you. And they still back you, so she is going to find herself extremely outnumbered, even if she's strong-armed some scaredy cats on the board to go along with her on holding a meeting."

"You're very good at this pep talk stuff, you know that?" Jack says. He lets out a big sigh. "Okay, I'm going to go take a shower, and what do you say we get out of here, go get some takeout, and have a picnic?" He stands up. "Sound good?"

"That sounds great," Lizzie says. "I'll be ready as soon as you're good to go."

He gives her a kiss. "Thank you, babe, for being so supportive of me, and being so steady. I'm glad this is all we've got going on, right? I don't think I could handle another surprise."

Lizzie sits alone at the kitchen table after he goes to take his shower and hopes, when all of this has calmed down, that the news that he's going to be a father will be happy news, and not one more thing to be stressed about.

Unable to decide what they each wanted for dinner, they decided to go to Bradford's to get some of their delicious and healthy offerings.

"I think I'm going to go with this amazing looking salad," Lizzie says, picking up a very bright and delicious looking bowl and grabbing a small container of vinaigrette next to it. She also picks up a small whole wheat baguette. Dinner isn't dinner for her without some type of carbs.

"What looks good to you?" she asks Jack. She knows him, and when he's stressed he loses his appetite, and she knows not eating and just existing on coffee—something he's known to do—won't help fuel him to get through this. "How about a burrito? You always like those," she says, pointing them out.

"Nah." Jack shakes his head. She can see him not really looking at the food and being in his head.

"Okay, you can go total comfort food with their house-made mac and cheese?" Again he shakes his head. "Sweetie, you need to eat something. It's not good for you to be stressed out and not eat."

"I know," he says, focusing again on the takeout case.

"Hey guys, fancy meeting you here!" They both turn and there's Eric. "What's going on?"

Lizzie looks at Jack with one of those "do we say something or not?" looks.

"Let's just say it's complicated..." Lizzie says, looking at Jack.

"Okay," Eric nods, not wanting to push and reading the room quite masterfully. "Well, I just came to pick up Jessie. We're going to go fly a kite down at the beach."

"Aw, that's really sweet, and fun," Lizzie says.

"Yeah, so I'll see you at the office tomorrow," Eric says, wanting to give them the space to deal with whatever is going on.

"Well, that was certainly awkward," Lizzie says. "I wasn't sure if you wanted me to say anything or not. Where are we with letting people in?"

"I don't know. Good question. I think we can certainly tell close friends, but I really didn't want to get into what's happening in the middle of Bradford's, you know?" Jack says, finally making a choice and picking up a margarita pizza sandwich on fresh ciabatta bread.

As they walk to the checkout Lizzie beats Jack to taking out her wallet. "I'm paying, and I'm totally going to be taking a bite or two from that sandwich," she says, putting her salad on the belt. "Hi," she says to the young man behind the register.

"Hi," he says back. "That will be $17.40," he adds.

Lizzie swipes her card. "Oh man, we forgot to get drinks," she says, looking at Jack.

"I'll go grab something. Seltzer? Juice?" he asks.

"Seltzer please. I'll meet you outside."

"Thanks so much," she says to…Kyle, according to his nametag, taking her receipt. "Have a good night," she says, picking up her bag.

"You too," he says as she heads outside.

"Okay, so where are we going to eat our lovely food?" Lizzie asks as they walk to their car. "Beach?"

"Nah, not really in a beach mood," Jack says, backing out of the parking space.

"Okay, town green?" she next suggests.

He shakes his head.

"You're not making this easy, honey. What do you suggest?" she asks, keeping her frustration in check, knowing what he's dealing with, but also having her own host of feelings about her life taking a dramatic turn as well.

"I'm sorry," he says. "I'm so distracted it's hard to focus. I've got an idea," he says, taking a turn, and, to Lizzie's surprise she sees that they're on their way to Terra Marique.

He pulls into a parking spot, and they both get out. Lizzie takes the bag of food. Jack has their sparkling waters in hand.

"Follow me," he says, smiling slyly at Lizzie.

"Okay, where are you taking me," she giggles. "This is not a path

I know at all," she says, feeling very happy that she'd chosen sneakers and not flip flops, given the uneven terrain.

"It's not far, promise," he says.

And then Lizzie sees it: a beautiful, elaborate grass labyrinth, surrounded by gorgeous plantings, four benches, a picnic table, and a pretty babbling water feature.

"What the heck?!" she exclaims. "How did I not know about this?" She's turning and looking around. "When? How? Who?" She doesn't know what to ask first.

"When," he says, putting the cans on the picnic table, taking the bag of food from Lizzie, and swinging his legs over to sit down, patting the spot next to him for her to join him. "It was completed three days ago."

Lizzie can't stop looking all around her. "Okay, so how and who?"

Jack laughs. "It was a very secret operation. Only the team who built it and the donor know about it," he says. "The person who donated the funds grew up here and moved away, and has lived in Ireland for decades now. Anyway," he says, unwrapping his sandwich, "she read about what we're doing here, and she wanted to contribute something in memory of her parents, who grew up and lived their whole lives on the Cape."

Lizzie takes the lid off her salad, but can't stop looking around. "This place is just...magical," she says, pouring the vinaigrette and gently mixing it in.

"Funny thing you should say magical," he says, putting down his sandwich and getting up. "We're going to have some fairy houses one of the artists who lives here is making, scattered all around," he says, showing her where they'll go, "and some gnomes too. We want it to feel like a beautiful, relaxing, magical place for people to come and take a breath. Walking a labyrinth is very calming," he says, coming back to the table. "The yoga teacher in the community center wants to do some meditation classes here, and kids' yoga too."

"See? This is not something some random VC who isn't part of the day-to-day life of this, Cranberry Harbor, or the Cape, for that matter, would ever make happen," she says. "This isn't a 'bottom line' kind of project. This is a heart project, a quality of life project.

Not everything is about numbers. Amanda doesn't know about that. Terra Marique and Cranberry Harbor are about so much more than bottom lines and numbers, and you are the one who made that happen."

"You know, if this whole journalism thing doesn't work out, you would be a pretty amazing coach," Jack says, leaning over and kissing her. "Thank you, I needed that. And you're right, damn it. I have done a good job. It may not be perfect, and I've made some mistakes, but nobody loves this place more than me."

"I think that's your pitch, honey, and just don't give her the power to take away what you've built," Lizzie says, looking him straight in the eye.

"Want to walk the labyrinth?" Jack says, standing up and reaching for her hand.

"I would love to," she says, joining him, secretly thinking she can't wait to bring their baby here, and finally feeling more excited than scared.

CHAPTER 31

With Jack's blessing, Lizzie had told Alexis about saving Jack's job, and she in turn told Ian, who had a plan to make sure Terra Marique wouldn't go the way of so many great concepts he'd seen over the years: the situation where one person with vision and skills comes in, creates something incredible, and then the people who had financed the project suddenly decide they know better and try to take over. Money sometimes has a weird way of making people delusional and think they know things they really don't, but because they have money no one says anything... Anyway, Ian was not going to let that happen with Terra Marique, and he was going to subvert Amanda's plan to get the board to agree to push aside Jack and bring her in to run it. And his secret weapon? His film. When he approached his producers and the studio who had financed it, they gave him permission for one public showing. They weren't dumb; they knew the publicity could bring great buzz before the movie would be streaming, so they were on board.

"Okay," Ian announced as he plopped himself down in a chair on the patio outside Sea Coast. "I just met with the town manager, and we've got permission to show the movie at the high school auditorium in three days at 4 pm. I've done some editing for this version, making it a bit shorter, and I've called in some favors and some folks I know from Boston are going to bring down a large screen and all the projection equipment we'll need, and they've offered to run it for us." He sits back and sighs. "Wow, I wasn't sure we were going to pull this off."

"Okay, wow, that's the same day as the Kind Fest on the town green. No worries, we'll make it all work," Lizzie says. "Thank you, Ian. I knew you'd make it happen, so much so that I have a full page ad ready to go in tomorrow's paper. All I was waiting for was final details. We'll also have it all over our socials." She takes out her iPad and shows him the ad they've created for the showing of *Terra Marique: A Blueprint for a Green Future.* "You okay with this?" she asks, a little nervous that Cranberry Harbor isn't exactly Hollywood and that her graphic skills are a bit lacking comparatively. "I'll just add the date and time now."

"It looks wonderful, Lizzie. Thanks so much for doing that," he says. "So from what I understand, since the town holds the deed to the land, they have a say in what happens there, right? This person, or even their board, can't push Jack out if the town doesn't agree?"

"Right, it's this pretty amazing loophole that Jack just learned about. He had no idea. His concern, however, is that Amanda and her fellow VCs will be able to snow the selectboard and other higher-ups that he's somehow mismanaged it and that they should take over," Lizzie says. "He feels fairly confident, but he won't relax until after the vote."

Alexis, laptop open, speaks up. "Yeah, so as Jack's rep at this meeting," she says, smiling, "he says that the plan is that the Terra Marique board will speak to the town and to the town selectboard, presenting their case for a change in leadership, and then we have our turn, which is showing the movie, which Ian will introduce."

"How long is the movie now, Ian? I know I should know this, sorry," Lizzie says, taking notes.

"It's 54 minutes," he says.

"Okay," Lizzie takes a deep breath. "And then Jack will speak, and then the selectboard will vote? In front of everyone?"

"Yup, they told Jack they want complete transparency," Alexis says.

"Okay, this seems like a plan," Lizzie says, hoping against hope that Ian's film is as impactful as Alexis and Ian seem to think. Jack had decided he didn't want to see it beforehand because he might second-guess himself, what he said and how he appears on film. He was already so stressed he couldn't add anything more to his never-ending stream of worries. He trusts Ian, and he trusts Alexis.

The three of them finished their meeting, and Lizzie rushed to the paper to get everything set up so they could get as many people as possible to come to the meeting. The print edition would be everywhere, but even more importantly in the online edition, and on all the surrounding towns' social media pages, and the Gazette's as well. Those were the places where news really spreads fast.

Eric had also, of course, been looped in and had done a great interview with Jack, and gotten some quotes from Amanda and another board member that he didn't want to use, but had to—journalist ethics and all. But Jack still came across as the competent leader, while the challengers had nothing of merit, or so Lizzie believed, to swing anyone in their direction.

"Okay," she says, sitting back in her chair. "I think the first round of dropping everything out there is done," she says. It was so hard to not be sharing her other news with any of her friends. There were times when she even forgot that she was pregnant. Since no one except her parents knew, it was easy to forget since she was never talking about it. That was until she felt nauseated, or extremely tired, and then she remembered, and felt guilty for forgetting.

"My story is up on the website, and I shared it, with no paywall restrictions, all over the place," Eric says. "No one in Cranberry Harbor will have an excuse for not seeing this, or knowing about the screening and the meeting. And I don't know anyone who hasn't had some kind of positive interaction with Terra Marique." He looks over at Lizzie, who looks exhausted. "You look so tired. I've got anything else that needs to be done. Why don't you get out of here and relax a bit?"

"You sure you don't mind?" Lizzie says, stretching. "I think I will take you up on your very kind offer." She closes her laptop, packs it into her carrying case, grabs her phone and purse, and stands to leave. "Thank you for everything, and I know this isn't the most ceremonious way to do this, but if you look at the masthead on the paper I think you'll see something I hope you like," she says as she walks toward the door.

"Associate editor? Really? I got a promotion?" Eric says, smiling.

"Yes, and I apologize that it took me this long to make that change. You are an integral part of what happens here, and I hope you accept the new title, along with a raise," she says, hand on the door.

"Yes, and thank you," he says, turning toward the door in his chair. "I appreciate this, more than you know. Have a good night."

"You too, partner," she says,

When she arrived home she was delighted to see her mom walking over carrying what Lizzie hoped might be dinner. It was hard not being able to tell anyone why she was feeling so tired, and hiding any nausea she was experiencing as well.

"Mom! Is that what I think and hope it is?" Lizzie says, walking from her car to the door. "If that is some of your amazing vegetable soup you will have totally made my day," she says, unlocking the door and holding the storm door for her mom to go ahead.

"I thought maybe you could use a little comforting," she says, carrying the bags into the kitchen and placing them on the counter.

"Oh, you have no idea! Thank you, Mom!" she says, giving her mom a big hug. "You don't know how hard it is not telling anyone, especially Jack, but I really want him to focus on this and this alone right now, and not be pulled off track thinking about or worrying about me, the future, any of that."

"It's very selfless of you," Gabby says, taking the covered bowl of soup and putting it in the fridge along with a salad. There was also some amazing looking bread, and a fruit salad as well.

"This is all so incredible, Mom, thank you. I'm so glad I have you and Dad to talk to at least," she says.

"Let me make you a cup of tea," she says to Lizzie. "Go sit on the couch and I'll bring it in."

"Thank you, Mommy," she says, smiling at her mom as she drags herself to the living room and plops down on the couch.

In just a few minutes Gabby is there, tea and some homemade, organic whole grain crackers in hand.

"Here, this will be good for anything that ails you," she says.

"Oh my God, Mom, these crackers are amazing!" Lizzie says after taking a bite. "I'm really loving being your guinea pigs for all your cookbook recipes," she says, sighing and sitting back, tea in hand. "It's hard because I can't let anyone else know why I'm maybe a little extra tired, my stomach feels iffy, or why I might burst into tears at the drop of a hat," she says, taking a sip. "I'll be glad when all of this is settled, and then—"

"And then everyone can spoil you and take care of you," Gabby teases.

"I would not mind a little bit of that," Lizzie says.

"So is everything ready for Thursday? It's all anyone was talking about at pickleball, and at Bradford's too. You're going to have a great turnout," Gabby says.

"Yeah, Ian has people coming to take care of the screening, all the ads are out there—I think we're all set. Now all we need is for it not to rain, and for the universe to be on our side," Lizzie says.

"The universe is most definitely on your side. I've had a word with them," Gabby says.

"Phew, I was hoping you would. I can check that off my to-do list now." She's quiet.

"Okay, honey, what are you thinking?" Gabby asks. "Like I need to ask."

Lizzie shrugs. "I just want life to go back to normal—well, our new normal with me being pregnant, but not looking over our shoulder worrying about something awful happening. Oh God, is that what the rest of my life being a mother is going to feel like? It kind of is, isn't it?"

Gabby thinks for a minute. "Kind of. But interspersed with the most joy, and love you never imagined feeling."

"So a bit of everything?" Lizzie asks.

"Yeah, I'd say that sums up being a parent pretty well. It's a bit of everything. Times ten," Gabby smiles. "You will love this baby more than you ever thought possible, and experience more joy over the littlest things than you ever have."

"But?" Lizzie knows there's a but.

"But it's also the hardest, most exhausting, worrisome job you will ever have. But here's another thought: it's all completely worth it and you wouldn't trade it for anything," Gabby says.

Lizzie takes a deep breath. "Sounds like quite the roller coaster."

"It is. It is most certainly the ride of your life. And I can't wait to get to be a part of you experiencing it," Gabby says, pulling her own little girl into a hug. "You and Jack are going to be great parents, and we will be right here with you every step of the way."

CHAPTER 32

Lizzie had mixed feelings about how fast the week was going. Lost in all the Terra Marique drama, the end of summer kindness festival wrap-up was feeling lost in the shuffle. Being on the same day, it was going to be crazy. One event would have been more than enough, but she'd already announced it and there was no turning back. Thankfully, Leah, Justine, Anika and Jay had taken over all that planning, so in theory all she was going to have to do was promote it on the paper's socials and show up. In theory. She was a little wary of relying on norms and theories these days. Between an investor trying to force Jack out as director and (surprise!) getting pregnant, there wasn't much that could shock her right now. As soon as she had that thought she knocked on her wooden desk, hoping to ward off any more surprises.

A very welcome surprise, however, was seeing her brother and niece come through the door bearing some gifts. That was a surprise she could handle.

She immediately stood up, and Sophie ran to her.

"Well, this is the best thing to happen to me today. To what do I owe this honor?" Lizzie says, giving her niece a big hug, standing and doing the same to her brother.

"We were out and Sophie said she wanted to bring you a present, so here we are," Matt says. "You doing okay?"

She shrugs as Sophie tries to get her attention.

"Yes?" Lizzie says, squatting down.

"I brought you a fairy for good luck!" she says, handing Lizzie the cutest little handmade fairy.

"Oh my gosh, I love her!" She hugs Sophie. "Thank you so much! You made this?"

"Yup! I made her at the library with Momma and some other kids. You like her?" Sophie asks.

"I love her!" Lizzie says, looking at the little stuffy with glittery wings and a sweet little dress. "She will bring us so much luck! I just know it! Thank you so, so much, sweetie!"

"Can I sit at the desk and pretend to be the boss?" she asks, having moved on from the gift presentation.

"Of course. Can I ask what you're the boss of?" Lizzie asks, smiling and looking at Matt.

"The whole world," she says, wiggling in the big chair.

"Wow, that's a big job. Let us know if you need anything, okay?" Lizzie says, gesturing to Matt to take a seat in the reading area of the office, meaning the well-worn couch and two overstuffed chairs.

Sophie nods, distracted now by the sundry papers, stapler, desk phone, and other office supplies on the desk.

"So how are you, really?" Matt asks.

She takes a deep breath. "Good." She pauses. "Good-ish? I'm pretty confident in what we have planned, but we have no idea what this woman who wants to take over has planned. And she has a lot of resources behind her."

"But you have all of Cranberry Harbor, and," he points to the fairy in her hand, " now a fairy on your side. No one can compete with all that."

"Good point. I'm sure they don't have fairies, and they sure don't have the town," she says. "But I won't be able to relax until it's all done, and we're partying it up with kindness afterward."

"It's going to be fine. Everyone I know plans to be there, stores are closing for that couple of hours, and people are saying they can't work from 4-6. It's amazing," Matt says.

"Really? I hadn't heard that," Lizzie says, buoyed by that news.

"Well, we should get going. Shannon has taken care of making sure there's childcare at the meeting, and I've got to get there to help her get that all set up.We just wanted to check on you first," he says, giving his sister a hug.

"Is Shannon doing okay? Everything is good with the pregnancy?" Lizzie asks.

He smiles and gives Lizzie a thumbs-up. "It's all good, very good," he says.

"Good, glad to hear it," she says.

"Soph, we gotta go. Give Aunt Wiz a hug, and we will see her later, okay?" Sophie reluctantly gets up from her big boss desk.

"You can come back another time and be the boss, okay?" Lizzie says. "Thank you again for my fairy! I love her. And I love you," she says, giving her a hug. "See you soon!"

"Bye," she says, walking to the door.

"I feel so disposable," Lizzie jokes with her brother.

"Hey, when she's over it she's over it." He opens the door. "See you soon, love you, and it's all going to be okay, okay? I promise."

"Well, as long as you promise... love you too," she says.

After they left Lizzie finished up a couple of things, and then, looking at the clock, decided it was time to go. She gathers up all her things - purse, keys, phone, and of course, her new fairy, and walks out of the office, locking the door behind her.

Lizzie thought she was pretty early getting to the high school at 3:30, but it was already filling up. She signs in, is given her remote voting device, and goes to find a seat. Her stomach flips a little. This is a lot, and then she sees Jack, which makes her feel a lot better.

"Hey, I've got you a seat here, right up front," he says, taking his things he'd placed on it to save it for her.

"Thanks." She puts down all her stuff, including a bottle of water and some more of her mom's crackers that she'd stashed at work. "How are you doing? Everything all set?"

"Yeah, we're going to open with the VC team making their pitch, show the movie, I'll say a few words, very few, and then we will take a vote," he says.

Lizzie nods. "Will Ian say anything? To introduce the film or anything?"

"Yes, he wasn't crazy about doing that, wanting the film to speak for itself, but I convinced him," he says.

"Okay," she says, sitting down in her seat. "You scoot. I'm sure you've got lots to do. I'm fine here."

Jack nods and turns to go finish getting ready.

"Hey," she calls after him, and he turns around. "I love you, and it's all going to work out."

He blows her a kiss and goes back to the stage.

When a group that had saved seats near her decided to move, she was able to snag seats for her mom, dad, Matt and Shannon. When they all arrive it feels a lot better having them next to her.

A hush falls over the crowd when someone Lizzie doesn't know takes to the mic.

"Hello, thank you all for being here. We're so impressed by how much all of you care about Terra Marique and Cranberry Harbor," he says. "I am Robert Miller, from Bragg, Anderson and Miller, an investment group that has helped fund Terra Marique."

Unbidden, some people start yelling out, "Team Jack Cahoon!" "Go back to Boston!" and the other more…colorful comments. Mr. Miller looks flustered and Amanda Solomon, the instigator of all of this, comes to the mic.

"Hello, I am Amanda Solomon, an associate with the firm, and I am here to tell you how much more Terra Marique could be if we were to change leadership."

The boos are practically shaking the room. Lizzie looks at her mom and can't resist smiling.

"We want Jack!" a few people start chanting, and then more and more join in.

Amanda is having a hard time getting any kind of control.

"What you can't see," she says, now shouting into the mic, "is what Terra Marique could be with a real experienced leader at the head. We could grow it even more, we could expand, and grow Cranberry Harbor even more. I have even been approached by some wonderful national businesses that would like to come here," she says, just sealing her own demise.

"We don't want your big box stores!" the crowd shouts over and over.

Giving up, she walks away from the mic, and Ian comes up.

"Hello, I'll be brief. I wanted to make *Terra Marique:A Blueprint for a Green Future* as both a wake-up call for the world and as a way to document the incredible project that this one man, Jack Cahoon, thought of, fought for and created. He didn't do this to get rich." He glances over at the collection of venture capitalists off to the side. "He did it because he loves this town, he loves Cape Cod, and he wants to see it survive into the future. One place like Terra Marique can't change the world, but it can be an example that others can build on, expand, and inspire others to do the same thing. To take a risk for the sake of their communities, and for the sake of the planet. I hope you enjoy the film." Ian then steps aside, the lights dim, and for the next 54 minutes you could hear a pin drop, except for the periodic applause and "heck yes" coming from the crowd.

Ian did an incredible job, starting at the very beginning, with Bud protesting, chained to the tree, and Jack convincing him Terra Marique was going to be good for the town. There was even an interview with Bud talking about how he now teaches woodworking to people at Terra Marique, and how vital it is to the town. "Jack Cahoon is a child of this town, someone who grew up here and cares about all of us. I'm grateful to him and can't wait to see what more he does to make Cranberry Harbor better and better. And maybe help save this planet too."

By the end, when Jack is playing with Terra, the puppy who got a new home there along with her human family, there isn't a dry eye in the house.

When the lights come up you can hear sniffling all around the room.

Sharon MacKenzie, town moderator, has now stepped up to the mic.

"Good afternoon, everyone, thank you for being here, and thank you, Ian MacFaydan, for that beautiful film. As you know, we have a vote to take. The board from Terra Marique has voted to replace Jack Cahoon as executive director of Terra Marique, to be replaced by Amanda Solomon." The entire room is filled with booing citizens.

"Shhh, please, let's just get through this," she says. "But as the deed holders of the land, our contract stipulates that we have control over who the director is because it is on town land. So we are here to vote. Do you wish for Jack Cahoon to remain the director of Terra Marique, or for him to be replaced by Amanda Solomon? A yes vote is a vote for Jack Cahoon, no is for him to be replaced. You may vote now."

The room once again falls silent as they all register their votes on their remotes, and within just a few minutes the votes have shown up on the large screen for all to see.

"We have 636 votes for Jack and hmm, and it seems, just one vote for Amanda Solomon. The ayes have it, Jack Cahoon will remain the director of Terra Marique." And with the crack of her gavel, it's done.

The applause is thunderous and Jack comes running down off the stage, lifting Lizzie up and hugging her.

"We did it!" he says, spinning her around.

"You did it!" she says, squeezing him so tight.

From the stage they hear a dramatic "I quit!" and see Amanda strutting out the door.

"Bye, Amanda!" everyone shouts, and then the room breaks into laughter.

The whole family and all their friends have gathered around, laughing and hugging. It was a very good outcome.

"So, what do you say we all go celebrate kindness at the town green?" Alexis says.

"I'm thinking Amanda will not be there," Eric says.

"Probably not," Jack says.

Jack is then approached by Robert Miller. He turns to him.

"Jack, I'm really sorry this happened. We actually fired her before she announced she quit, and this will never happen again," he says. "No hard feelings?"

Jack pats him on the shoulder. "Actually, Bob, your whole firm has been fired. I have a new team that's going to be working with us. So thanks for everything, but we're done. No hard feelings?

Right?" And with that Jack turns to his crew, and they all walk out, leaving Robert Miller speechless.

"Let's go celebrate!" Jack says, as they all exit.

CHAPTER 33

Things were already hopping when they got to the town green, and this being the era of social media and cell phones, news had already spread that they'd won, and all was good.

Lizzie wanted to find the right time to tell Jack they were going to be parents, but this clearly wasn't it. There were people everywhere, music was happening, thanks to a wonderful band from Wellfleet, a juggler was entertaining a group of kids, and ice cream was being handed out for free. It was pretty darn magical.

"Oh, I see Leah and Alexis," Lizzie says to Jack. "I need to check in with them and see what's going on."

"Got it. I see Sean, Ben and Ollie over by the gazebo. I'll be over there," he says, walking toward their friends.

"Hey! Congratulations!" Leah and Alexis both exclaim, pulling her into a hug.

"I hated not being there to be able to vote, but I was more than certain that it was going to go the way it did," Leah says.

"No problem. Thank you for holding down the fort here—well, for actually building the fort and making all this happen," Lizzie says.

"I loved it when I caught the moment, albeit from a little bit of a distance, when Jack fired that whole firm," Alexis says, choking up. "I am so glad we're not going to be working with them anymore. They were not our people," she says, smiling.

"No, they were not," says Lizzie. She stops and looks around at all the handmade signs, the people of all ages smiling, dancing, crafting...all in the name of kindness. "This is just remarkable, you guys. Thank you for making this so beautiful. It's just perfect."

"So what happens next?" Alexis asks.

"You mean here? Now?" Leah says.

"No, I mean long-term. I can't stand the thought of giving this up. I think that Cranberry Harbor needs to keep being a place where kindness matters," Alexis says.

"Oh, I like that tagline, Alexis," Lizzie says. "'Cranberry Harbor: Where Kindness Matters.' I think that's a keeper, don't you, Leah?"

"Yes! I think we keep the signs up, maybe refresh a few things as the fall comes, but I don't see why we can't keep working on keeping Cranberry Harbor kind year-round," Leah says.

"Sounds good," says Alexis. "In the meantime, we have a few speeches to be made. There are things to say," she says, taking Lizzie by the hand and leading her toward the gazebo, where the band is winding it up.

"Uh, what do you mean, 'things to say'? No one told me I was going to have to say anything. I'm not prepared." Lizzie feels her heart start to race and her palms sweat. "I'm a writer, not a public speaker."

"Oh come on, sure you are. You convinced this whole damn town to do this, now it's time to thank them and inspire them to keep it up!" Alexis says.

"You seem to have your cheerleader hat on; why don't you do it?" Lizzie says, trying not to panic. There are so many people there, and she doesn't want to sound like an incoherent idiot in front of what looks to be hundreds of people. And what if she throws up?

"I am not the one who thought of it, who made it happen, that's why," Alexis says. "You will be fine. I'm going to introduce you, and then just thank everyone. It doesn't have to be a speech worthy of Lincoln, just say something from your heart."

Speak from my heart, okay, I can do that, she thinks. *Speak from the heart and be sincere. Does trying to be sincere come across as insincere? I don't want to sound fake; what if... Oh my God, you're spinning; take a deep breath. What is wrong with me?* She's beginning to calm down a little when she sees that Alexis is now standing at the microphone, about to introduce her.

"Hi everyone, thank you so much for coming to our end of the summer celebration of our kindness project. We're thrilled to see so many of you here having fun, and," she pauses, "being so kind to one another. My name is Alexis Johnson, and I work for Terra Marique as the program director, and I would like to introduce the woman who made this all happen, the editor of the Cranberry Harbor Gazette and my dearest friend in the world, Lizzie Martin."

Jack has made his way to the front of the crowd and is beaming, while applauding with everyone else. Lizzie is happy to have him to focus on as an anchor.

"Thank you, thank you so much," she says, as she steps next to Alexis, who quietly moves aside.

"I am fairly speechless right now, but I will try to pull myself together," she says, laughing a bit, which helps her relax. "Ten or so weeks ago I had an idea. It was just an idea, but I shared it with my friends, Alexis," she points to her, "and Leah Alden of Sea Coast Coffee." There's thunderous applause for that. "I was seeing so much impatience and lack of consideration, and yes, a lot less kindness around town, and I wondered if there was anything we could do to fix that. So I turned to my friends, who didn't think I was crazy, and we came up with the idea of creating a kindness project across the town."

There's more applause and people calling out, "Thank you!"

"What is truly incredible is that our whole wonderful, amazing town went along with it, and visitors too. I really like to believe we've created something here that can catch on. I've already heard of towns in other places doing this as well. You have all been on the ground floor of a kindness revolution. We have become the ambassadors of kindness, of civility, and of thoughtfulness. We've made being kind cool!" she says, now getting fired up. "And we're not done; this project will continue because Cranberry Harbor is where kindness matters," she says, winking at Alexis. The crowd loves it; clearly they've got a winning message. "Thank you for coming tonight, and for carrying on the message of kindness. And remember, stay kind. Thank you!" The crowd erupts into applause, whistles and cheers. Lizzie is shocked at the response, she can't believe it.

Jack scoops her up and hugs her. "Look at what you created! This is incredible!" He kisses her as the crowd moves down the green toward what seems to be a magic show about to begin.

"And look at what you did tonight! It really is amazing!" Lizzie says, kissing him back.

He shakes his head. "I know, right? I cannot imagine how anything could top these two events!"

They're alone now, the crowd having moved to watch Caleb Wells, a Cranberry Harbor high schooler, do his magic show before there's some kindness storytelling.

Lizzie looks at him. "Well, there may be one thing that could top all this," she says.

"Really? I can't imagine what!" Jack says.

She lets out a deep breath. "I'm pregnant," she says, wondering what his response will be.

"What?! I, what, when.. Oh my God!" he says, picking her up again. "Oh, wait, maybe I shouldn't do that!" he says, gently placing her down.

"No, sweetie, it's fine, I'm fine, we're fine," she says, smiling at him.

"Did you just find out?" he asks.

"No, last week, but you had so much going on, I didn't want you worrying about your job *and* becoming a dad. Are you mad at me?" she asks.

"Mad? No, of course not, that was really thoughtful and caring of you. Does anyone else know?" he asks.

"My parents. I threw up at their house, as one does after eating a banana," she jokes, "and my mom, being the sleuthy doctor she is, nailed it."

Jack sits down on the steps of the gazebo and Lizzie joins him.

"Wow, we're going to be parents," he says, looking a little overwhelmed.

"I know, believe me, I've been flipping out about it all week. We don't even have a dog; do you think we can handle a kid? What if we really mess it up? Forget to feed it or something?" she asks, looking for reassurance.

He shakes his head. "We're not going to mess it up," he says.

"You sure of that?"

"Yes, and when we don't feel like we can handle something, we've got family, we've got friends—hell, we've got this whole damn town." He gestures to the people cheering on a 14-year-old doing magic.

"True, there's no place I'd rather be scared new parents than here," Lizzie says.

"Me either." He puts his arm around her and pulls her in tight. "Let the next adventure begin!"

"I mean, how badly could we mess it up?" Lizzie says.

Jack looks at her and they both immediately knock some wood, and then laugh.

"Better safe than sorry," Jack says.

"Always," says Lizzie.

The End

ACKNOWLEDGMENTS

I am ever grateful for the amazing team at Sea Crow Press. I am so fortunate to have found a home for my books that feels more like a family than a business. Thank you for partnering with me to bring my books to life.

To my early readers who always set me straight—Sarah Shemkus and Jean Baxter. Thank you so much for your notes and catches. Maybe someday I'll figure out where the commas go.

My partner in life, Frank Poranski, you are so steady and help keep me from wobbling too much. All my amazing children and partners who don't think I'm too crazy—or at least keep it to themselves. Dylan, Ben, Constanza, Emma, and Ross. You are all the best.

And last but not least, I'm so grateful that when I was 14, my mom decided we should move to Cape Cod. This is home. I hope my books do at least some justice to a place that I, and so many others love.

ABOUT THE AUTHOR

Candace Hammond grew up and still lives on Cape Cod, but will forever be considered a washashore for not having been born there. She is a journalist, playwright, and novelist, who also hosts an arts podcast/radio show on WOMR out of Provincetown, because people in the arts have the best stories. She is the mother of three adult children who are scattered around the globe, and grandmother to one amazing little girl. She lives with her musician partner and their very large cat on the Lower Cape.

ABOUT THE PRESS

Sea Crow Press is an award-winning woman-run independent book publisher based on Cape Cod in Massachusetts committed to amplifying voices that might otherwise go unheard. We publish creative nonfiction, literary fiction, and poetry. Our books celebrate our connection to each other and to the natural world with a focus on positive change and great storytelling.

www.ingramcontent.com/pod-product-compliance
Lightning Source LLC
LaVergne TN
LVHW030910080826
845145LV00010B/2838

* 9 7 8 1 9 6 1 8 6 4 5 6 6 *